Sudden Death
&
Old Goats

SUDDEN DEATH
&
OLD GOATS

BY

STEVEN G. SHANDROW
&
GREG E. RIPLINGER

Bookstand Publishing

www.bookstandpublishing.com

Published by
Bookstand Publishing
Morgan Hill, CA 95037
4406_2

Copyright © 2016 by Steven G. Shandrow and Greg E. Riplinger
All rights reserved. No part of this publication may be reproduced or transmitted in any form or by any means, electronic or mechanical, including photocopy, recording, or any information storage and retrieval system, without permission in writing from the copyright owner.

ISBN 978-1-63498-315-0

Printed in the United States of America

Dedicated to past, present, and future Armed Forces men and women.

PREFACE

The late winter day was typically Seattle: long, cold, wet, and windy. Master Chief, Bob Kensey, (Retired), plopped down in his overstuffed recliner and took a sip of Chimeaud brandy that was a gift from his lady friend, Lois. It was a reminder of their upcoming date at the ballet.

Bob Kensey closed his eyes to give that some thought. *"The brandy is wonderful but I'm not so sure about a bunch of people dancing around in frou-frou tutus. Although . . . the ballet might not be so bad; it is the 'Pirates Of Penzance' and I have some experience with Somali pirates."*

Instead of concentrating on tomorrow's christening of the radio room addition to his favorite waterfront hang out, Safe Haven Tavern, or looking forward to a night out with Lois, Bob settled into his lounge chair, closed his eyes, swirled his brandy to warm it, and drifted back a year or more to his ship, **Goat Locker**, and **'The Raid'** that shook up Washington, D.C.

"The crew . . . Nine better men would be hard to find: Masters, Boats, Fritz, Greasey, Sparks, José, Preacher, and the Gonzales brothers, Jorge and Manuel." Bob smiled and took a sip of brandy.

"Yup, that was quite a crew!" Bob surprised himself speaking out loud. He nodded his head, closed his eyes, and savored the excitement he felt just before executing his battle plan.

*"All stations combat, T-10 minutes! Bridge, when I go weapons free engage HYCATS, (Automated Navigation System), and close your eyes. Gun control; make sure **'everyone'** is clear of rotating machinery!"* He would never forget that order.

Bob took a sip of brandy and let the emotion wash over him. He steadied his shaking hand. *"Jesus, it's just like the fear and surging adrenalin when I opened fire on a harbor full of blood thirsty pirates at T-6."*

Bob grinned; he vividly remembered José's initial report from the bridge. *"Holy shit!!!! My ears are ringin' and the place is a . . .a . . . inferno!"*

Bob momentarily relived the assault he and Boats made on the hijacked yacht, **High and Mighty**, and **Goat Locker's** narrow escape from the harbor. *"Boats lying wounded on the schooner was a dark moment punctuated by exploding artillery rounds! We shouldn't have made it out of there . . . but that shit was easy! Those damn helos just about did us in!"*

The last of the brandy went down smoothly. Bob rose and started for bed and a good night's sleep. He saluted the bottle of Chimeaud and made a toast. "I'm damn proud of my crew, my ship, **Goat Locker**, and what we accomplished!"

"Well, shit! Those days are gone forever . . . We got stabbed in the back by a feckless Administration led by an incompetent President. '*He*' made us scuttle the best damn fighting' ship that ever sailed the bonny blue!" Bob spoke with remorse and regret, and sadly shuffled off to bed. Tomorrow was another day . . .

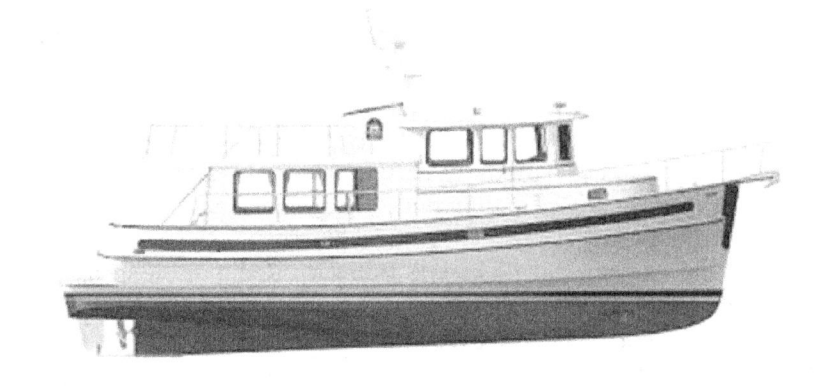

Dead Eye (Springer)

INTRODUCTION

The Character, Master Chief Bob Kensey, embodies the experiences of both authors' many years at sea and interesting shore duty stations. They served on the finest, most powerful, ships of the cold war and Vietnam era. These ships included: *USS Chicago (CG-11)* where the authors and some notable characters served together.

FTMC Shandrow moved on to the much loved *'Dirty Dozen' USS Columbus (CG-12)*, and later the *USS Albany (CG-10)*.

FTCS Riplinger moved from the *USS Chicago* to the *USS Long Beach (CGN-9)* and later the *USS Bainbridge (CGN-25)*.

FTMC Shandrow served with Mobile Technical Unit MOTU-7 and MOTU-13 keeping the NATO Sea Sparrow and BPDMS missile systems working on every ship type imaginable throughout the Western Pacific. He served a stint at Mare Island, CA teaching the next generation of Fire Control Technicians how to keep their gear operational. He retired as the Self Defense Division Chief at Naval Ship Weapon System Engineering Station, Port Hueneme, CA.

FTCS Riplinger was shanghaied and spent one fascinating stint at NAS Alameda, CA working as a Navy peace officer. Other shore duty assignments were more in character and included a tour with Fleet Training Group San Diego, CA where he trained every ship type and ran gun and missile live-fire exercises. He retired from Fleet Combat Systems Training Unit Pacific, (FCSTUP), San Diego, CA

This novel is steeped in naval lore gleaned from more than forty years of combined navy service and experience. Read it and enjoy!

Derdrake

CHAPTER 1

THE SAFE HAVEN

Jim Billings called some time ago, made contact, and then went silent. On two occasions, I tried the one-number cell phone he gave me a year or more ago. It connected to no one nowhere. I pitched it back into the kitchen junk-drawer and did not give it a second thought.

I kept busy throughout the winter working on the 'Radio Room' addition to the Safe Haven. I was adding the finishing touches today. As soon as I hung *Goat Locker's* ships bell I planned to test the newly installed Hallicrafters Cyclone III transceiver. The bell inscribed *"Goat Locker One Hell of a Ship"* was mounted on a beautiful padauk plaque made by an old Air Force friend. I hung it above the radio operator's desk made of teak. **"Yellow Submarine"** just finished playing and the Wurlitzer was queuing up **"Paperback Writer"**; I carefully drove the last brass screw into place.

I stuck my head through the narrow doorway located behind the bar, and asked Gunny to shoot a short video while I christened the Radio Room. He said he was never too busy to help a Squid, I owed him for two San Magoos, and he would be more than happy to lend a hand. *Goat Locker's* CIC, (Combat Information Center), clock displayed 1430, I rang five bells and announced, "The Radio Room is officially open!"

I scanned frequencies listening for chatter in English. I picked up numerous foreign language transmissions until I reached the middle of the ten-meter band. A conversation just signed off with seventy-threes.

I keyed the mike. "CQ, CQ, CQ, this is SGS three-niner-zero in Seattle, over."

A bit of static followed by, "This is GER five-three-six in Hawaii. I read you five-by-five, over." pealed from a meticulously resurrected AR-5 speakers and filled the Radio Room.

We were up and operating in both receive and transmit modes. "I've got you five-by-five. I hope your weather is less dismal than our incessant rain!"I answered.

"I can guarantee the sun is shining here, but I'd kill for a good cup of coffee. I'll send you a box of macadamias if you send me a couple pounds of course ground, Seattle's Best."

"Make 'em chocolate covered and you've got a deal."

We exchanged addresses and arranged shipping details. Just before signing off, I heard a thump near the Haven's boat landing and felt a distinct jolt.

Gunny ran into the Radio Room, looked out the window, and exclaimed, "What the fuck! Would one of you squids teach that ground-pounder how to drive a boat! I just got the dock fixed from the last Black Cloud visit. Shit!"

"You can't teach an old dog-face new tricks." I laughed. "He did manage to get *Dead Eye's* bow on your dock. That 'is' tough to do! Hey, check out that unique cameo pattern on his new bimini."

Gunny frowned, went directly to the beer cooler, picked out a can of Busch Bavarian, gave it a disgusted look, and then shook it like a martini. "No sense changing his luck." he mumbled under his breath and replaced the brew back into the cooler.

"Hey Gunny, you got any duck tape?" rang through the Haven when the door flew open. Black Cloud, not so well known as Mike Smith, sounded in a hurry.

"*Dead Eye must be taking on water.*" I thought. "*Wouldn't be the first time!*" I shut down the Hallicrafters, and then stepped out of the Radio Room and took up station behind the bar.

"It's 'duct' tape and yes. Nice job parking your boat. You want a beer?" Gunny asked.

"Does a bear shit in the woods? Don't give me any of that piss Kensey drinks but put it on his tab! Oh, hi Kensey. And I want to 'tape' those fuckin' ducks that slept on my neighbor's newly tarred roof before waddling all over my new canvas to the leather seats in his Beemer!" Black Cloud was in a dark mood; he scowled and absently popped the top on his icy cold Busch Bavarian brew.

"Bull shit motherfucker!" was all he could splutter between dabs of beer and foam oozing off the edges of his beat up, faded, jungle cover (cammo patterned crusher hat). Gunny and I could not maintain straight faces. At first he, then I doubled over with laughter.

Regulars, Burt and Harry, retired Chief Coasties, (Coast Guard members) who were engaged in a perpetual penny-a-point cribbage game, joined in the laughter.

Harry put in his two-cents, "It ain't Saturday Mike, but you did need a shower!"

"You two shallow water pukes just wade ashore? Wanna go for a real boat ride?" Mike studied them with the look a sniper uses to size up his target.

"Not with that black cloud that follows you around!" Burt added. "But I will buy you a San Magoo if you need to rinse off."

Gunny threw a bar towel to Mike and said, "Hey guys, Kensey finished his project. Come check out the radio room." He broke out a round of San Magoos. "Beer's on Black Cloud."

Most all of Haven's regulars worked on the radio room at one time or another. The walls of our ten-by-fourteen foot hideaway were decorated, nearly floor to ceiling, with memorabilia from every branch of the service, most of Seattle's fishing fleet, and merchant ships from around the world.

Centered on the wall, adorning the place of honor, was a large satellite photo of the heavy lift ship, *Scrap Dealer*, with a small, armed, ship sporting a huge 'egg' like dome, nestled in the skids on her deck. Gman, who scrawled a caption in one corner, sent the photo. It read: Loose lips sink ships! This photo spoke volumes: it explained how someone found a speck on the Indian Ocean and why I would not be so kind to the next Richard Kopf* I ran across!

Centered on the opposite wall, and my personal favorite, hung a grainy, black-and-white, eight by ten, photo of "Hanoi Jane" perched on a Commie anti-aircraft gun with cross hairs and range marks superimposed on her. This personal photo was a gift from Black Cloud's mentor, himself a seasoned sniper instructor. The caption read: **Micro management sucks!**

The radio room was self-contained. I installed a ductless heating and cooling system, electro-magnetic interference shielding, soundproofing, chemical toilet, and a coffee making system plumbed directly into the water supply.

Harry and Burt, both licensed HAM operators, flipped open the transmit/receive log and nodded their approval at the first entry.

Burt looked around approvingly. "It's a beauty Kensey. We can all **Skype** around the world but talking over the airwaves is . . .

3

just better! I'll build a special file cabinet for our QSL cards. There isn't any room left on the walls to hang them. Now that this is finished what are you going to do before the fishin' gets good?"
"I haven't given that much thought. I have an invite to christen the three-masted schooner, ***Derdrake***, down south in a month or so and Lois is complaining that I don't spend enough time with her. Me and Black Cloud are takin' my new boat down to Portland to chase Springers for a few days . . . but other than that . . . Don't know..."

CHAPTER 2
INVITATION

Any fishing trip with Black Cloud is an adventure. Chasing Springers, (spring run Chinook salmon), in sideways rain on the Willamette River was no exception. We christened my new North River Commander, *Ketch Em' Too*, with salmon blood and decided she was twenty-one feet of mean, fishing machine! Three days of fishing netted us five bright Chinooks; two were slab-sides. I anticipated filling the freezer and smoker with enough salmon to last well into the summer months.

We arrived back in Seattle and my new digs near the Haven around five. It took several hours to erase the blue *Arima, (fiberglass fishing boat),* paint from *Ketch Em' Too's* portside. Playing chicken with a bigger boat, especially one piloted by Black Cloud is always a losing proposition. A little elbow grease and one more hour of work saw *Ketch Em' Too* ship-shape and stowed away.

Lois, my current lady friend, stopped by and Black Cloud, feeling guilty for scratching my new boat, barbecued salmon and put on a feast for us. The sun shines when he cooks. If he was not hiding out from the IRS, he could write his own ticket in any five-star restaurant. After our late dinner, I saw Lois home and did not feel a bit guilty about leaving Black Cloud with the dishes. I considered scullery duty a down payment on the extra work needed to remove *Arima* memories from my new boat.

Black Cloud was asleep in my easy chair when I returned a little after midnight. I was beat! I tossed a throw rug over him and hit the rack. I was in bed five minutes when the insistent, annoying, dingdong tones of the landline woke me.

"Hello, what can I do for you?" I mumbled, still groggy and half-asleep.

"Kensey, this is Bill Masters. You weren't sleeping were you? Boats and I take delivery of *Derdrake* in four days. Get down here as soon as you can. Fly down to Cabo and Boats will meet you. We are looking forward to seeing you. Mamma Maria sends her love and says she will cook something special just for you." Masters sounded entirely too chipper for the hour!

"FMTT (Fuck Me To Tears)! I just got back from fishin' down in Portland! I'm dead on my feet. You guys are taking delivery of your schooner a might early aren't you?" I was fully awake and thinking, "*OK, this isn't unexpected. I can be there in two days. I certainly do not want to miss one of Mamma Maria's fiestas!*" Masters waited patiently for my answer; I made a snap decision. "I'll be there in two days. I will email my travel details later. Now let me get some sleep!" I hung up without waiting for an answer.

Derdrake, I had to smile about that. Very few people knew John Derdrake master of the pirate ship **Sudden Death** inspired my middle name. I was extremely honored that Bill and Boats named their schooner to honor me, **Goat Locker,** and our successful mission against Somali pirates. Delivery was sooner than expected, but I would not dream of missing her debut and, sure as hell, I wasn't going to miss *Derdrake's* maiden voyage.

"*That settles it; I'll book a flight to Cabo first thing in the morning! A vacation in the sun will be a welcome change. Lois is checking Opera listings . . . Baja here I come!*" Those thoughts were my last before drifting off to sleep.

0730 rolled around too soon but the aroma of fresh brewing coffee and sizzling bacon convinced me to get out of bed. Black Cloud was busy in the kitchen.

"Pull a stool up to the counter. Breakfast will be ready in ten."

"Good. That gives me time to book a flight to Cabo." I replied.

"We're going to Cabo?" Black Cloud, looking like a puppy with his first doggie treat, asked.

"Not we Kemosabe! I wouldn't dare get on a plane with you. Hell, you can't even leave the country without a passport or enhanced driver's license. And besides, you have to pick up Varmint, *(Mike's large, scary, specially schooled, Alsatian),* from advanced training today." I ignored the dirty look and booked a flight to Cabo the next afternoon. That gave me ample time to pack and arrange for Gunny to keep an eye on the condo.

"What's in Cabo?" Mike asked while I typed and sent an email with my flight information.

"I'm flying into Cabo but I will be staying on Isla Cedros a little to the north. I want to be there to help christen the three-masted schooner **Derdrake** and sail on her maiden voyage." I gave my watch an exaggerated look. "Hey, Mike, it's goin' on thirteen minutes and I'm fuckin' hungry! What's the hold up?"

"Keep your hair on gramps! What sort of silly name is **Derdrake**?" Mike lifted the frying pan from the gas burner and expertly flipped two perfectly cooked eggs high into the air. They landed with a plop on the edge of the granite counter before sliding majestically onto my bamboo floor.

"Derdrake is my middle name you dipstick and those pathetic cackle berries on the floor are yours! Bet you wish Varmint was here to clean up after you."

"Yeah, yeah, yeah . . . you navy pukes all have weird names and I'm teaching Varmint to bite squid ass every time he sees you. Put some toast in; eggs will be up shortly."

I spent the rest of the day securing my little condo and **Ketch Em' Too** for an extended time of inactivity. Gunny was all primed to take care of the condo and keep all the junk mail from accumulating on the front porch.

I made a quick call to Lois; I hung up and Mike yelled at me from the kitchen. "I'm leavin' now to get Varmint. Hope he didn't tear up any instructors this time! That dog gets smarter and meaner every day! Talk to you when I get back." I did not have a chance to answer; the back screen door slammed shut.

I was not looking forward to seeing the new, stealth-trained, Varmint. He is sneaky, cunning, and deadly; he gives me the heebie-jeebies every time I see him. I hurriedly packed a small wheelie suitcase and staged it next to the front door in case I had to beat a hasty retreat.

I had time to kill before Black Cloud's expected return and decided to start a new journal to chronicle my upcoming adventure. I sat on the couch and tapped out a couple of paragraphs on the laptop. I finished, shut the laptop down, and set about stowing it. I stopped in mid motion; my sixth sense informed me that someone was stalking me.

I turned my head slowly; Varmint sat right next to me, staring. He entered my house, walked through the kitchen into the study and sat down next to me without making a single sound. *"Varmint, you are one scary hound!"* instantly crossed my mind.

"Hi Varmint, glad to see your instructor didn't euthanize you." I said that through gritted teeth.

He curled his lips, bared his teeth, and rumbled deep within his chest.

"Varmint, heel!" Mike's commanded instantly changed Varmint's demeanor.

He turned slowly and silently padded to the kitchen.

My immediate thought centered on relief. *"My heart wouldn't take many more surprises like that! I looked forward to a restful, Varmint free, vacation cruise and fishing trip aboard **Derdrake**."*

*See book "***Goat Locker*** Strikes!*

CHAPTER 3

FLIGHT TO FORTRESS

My US Air flight departed SeaTac an hour late due to mechanical problems. I immediately regretted spending time with Black Cloud. In spite of that, the flight to Cabo San Lucas was uneventful. We landed in bright sunshine, forty-two minutes late. I cleared customs without a hitch and entered the terminal. The heat of the day hit me like a blast furnace and I felt the sweat trickling between my shoulder blades and down my back. The heat, to my frozen-north acclimated body, was oppressive. The terminal's air conditioner was working overtime but could not keep up.

"Maybe forty-five degrees and rain wasn't all that bad!" dominated my thoughts.

Retired Master Chief Boatswain Mate, Ronald Clark, better known as Boats, a large barrel-chested muscular man in his mid to late 60's, is easy to spot in a crowd, but I didn't expect him to be blocking the exit wearing a Hawaiian print shirt, raggedy assed cutoff jeans, huarache sandals, and a **Goat Locker** ball cap.

He had an ear-to-ear smile and greeted me with, "Where's the apron? You're lookin' good Kensey. Why the fuck did you keep me standin' here for so long?"

"I know you hate waiting for anything except paint to dry and you're looking... different. And better I might add! Still a bit grumpy though. Good to see you Boats. You could have painted something or swabbed the deck while you were waiting. You in a rush?" I asked while vigorously pumping his hand.

"We take delivery of **Derdrake** tomorrow afternoon and Bill wanted you here when she arrives. I have a helo waiting so we've got to get the fuckin' lead out. How many bags you got?" Boats seemed annoyed or anxious and he motioned for me to hurry.

"Only this one. No checked baggage. Why the big rush?" I was curious.

"We have to be out of here before the sun goes down. We don't want to be anywhere around here after dark. Fuckin' cartel is just itching for a chance to avenge the ass kickin' *Goat Locker** laid on them! If they had a good sniper we'd probably be toast right now. They sure as hell know the value of a Stinger missile and wouldn't hesitate to use one on us! So let's scram out of here before they try something stupid!" Boats pretty well answered my question, but he added amplifying information while we scurried for an exit.

"They took a few potshots at Miguel and Jorge. Miguel was hit pretty badly. That was six months ago and he has fully recovered. I know why Jorge is so good on the 20mm. He dropped a rifle-totin' dick at fifty yards with his Glock! The druggies don't bother them much anymore." Boats stopped talking and concentrated on snaking us through the terminal. He continuously scanned the crowd until we exited through a side door where a jeep sat idling on the tarmac.

I barely had time to close the door before Boats hastily hung-a-uie and then sped across the taxiway toward a pair of hangers on the far side of the airfield. He reached under the seat, pulled out a Smith and Wesson, model 629, Stealth Hunter, .44 Magnum, fitted with a Leupold, Fx-II scope, and handed it to me and said, "There are four speed loaders in a box under your seat, and an M-16 on the floor behind you, and that baby is dialed in at one hundred yards. Don't look surprised. We don't take any chances. The druggies are less than happy that Bill and I moved down here. Those bastards have been harassing the shit out of us as well as our customers, friends, and families on the mainland. I'm not sure, Kensey, but we think someone informed the new leader of the Cartel, Don Marcos, that we were responsible for killing his predecessor, Don Escobar. This is something new and it started about six months ago when Jorge and Manuel were ambushed."

This was surprising and alarming news. I knew there was bad blood between the Cartel and the Masters' after we destroyed a few of their boats, but open hostilities was something completely different. I hefted the .44, tested the scope, reached under the seat and picked up two speed loaders and set them on the seat between my legs. "Nice piece! We goin' moose huntin'?" I didn't wait for an answer.

The newspapers I perused at the airport were full of caustic national security details. The New York Times did two full-length features that were pretty damaging to the Administration. The articles laid out how our southern borders were a mess. Armed drug smugglers from several Mexican and South American Cartels came and went across the border with impunity. Along with them flowed a river of unaccompanied children from Honduras, migrant farm laborers, and most likely Jihad driven terrorists. That information backfilled what Boats told me and added some perspective to the way we were armed.

I started thinking out loud and Boats nodded his head in agreement while I spoke. "I wouldn't be surprised if it was Dick Head's* boss who passed info about **'The Raid'** to the Marcos Cartel. According to Gman, DC is plagued with leaks and the current Administration is in overdrive trying to plug them." I flipped the .44's cylinder open for emphasis and to check the cylinder; it was loaded with six rounds.

Boats did not say another word; he concentrated on breaking the land speed record driving toward a hangar across the tarmac where a bright red, MD 530F, helicopter sat just inside the large hanger door with rotor blades already turning.

We skidded to a stop with Boats shouting, "Jump out and haul ass for the chopper!"

No sooner did my feet hit the tarmac than the jeep's windshield spider-webbed and showered me with glass. I crouched behind the jeep and scanned the area looking for the shooter. Boats yelled to get my attention and pointed to the next hanger over. I saw motion on the catwalk that ran up the side of the hanger about one hundred yards away.

I glanced at Boats, he nodded and raised his 9mm. He did not have time to get the M-16! "Boats, you see that patch of blue behind the vent? Try to get the asshole to move and I'll take him out!"

I laid three rounds in and around the vent. The reports from the .44 deafened me. Boats peppered the area with fifteen more. The fool in blue exposed his head and shoulders firing at us in full auto. Concrete chips and the rest of the jeep's glass pelted us. The helo's engine revved up and I heard some heavy-duty gunfire from that direction. I laid prone under the jeep, carefully sighted and fired three rounds as fast as I could. One of my rounds or someone from the helo nailed the bastard.

Boats yelled, "Let's go! Get aboard!"

11

I didn't need a second invitation! I ran towards the helo with Boats right behind me. I try to keep in shape but I'm not nearly as fast as I once was. It felt like a lifetime elapsed before I plopped into a helo seat and started to untangle the safety harness.

"Strap up. Put this skull cap on so we can talk on the intercom." Boats yelled at me over the whine of the engines. I glanced back over my shoulder, saw a man in a uniform get in the jeep, and drive away.

I fumbled with the safety harness, and then struggled into the cranial. I was greeted with, "Welcome aboard Meester Kensey!"

"Damn! Is that you Jorge? When did you learn to fly an eggbeater?" This certainly was a surprise!

"Si Skipper! I always want to fly one and Mr. Billings pull some strings for me and Manuel."

"Bueno verte Skipper!" Manuel spoke up from the copilot seat. "I ride shotgun today," he pointed to a wicked looking, smoking, FN-FAL holstered between the front seats. "But I fly too."

"I'll have to tell Preacher the two finest gunners he ever trained saved my ass again but they have new occupations. Damn good to see you both. What's with the smelly fucker in the back?" A goat wasn't something one expected to share a helicopter ride with...

"The goat she be a new breeder for our herd. Don't fuck with her. She bites! It's about tres hours to Fortress; so sit back and enjoy flight. There's cerveza, bottled water, and fresh fruit in the cooler." Manuel did a pretty good job as flight attendant but he wasn't near as good looking as the bouncy purser on my US Air flight here.

"Goat herd...?" I thought. "What have these two boys been up to?"

We lifted off, sprinted a short distance, then shot straight up. The goat, I named her Playgirl, protested mightily, "Na! Na! Naaaaaaaaaaaaaaaaaaaaaa!" and then she shit all over the helo.

"Mother fuckin'stinkin' motherfucker!" Boats, closer to Playgirl than me, shouted down the intercom and thumbed his 9mm's safety 'off'.

All windows that could open flew open. "Many apologies Signors! That goat."

"Playgirl." I interrupted.

"She is very important goat." Jorge pleaded.

"She's fuckin' dinner if I have anything to say about it!" Boats' muffled voice announced through the red paisley scarf wound around his mouth and nose.
"You got another hanky Boats? That *is* some stinkin shit! Anywhere we can land and hose this shit out Jorge?" Boats shook his head and Jorge said no. This was going to be a long three hours. Maybe longer than the **SS Minnow** tour!
"Nice evasive take off? Expecting any more trouble Boats?" I said into the mic attached to my helmet.
"You never know. I am always expecting trouble around here." He answered and said nothing else for the next agonizing two hours and fifty minutes.
I thought to myself *"There is more going on than just taking delivery of the schooner."*
Finally, after an eternity, Jorge started gesturing for us to look down. Off to our right and below, laid out like a satellite photo, was the Isla De Cedros, and the Fortress and its airfields and hangers.
"Thank God!" I thought. *"I will soon be on the ground and out of this flying sewer pipe!"*

13

Chapter 4

THE FORTRESS

Jorge quickly landed the helo close to the hanger. A dark blue van was waiting for us. Jorge and Manuel talked to the driver, motioned for Boats and me to get in, then returned to the helo. I guessed they were making sure the bird was secure, cleaned, and no one plugged Playgirl.

Boats thought they wanted to drag Playgirl to the hacienda with us and voiced his disapproval. "The quickest way to have goat for dinner is to get that stinkin' motherfucker anywhere near me! Three hours with that piece of shit is too long. I never want to see her again. Period!" He pointed his 9mm in her general direction for emphasis.

Jorge and Manuel put their hands in the air and Jorge said, "Si Boats, we get stinkin' goat far away and hose out helo." Boats nodded his head and stuffed the 9mm in his waistband.

"Good call Boats. I'd a plugged that damn goat if you didn't." I wasn't thrilled with Playgirl and the farther away she was the better I liked it.

The driver was hesitant to leave but Jorge and Manuel waved him toward the hacienda. We entered through the gate and Mamma Maria came running down the walkway crying and waving her arms. She ran up to us, threw her arms around me, and almost broke me in half with a bear hug.

"Is so good to see you, Meester Kensey. What take you so long to visit?" She backed away and wiped a tear from her cheek. " I so proud you make my boys successful ranchers!"

"I'm pleased to see you and apologize for not coming sooner. And . . . I can't wait to dive into your famous cooking."

I gently extricated myself from the vice like hug and carefully listened while she motioned for us to follow her. "I feed you well. Please, please come in. Meester Masters is waiting for you and Meester Boats in the library."

We made our way to the library. Boats opened the door and I took a moment to look around before entering. It was as I remembered; nothing had changed. The books, chairs, tables, and furniture were arranged as if no time had passed since the last time we gathered here.

Bill arose from his large leather chair and walked toward us with a cheerful greeting on his smiling lips. "Kensey, it's so good to see you! Glad you could get here so soon. How was the trip down?"

Boats answered before I could get a word in. "We were ambushed at the airport for Christ's sake! Luckily, we weren't killed. As it stands, it is Cartel zero, Fortress two. One of these days they are going to hire professionals and we will be in a world of shit! For now they need to hire at least one more soldier."

"Nice reception you guys arranged for me. You do this for all of your guests?" I sarcastically asked.

"Certainly. Wouldn't want you to feel neglected would we?" Bill replied smiling and pumping my hand in an enthusiastic welcome. He quickly sobered up and asked serious questions. "Anyone hurt? Any damage to the helo?"

"Boats answered quickly, "Yes and no. No one shot up the helo but Manuel and Jorge's stinkin fuckin goat crapped it up. We may never get the stench out! The jeep was shot up pretty good but Tejo drove it off the tarmac and will have it repaired."

Boats hesitated a moment, turned toward me and then continued with an explanation. "Tejo is our man in Cabo and works directly for another good friend, Miguel Olmos. He and Miguel smoothed things over with airport security. Remember Tejo if you ever need help down there." Boats turned back to Masters, "I find it odd that airport security didn't jump into the fray. We did leave real sudden like though. They contact you?"

Bill handed Boats and me snifters of fine Napoleon Brandy; he was deep in thought for a moment. "Airport security and the Cabo police and the Federales *'all'* contacted me." He motioned for us to sit and continued. "All were concerned about our safety and not so much about a body. I consider all three allies in this war we seem to have with Don Marcos. We have always followed the *'trust but verify'* code and I think we should kick the verify part up a notch or two." Bill nodded his head for emphasis. "Yup, verify! For now, though, our schooner will arrive tomorrow afternoon. Bob, I think you will be surprised when she gets here. The only thing we have scheduled occurs after dinner; Boats and I want to give you the grand tour. You know about all the improvements but seeing them is much better than paying the invoices and viewing *.jpg* picture files. I think you will be impressed with the workshops, magazines, and communications equipment. I think more impressive, though, is the feast Momma Maria has been preparing all day!"

"I can hardly wait. It's been a while since I sampled Mamma Maria's cooking. Too long! I'm itching to see what you've accomplished. I hope it's completed since we depleted the remainder of **Goat Locker's** advance money. We'll all have to go back to work if you need to build anything else. By the way Bill, have you heard from Gman lately?" I asked as I sipped the last of my brandy and held the snifter out for a refill.

"As a matter of fact I have. I received a message over secure comms shortly after we had it up and runnin'. All he said was *'consider this contact'*." Bill replied, and then added, "To coin Boats' thoughts, I found that a bit odd... Can you shed some light on what he's up to?"

I sampled my brandy before answering. "Not really; I got the same message. Knowing Gman, something is in the wind! Wonder what he is up to? Guess we will find out whenever he's ready." I replied.

Bill nodded in agreement. "Yeah, Gman moved up a few rungs on the ladder after the raid so whatever he's up to should be interesting. He didn't squawk about us spending the two-million slated for **Goat Locker's** upkeep and outfitting. He either has something up his sleeve or he feels responsible for sending her to Davy Jones." Bill stared into his brandy before ending on a sour note. "We all still feel the loss of **Goat Locker!**"

Before anyone could comment, the silence was broken by a discrete knock on the door. Manfred poked his head into the library and announced in his cultured British accent, "Dinner is served. Please follow me."

It was an awkward moment; each of us was lost in our own memories of **Goat Locker**. We silently stood and followed him down the hallway. He led us out onto the veranda where a long table was heaped with Mexican favorites and pitchers of frosty beer. Several BBQs belched smoke and the smell of grilled meat filled the air.

17

"I hope I'm smellin' that stinkin' fuckin' goat of Jorge's and Manuel's being grilled!" Boats said under his breath.

"You mean Playgirl? Not a chance." I said and laughed while thinking, *"This defines fiesta!"*

There was enough food spread atop the long table to feed a small nation! The beer was flowing and our moods changed from somber to grateful for surviving where **Goat Locker** had not...

The entire Fortress staff attended. Security forces and their families mingled with Bill and his mother, Joyce. Both Gonzales Brothers and their wives were present. I'd never met either Selena or Julietta and started in their direction twice to introduce myself. I'd been waylaid first by Bill who introduced me to his mother, Joyce, and now by Boats. I did notice both Selena and Julietta retreated to the other side of the veranda when I started their way and mentioned that to Boats.

"They don't trust you." Boats stammered before continuing. "Selena thinks you're responsible for the ambush that nearly got Manuel and her brother Miguel killed, and Julietta thinks you are here to recruit Jorge and Manuel for another death-defying mission. And oh, by the way, Playgirl is her goat! You can see the daggers she is staring at the two of us. She's convinced we're gonna have that stinkin' fucker for dinner some day. I hope we can smooth this over." Boats waved to Julietta to come over and meet me. She did an immediate one eighty and engaged Jorge and Selena in an animated conversation.

"Oh . . . stick around Boats. I may need more back up than you gave me on **High and Mighty!**" I pleaded as Manuel with Julietta and Selena in tow headed our way.

"Remember that fuckin' pink apron? See ya!" Boats made a beeline for a frosty pitcher of Dos Equis.

I stood there with trepidation. Jorge approached tightly holding Selena's arm with Julietta one pace behind, "Meester Kensey, I would like you to meet my beautiful wife Selena and my Brother's beautiful wife Julietta. They are first cousins and have heard a lot about you." He turned to Selena and pulled her forward.

"I am proud to meet both of you." I said meekly. "Your husbands saved our lives more than once and are owed a great debt of gratitude. I am proud to know them."

I bowed slightly and offered my hand. Selena brushed it aside and asked matter-of-factly. "Are you here to take my husband away and get him killed?" Her English was accented but near perfect.

"No." I replied. "I came down to see the new schooner arrive tomorrow afternoon, sail with Bill and Boats for a few days, maybe do a little fishing, and then return to Seattle."

Both women glared at me as if I was a politician and incapable of telling the truth. Selena dipped her head to say, "Ok . . ." took Juliette's hand and walked quickly away.

Jorge looked down and stammered a bit making apologies. "I so sorry for my wife's behavior. She worries you here to hire me and Manuel again. She sees all the building going on and that ambush attempt really bothers her. She afraid I be off again and no come back. Please forgive her rudeness."

That conversation put a damper on my spirits but it wasn't Jorge's or Manuel's fault their wives were less than cordial to the guy who recruited them. I noticed that Bill also steered clear of them. I needed to put Jorge at ease. "I understand completely, Jorge. I envy you. It must be nice having someone who worries about you. Please ensure Julietta that my only intention is to vacation and party. No hard feelings! Enjoy the party."

I sipped a Corona and watched a dozen or so kids bash a goat shaped piñata. I smiled at the thought of it being Playgirl. I met most everyone. Our conversations seemed strained. *"He is on a recruiting mission,"* must have been on the back of everyone's mind. Mamma Maria, Julietta, and Selena were in an animated conversation across the room. Every few seconds one of them would glance my way. My ears burned. Luckily, Boats and Masters rescued me and we retired to the Library for after dinner drinks.

Masters opened the conversation with, "Bob, Boats tells me you think Dick Head's controller may be feeding info to the local Cartel? I'm with you there, and I'm sure revenge is on their collective mind! I wish I knew whom Kopf worked for . . . Even Gman couldn't find out or he isn't saying. Maybe there is some pertinent information buried in our 'insurance policy'. You have a chance to study those CDs (booty from '**The Raid**')?" *

"Yeah, a little, but I just skimmed over them. I wasn't looking for anything in particular." I answered, gave it some thought, and then continued. "You know, now that I think about it, might be a good idea to closely study that material. Maybe we can get a lead on who Kopf worked for and pass that info to Jim. I'm sure he and his geeks studied the shit out of those CDs but not with our point of view. We live in a different paradigm and something obscure to them may glare out at us." I paused tapping my fingertips together thinking about Kopf.

"Let's take a look at that, Bob, and you too Boats, when we get back from sailing. We need to stop the flow of information about us. Your reception at the airport makes that clear! Anything making the Cartel's life more difficult helps us here. Eradicating them is probably a pipe dream but crippling them would be nice. Even a peaceful co-existence would be better than what we have now."

"Fuckin' A!" Boats chimed in. "But right now we are burning daylight. You guys ready for a little jaunt?"

"Sure, let's go. I'm curious to see what **Goat Locker's** money bought." I replied.

CHAPTER 5
INSPECTING THE AIRFIELD

I was anxious to see the new facilities. I followed Boats and Masters to a parked jeep. I managed to squeeze into the back and Masters rode shotgun. We quickly cleared the manicured grounds and three-rail fences surrounding the hacienda.

Boats cautioned, "Hang on!", and proceeded to a bumpy shortcut across an open field and then across the runway to a pair of large hangers.

I noticed several small concrete blockhouses directly across from where we momentarily parked between the hangers. They were well suited to protect anyone inside and commanded a field of fire that would be hard to get by. To compliment the blockhouses, dirt revetments were built to protect everything from a seaward assault. Boats, pointing to the blockhouses said, "They double as guard huts. We put armed guards in there whenever we fly. Anyone inside has an unobstructed field of fire and, as an added bonus, they protect each other. I like to call them a defense in depth. The roofs are hardened and we placed mounts for fifty-cals up there. We are on the lookout for a pair of 20mms to make sure anyone thinking of a seaward attack will think twice! No one in their right mind would charge those mean motherfuckers! Look to your right, next to the hangers, you see that small building? That's the communications hut. We installed an HF transceiver and SatCom. We can securely communicate all over the world." That was quite a long speech for Boats but there was a lot here to show off.

Masters motioned for Boats to continue on and drive into the first hanger. "Boats and I turned this hanger into a mini-shipyard. We can repair or fabricate most anything we might need to keep our charter fleet afloat. We even have a damn good electronics repair shop outfitted and ready to go. Most of our security force personnel spent time in various shipyards and are well versed in repairing all sorts of ships. And, of course, that was and will remain a major consideration for who we hire to work for us. The entire port side of the hanger is an engine shop. We can repair diesels as well as state of the art gas turbines. Over there, on the right, is the hydraulics and machine shop and a full-blown carpenter shop. We can do anything needed above the water line. We don't have a dry dock but we have most everything else, including a sail shop! Boats and I are jazzed about our new facilities. Not only can we maintain our charter fleet, well, just one schooner for now, but we plan to build the rest of our fleet right here. Bob, we used practically all of what remained of ***Goat Locker's*** maintenance funds.* I don't feel right about that. Two million didn't buy everything you see here. Some of the heavy equipment just showed up on our doorstep. Secure satellite communications equipment and an installation team followed the same routine. I still don't know exactly who paid for that. All of my inquiries about funding and where all this equipment came from have been stonewalled. Most everyone here thinks all this is your doing and that's why they are uneasy about your presence. That is especially true where Selena and Julietta are concerned! They are certain you are building a base and looking for recruits."

"Bill, this is fantastic, but I didn't have a thing to do with the extra equipment. I'll be sure to ask Gman about it if he ever contacts me. I like the way this facility is laid out. It gives you quite a base for working on your charter fleet. Don't *even* feel guilty about spending ***Goat Locker's*** money. Uncle Sam said it was for upkeep and repair. We didn't scuttle her they did. Consider the extra equipment and money spent as payment for that! I don't think the crew we sailed with minds a bit. Their payoff was substantial and besides, I've kept them informed about what you and Boats accomplished here. Sweet Cheeks might bitch but only to weasel a vacation here and a ride on ***Derdrake***! If you invite Fritz down you may never get rid of him once he sees the engine shop. You and Boats really out did yourselves. This entire facility is far out cool! What's behind the green armored door?" I pointed to a heavy steel vault door.

"You are observant. That door leads to the armory. I off loaded all the leftover M60s, M-16s, Stingers, LAWS (Light Anti-Tank Weapon System), 9mms and ammo, 76mm ammo, and all the 20mm rounds from ***Scrap Dealer*** and had the armory specifically built to house both ordnance and a variety of firearms. I do wish we still had the 20mms but they went down with ***Goat Locker***. I'm lookin' for a couple to install here, but so far no luck. I made the armory big enough to hold twice what we carried on *Goat Locker*. The building will withstand armor piercing rounds as well as a 500-pound bomb. A 1000-pound bomb might trip the sprinkler system and flood the magazine!"

"You don't fear an attack from the Cartel, I see!" I said with mock surprise.

"What? Me worry!" Masters deadpanned a passable impression of Alfred E. Neuman and then continued, "Not really. We have enough firepower and supplies to withstand a major assault. I think they know that too. That's why they plan their attacks on us when we are away from here. Let's jump back in the jeep. I'll show you what we've done with comms." (Communications, radio, satellite, etc.)

Entering the air-conditioned comms suite was a welcome relief from the residual heat trapped in the hanger. On the way here Boats explained that the communication hut was a hardened building much the same as the armory. Some of the gear I recognized. Some of the modern stuff I didn't.

"Where the fuck did you get the Cyclone III?" I immediately spotted the HAM, (armature radio), radio set and was pleased and flabbergasted!

I walked over to the SA400A, lit it off, and dialed in a memorized frequency in the ten-meter band. "I should be able to raise the Haven when this comes to ready. Back in Seattle, I installed a scanner that would log and record any traffic on preselected frequencies. As an added bonus, it was set to contact my iPad or iPhone and patch the traffic through if it was anywhere near a WiFi, G3 or G4 service provider. We got any of that around here?" I asked.

"Yup." Masters piped up. "We have a wireless network set up and a wired network as backup. Both are connected via satellite to the internet."

"Ok let's see if anyone is awake at the Haven. CQ, CQ, CQ, This is SGS Three Niner Zero, Over."

"This is GER five three six in Honolulu. Does the weather in Seattle still suck? Me . . . I'm enjoying the fine sunshine and a steamy mug of Seattle's Best." Crackled from five or six speakers in near perfect 5.1 surround sound.

23

"Eat your heart out. I'm enjoying eighty degree sunshine, cold cervesa, good company and about to take a cruise on a three masted schooner. " Hawaii didn't hold a candle to Baja this time of year.

"This is Hotel-Alpha-Victor-Echo-November and it is colder than a well diggers arm and raining cats and dogs! Come home Bob we know you miss it!"

Harry was in the radio room. I could hear Billy Joe Royal on the jukebox in the background. "Don't miss the rain. When did the new call sign come in? The Jarhead around?"

"Just got the new call sign from the FCC today. Frank's ridin' heard on Black Cloud while he's fixin' the float. He wants it done right. Julie's tendin' bar and I was just fixin' to shut down for the night. What are you transmitting on? I've got you five-by-five with no static."

"The prettiest damn Cyclone III you've ever seen!" I just had to rub it in. Ours at the Haven functioned perfectly but was shabby and well used.

"Jeez . . . If you guys get tired of them send one here. Hawaii Over and out."

"Burt might consider it for a lifetime supply of chocolate covered macadamia nuts, but no dice on this beauty." I was surprised that Hawaii came up on our frequency. HF comms worked and it was time to sign off. " Good talkin' to you Harry. I'm going to do a little experiment and see if our scanner will pick up, log, and connect to a CW only signal. I'll send SGS in Morse code. Email me if it works. This is SGS Three Niner Zero. Over and out."

"Don't have too much fun. Send a good .jpg of the ***Derdrake***. Hotel-Alpha-Victor-Echo-November. Over and out." That was that. The comms suite was great. I was sure Bill put the Hallicrafters transceiver in just to make me happy. Before shutting the set down, I turned off the modulation and keyed SGS in Morse code twice.

"Thought you'd like that Bob. Boats and I looked all over hell's half acre for it. I contacted Sparks. What's he doin' in Thailand? He gave me an ET Chief Hancock's number. Hancock located the Hallicrafters for us. Said he knew you . . . Talk about six-degrees of separation." I did a double take and both Masters and Boats gave me one of those, WTFO looks.

CHAPTER 6
ANTICIPATION

*D*erdrake was due in before 1300 tomorrow afternoon. I knew very little about her. I knew she was a three masted schooner with a black hull but not much else. I talked to everyone at the fiesta but no one knew much or was keeping quiet and the most Boats or Bill would say was a nondescript, "Wait and see."

We returned from the grand tour a little before 2000. Fiesta guests started drifting away and most were gone by 2300. Almost everyone apologized for leaving early. I did not feel apologizes were necessary since we all knew tomorrow was going to be a very busy day and a working one at that. I was happy to slip away at 2330 (eleven-thirty pm) for some much needed sleep.

I had one chore to accomplish before hitting my rack *(climbing into bed);* I logged my iPad onto the hacienda's network and checked for new email. My iPad chimed and the dulcet tone of Holly's *(obstinate computer from the British telly program, "Red Dwarf")* voice informed me, "You have mail from the Cat, Lister."

Pressing the mail icon immediately played an mp3 file sent from safehaven.org. Even to my untrained ear, the Morse code was pretty raggedy. Regardless, S-G-S came through loud and clear. I made a mental note to practice keying Morse code to improve my fist!

I slept in 'till 1030. A light breakfast, a short workout, and a few minutes in the pool revived me. This was much more pleasant than my ritual mile walk to Starbucks in sideways, frigid, Seattle rain each winter morning. I thought to myself, *"I could get used to this!"* I returned to my room just before eleven, shaved, and then climbed into the rain locker to wash off the pool chlorine and shaving soap.

I had the shower temperature just right and started the second refrain of "Norwegian Wood" when Manfred, the butler, knocked on the door, stuck his head into my room, and shouted, "Mister Masters says come to the library and hurry please."

I turned off the tap and shouted back, "Roger that. Tell Bill I'll be there in about ten."

I thought I'd get everyone's attention this morning so I dressed in khaki cargo-shorts, a Hawaiian print shirt decorated with woodies and palm trees, slipped bare feet into a pair of Sperry Topsiders, and completed the ensemble with my *Goat Locker* ball cap. I had three minutes to spare before being late to the library. I slipped the strap of my Mk. I Mod. II TDT binoculars over my head, stole a quick glance at myself in the full length mirror, and thought, *"I sort of look like Troy on the Tiki III . . . Maybe an older Troy."* and hustled my way to the library whistling a Carly Simon tune.

Bill was in the library studying a printed sheet that I took to be a recently received message. He gave me an amused once-over before informing me, "*Derdrake* is less than twenty miles out. Jorge flew out to her a few minutes ago and will pilot her in. We have to get a move on. I want you to see her under full sail."

"What are we waiting around for? Let's go!" I was keyed up and did not want to miss a moment of *Derdrake's* arrival.

We all but ran to a waiting jeep. Bill jumped into the driver's side and before I could get fully settled, he tromped on the gas and threw me back against my seat. I grabbed my hat and held on for dear life. We skidded to a stop at the head of the pier. Bill jumped out and was halfway to the end before I even got out! It was obvious: he was anxious to take possession of his new schooner.

"Nice duds Twidget! It's about time you showed up." Boats quipped as I approached him.

I did a quick spin-around so Boats could get the full impact of my wardrobe. "Yeah, no thanks to you. You bugged-out and left me at the mercy of Julietta and Selena last night. I'm lucky to be here at all!" I quipped with mock anger.

"How much longer?" Masters asked changing the subject. He sounded impatient.

"Five minutes until you should see the masts above the horizon." Boats answered.

There was a cackle of static on the small walkie-talkie that Boats had in his hand, and Jorge's accented voice came from the speaker, "She handles like a dream Meester Masters! We had one small problem. The pennant and Flying Jib got a bit tangled on the forestay but we got that straightened out. We should be in sight right now."

Suddenly Masters started jumping up and down and pointing, "There she be. I can just make out the tops of her sails!"

I adjusted my 10 x 50 binoculars and scanned the area where Masters was pointing. *Derdrake* was magnificent! She was heeled over; every inch of canvas was straining as she beat into a freshening breeze. A bow wave climbed half way to her scuppers. "Christ! She must be making a good seventeen-knots with half a square mile of canvas out! That is phenomenal, just fuckin' beautiful! She looks to be bigger than **Goat Locker**!" I realized I was the only one talking. Everyone else had binoculars glued to the best looking sailing ship since the ***Cutty Sark***.

Her ebony black hull stood out in stark contrast to chalk white sails. It gave her a sense of power and mystery. She rapidly approached and I could see more and more detail. It looked like her main deck was teak and railings were mahogany. The Stars and Stripes flew from the top of the main mast and a pennant flew from the forestay. I couldn't make out what it said. When she was within half a mile, she suddenly came about directly into the wind. Her sails dropped and automatically furled. I had a million questions to ask Masters and Boats but they were busy pacing up and down the pier as excited as a couple of kids on their first trip to Disneyland.

Derdrake effortlessly shifted to diesel power and slipped gracefully into her berth. I made myself available as a line handler for the forward spring-line. It wasn't until I had my line firmly secured that I realized she was a steel-hulled schooner! I wondered what other surprises she held.

"Isn't she the most beautiful ship you ever saw, Kensey?" Bill said quietly as we stood there and admired her. He continued, "She is 103 feet long, 20 foot beam and has a 7.5 foot draft. I had her equipped with 671N Detroit diesel, the newest model radar, and GPS navigation systems on the market. She has a steel hull, with teak and mahogany decks and woodwork. I had the plans modified from ***Tom Colvin*** to accommodate us here. All the sails were hand made by a friend of the family so were practically free! Let's go aboard!"

"You bet. I'm looking forward to checking her out!" I exclaimed.

The fluttering pennant flying from the forestay caught my attention. I stopped to read it's message: "DEDICATED TO ONE FINE SHIP: *GOAT LOCKER*." I felt my eyes water a bit but shook it off and continued up the gangplank following Bill and Boats. Bill led us to the main salon and down to the Captain's Cabin. The door was open. *"Do the surprises never end?"* I thought. A good friend stood up and grasped my hand shaking it with gusto.

"So good to see you again Mr. Kensey. How have you been for the last year?"

"Captain Shaw, what a pleasant surprise. You are the last person I expected to see aboard a sailing schooner. I've been fine. How is *Scrap Dealer*? Did you bring *Derdrake* from the yard?" I asked.

"I earned my sea legs on the deck of a two masted schooner. When Bill told me about the *Derdrake* there was no way I wasn't going to sail her down here! We put her through her paces on the way. A few minor things need adjusting but the sails, diesel, and navigation are all dialed in and spot-on. Jorge helo'd out early this morning. He wasn't thrilled about being dumped in the ocean and having to swim to us but there is no way a helo could get close enough to drop him on deck. He wanted to pilot the ship into port. That young man has many talents. I expect seeing *Derdrake* with every inch of canvas straining was quite a sight. That was all Jorge. He wanted to have the windward railings awash before we hove-to!" Captain Shaw said with a twinkle in his eye.

We inspected *Derdrake* from stem to stern. Boats, Bill or both, opened every hatch, cover, and door. Everything from the engine and generator room to the staterooms was spotless. I noted with interest that she had a small communications room with an HF transmitter combined with modern VHF and satellite transmitters and receivers. That wasn't the only notable oddity; she had an auxiliary navigation station and wheel mounted in a bubble amidships to compliment her more traditional station forward of the mizzenmast. Whoever had the helm on a cold rainy night was going to love that! She boasted a closet sized armory. *"Something else you don't see on every charter yacht."* I thought. It looked like a dozen or so rifles and other small arms could be stored there with ease.

No one wanted to leave but Bill finally said we had to make preparations for the maiden voyage scheduled to start about 1000 tomorrow morning. I, for one, was looking forward to five days aboard this magnificent sailing ship. Boats stayed aboard to organize things and make sure we were ready to sail tomorrow while Bill, Jorge, Captain Shaw, and I returned to the hacienda. Tomorrow was going to be an adventure...

Chapter 7
MAIDEN VOYAGE

Bill, Captain Shaw, and I were the last ones up at 2330; we talked comfortably in the library waiting for Boats to return and report *'ready for sea'*. We spent the time discussing the ins and outs, and attributes and quirks, involved in sailing ***Derdrake***. We finished talking about important things and began trading sea stories about our last voyage and adventure. That excursion took place a little over one year ago but reminders of what we accomplished popped up every month or so when a story about this or that politician or high government official resigning or being reassigned ran in obscure newspapers or the "E" section of the "New York Times." I was about to call it a day when Boats found us in the library and reported we were provisioned and ready for sea at first light.

Bill dribbled a splash of brandy in each of our snifters and a shot in Boats', raised his glass, and toasted, "To our maiden voyage! Cheers."

Captain Shaw followed with, "Fair winds and following seas."

I finished up with, "May this voyage be less strenuous than our last." That earned nods all around; we clinked snifters, drank down the brandy, and retired for the night.

****

Derdrake completed her last training jib; I set sails and prepared to come into the wind. I looked forward to beating into a light breeze. Running was peaceful and quiet but hot. Air across the deck would cool things down nicely. Each of us, Masters, Boats, Jorge, Manuel, and I worked our way through two watches. We ran her on bare polls with the diesel, beat her into the wind, tacked her port and starboard, ran her down wind and jibbed, and rigged and trimmed sails when off watch. In addition, each of us ran ***Derdrake***

several hours from the secondary conning station. Any one of us could sail this fast modern schooner on the open seas.

We cruised North by North-West, more or less, for two days. Our goal was to be fifty or sixty miles off Isla Guadalupe when we finished training. Boats said there was some killer yellowfin fishing in that area and we would hang around there for a day and a half then before sailing back to the fortress.

We worked our electronics mercilessly! Radar, comms, navigation, and our side-scan sonar operated flawlessly. I regretted leaving my iPad at the hacienda, but we had the internet and Netflix on the big screen TV in the salon. I was falling in love with the side-scan sonar and thought I would see if I could cram one aboard ***Ketch Em' II***. Jorge swore jellyfish marked on the screen and I was convinced he was right. I couldn't wait to get a feather trolling to see how well it found fish! It looked like we were in a school of something so I dropped and furled all but the main and was pleased when we settled out at four-knots in a gently rolling sea.

Masters popped the forward hatch and padded back to the cockpit. "See something on radar Bob?"

"No Captain, just fish on the sonar. Isla Guadalupe paints nicely sixty miles north and east of us, but other than that, not a thing since Boats logged a contact at thirty-five miles south, steaming east. That was around 2345 last night. Once this fog burns off, we should be able to see clear to the horizon. It looks like we have an eighth of a mile of visibility right now so we shouldn't ram anyone."

Masters gave me thumbs up and said, "See that you don't! I'm surprised there aren't any tuna clippers out here. Fishin' is supposed to be hot. I'll have deckhands Eduardo and Federico get half a dozen rods over the side, and we'll change the watch every two hours. Miguel will relieve you at 1000 instead of 1200. I know you are dying to get a feather wet!" That news was welcome but I really did enjoy sailing this ship as much as fishing!

I watched Federico set-up two large rods and two fighting chairs. He rigged a couple of tuna-tacos and got them fishing for yellowfin. Eduardo rigged four rods off the fantail fitted with various lures for blue fin and albacore.

At 0935, Miguel came out on deck munching a breakfast sandwich and carrying a mug of coffee. "I relieve you. Anything special I need to know?"

"Negative. We're on a northbound heading, making three-point-four-eight knots. I'm looking for fish on the sonar. Nothing on radar and no one squawking on HF or VHF. Looks like a glorious day!" I checked my log entries and then signed the deck log. I gave Miguel a smart salute and said, "You've got the deck; I'm going to grab a bite to eat then show you how to catch yellowfin!"

"Si, Meester Kensey. Your last fix correct?" Miguel was worried about being lost. This was his first time this far out to sea.

"Think so." I answered. "Take another fix then log it. That way you'll know for sure."

"Si, aye! Meester Kensey you got Rolaids? Boats is galley rat."

"Thanks for the warning!" I laughed, and negotiated the three steps down into the salon.

Miguel maneuvered deftly while chasing down fish that he probably spotted on sonar. I felt ***Derdrake*** heel into a well executed starboard tack as I poured a cup of coffee and asked Boats to cook up a sandwich for me. I didn't want to spend the time waiting for a full breakfast. I wanted to get back up on deck and fish for tuna! I waited for Boats to finish putting my breakfast together before commenting, "Jeez Boats. You'd look a whole lot cuter in an apron. I know where I can get a spiffy pink one . . ."*

"Fuck you Twidget! You want to wear that breakfast?" That was more or less the answer I expected as I ducked a wet sponge and dishrag pitched at my head.

Miguel, just finishing up a log entry, smiled at us and said, "We have fish on sonar. We should hook up soon."

That was good news. "Boats and I will be on deck shortly." I said to Miguel and he returned to the topside helm.

I turned my attention to Boats. "I'll give you a hand securing the galley then let's go fish!" I retrieved the sponge and winged it back scoring a direct hit. "Easy target! Couldn't miss that oversized beam."

"Fuckin' Twidget! I'll have you holy-stoning the keel if you keep it up!"

Once we got the galley ship-shape, Boats and I took up positions fishing off the stern. We bantered back and forth about how quick and smooth ***Derdrake*** responded to the helm. A smattering of salt spray pelted us as the deck rolled under our feet. I commented

33

about the fishing being sluggish. Boats said we might be trolling a tad slow and asked Miguel if he could add a knot or two to our speed. Jorge and Manual came up from below and informed me that real coffee was brewed. Boats, galley-rat for the day, glared at them but did not comment. Deckhands Eduardo and Federico stifled a laugh and looked busy tending rods.

I dumped two-thirds of a cup of Boats' mud over the side, winked at Jorge and Manuel, "You guys take over. You're bound to have better luck than us."

"Na we've been up all night. It's the rack for me!" Jorge answered. "How about you Manuel?"

"Yeah me too. I'm beat." He waved his arms around to Federico and Miguel, "These guys can watch the rods." The brothers I'd grown very fond of plodded forward and down to their berths through the forward hatch.

I turned to Boats, "Let's go below and get a decent cup of coffee."

"I got a pink apron for any fuckin' twidget thinks he can do better!" Boats bellowed loud enough to be heard back at the Fortress and then followed me below.

I drew a cup of coffee from the urn, inhaled deeply and loudly of the steam, and then commented on the un-mud-like aroma. Before Boats could react Miguel yelled, "Radar contact 35 miles to the east. Don't look to be closing. Looks like she . . . between Isla Guadalupe and us. Most likely is tuna fisherman."

I acknowledged Miguel, told him to log it, and continued savoring my delicious brew. Bill was in the galley brewing a cup of Earl Gray tea. I asked him if he heard Miguel.

He said yes, and he'd keep an eye on it, but agreed with Miguel about the radar contact being a tuna clipper.

Before I could needle Boats about the coffee being drinkable, Miguel's excited voice blasted from the PA speakers, "It looks like a couple of fast boats approaching. No idea where they came from. Better wake rest of crew. Don't like this one bit."

Bill motioned at Boats and said, "Go wake the brothers."

My Spidey senses tingled and I started aft without a word. *Derdrake* shuddered and shook; a thunderclap rolled over her decks!

"What the fuck was that!" I yelled. Bill lay crumpled in a heap near the galley stove and Boats was in the passageway crawling on all fours. I felt lucky. I was knocked to my knees a bit stunned but not seriously hurt.

I felt ***Derdrake*** luff into the wind and heel over. I may never forget the horror of Miguel staggering into the salon holding a belaying pin that skewered his throat. There was little blood. The belaying pin formed a perfect cofferdam. I could hear Federico screaming in agony as Miguel crumpled into a heap on top of me. I rolled out from beneath him and felt his neck for a pulse; there was no hope.

I glanced forward in time to see Boats prop Bill up against the bulkhead and run toward me yelling, "Let's get up on deck!"

I started up the ladder and another explosion near the bow rocked ***Derdrake***. I turned to Boats and yelled as loud as I could over my ringing ears, "Better get forward and see if anyone's still alive and make sure we are aren't taking on water!"

I popped out of the hatch just in time to see the foremast rigging and sails splinter off to the starboard side and a fireball erupt on the fo'c'sle. Eduardo was nowhere in sight and Federico was tangled in the starboard lifelines, lifeless, limp, and bloody. I reversed course and went directly to the auxiliary conning station, fired up the diesels, and put the ***Derdrake*** into following seas hoping to keep the fire away from the salon.

I engaged the autopilot and ran aft. I stepped out on deck and spotted a high-speed boat flying by the port side. Two men riddled ***Derdrake*** with automatic small arms fire. I felt a horrible pain in my right arm and it went limp. I flattened myself on deck and Boats, crouching low, ran past me carrying a Barrett .50 cal. Manuel, wearing nothing but his skivvies, followed close behind carrying his FN-FAL at the ready. Bill staggered by trailing an M-16 in one hand and holding his head with the other. I pulled him down beside me and shielded him from another jolting explosion just aft near the water line. Salt water cascaded down drenching us and the diesel shut down. We were dead in the water!

I heard the Barrett and the FN-FAL start firing. Incoming small arms fire was still fierce. Bullets struck the hull with a definite ting and whine as they ricocheted. Jorge appeared out of nowhere with a pair of M-16s and a Stinger. He handed them to me then ran back toward the armory. A heavy machine gun started firing from

our fo'c'sle. *"Thank god!"* I thought. *"We have a chance with Jorge on the M-60!"*
My right arm hurt like hell but the numbness was gone and I could use my hand. I tightly wrapped the wound with my shirt and Bill tied a square knot to keep it in place. He didn't look right and was functioning well below par. I took up a kneeling position, rested the M-16 on the gunwales and commenced firing. I could see two Zodiacs with five attackers, laying off about 250 yards, pouring AK-47 rounds into ***Derdrake***. Thank God for steel gunwales!
Boats had the range and a well-positioned and stable Barrett. He squeezed off two rounds that literally exploded a pair of attackers and their outboard motor. Manuel, firing short bursts, eliminated three attackers in another boat. Everyone's attention refocused on the last boat. Jorge laid into them with the M-60 machine gun. They all but disappeared in the mist kicked up around them. Manuel had to reload and the Barrett barked. The single attacker alive, revved his engine, spun the Zodiac about, and attempted his getaway. I grabbed the Stinger, aimed, heard the Doppler lock, and fired! The small missile ran straight and true; it struck the outboard motor, and the boat disintegrated in a bright fireball.
The ensuing silence was deafening. Boats was lying on deck holding pressure on a nasty, bleeding, wound in his left leg. Jorge was helping Boats stop the bleeding. Jorge wasn't unscathed; it looked like he suffered from burns on his hands and legs. He must have pushed burning rigging and sails over the side. Manuel used his rigging knife to cut a sling from ragged remnants of the mainsail and gingerly slipped his left arm into it. Bill, still sitting on deck beside me, appeared dazed and confused. Rivulets of blood dripped from his nose, ears, and right temple. Miguel was dead in the salon and there was no sign of Federico or Eduardo anywhere. My right arm was bleeding and hurt like hell but I was thinking clearly. I carefully studied topside to see what it would take to get us back to the Fortress. Of all the luck! One rod set up on the port fighting chair was bouncing up and down wildly! We had a yellowfin on . . .

CHAPTER 8
COMMUNICATING

"Bill, Bill you got your hearing back?" Bill turned toward me rubbing both ears, and nodded his head yes. "Speak to me! I need to make sure we aren't sinking and to see if we've got comms. You gonna be ok if I leave you here?" One of Bill's pupils was noticeably larger than the other and he was still rubbing his ears.

"Yeah, I think so. I don't think anything's broken but I'm a bit dizzy. I should be able to make it to the salon. Check on the others first. Did we lose anyone?" Bill was talking loudly over the buzzing in his ears.

"I'm afraid so. Miguel is dead in the salon, Federico took the full force of the initial explosion, and Eduardo was blasted overboard. Right now Boats is down with a leg wound, Manuel has his left arm in a sling, Jorge suffered some burns, and I got hit in the arm but still have use of it and my hand." I delivered this bad news in a loud, gruff, harried voice. Things needed to get done.

"If Boats is down you've got the ***Derdrake***! Get us the fuck out of here before someone else comes looking for us!" Bill was definitely thinking straight.

"Señor Masters! Let me help you to your cabin." Jorge said with genuine concern. "Señor Kensey I'm pretty much ok. The burns are mostly third degree with a few second. Boats and Manuel are gonna stay on deck with the Barrett and M-60. What you want me to do once I get Señor Masters taken care of?"

I thought a second. "Make sure we're not sinking and then get the spare mainsail rigged and get us moving! Head north. Go easy on the sail trim. We are missing the forestay and the aft-stay is shaky at best! The aft helm and binnacle are destroyed. You'll have to isolate the hydraulic lines before you can use the rudder! I'm gonna try to rig the long wire and see if I can raise some help on HF."

Time was marching on and I feared whoever attacked us would try again; I hollered at Boats. "Boats you two stay put! Keep your eyes peeled. Any of those shitheads come back shoot first; don't ask questions. I've got the *Derdrake* and I'll be below trying to get comms up." With that said, I vaulted into the salon and ran forward to the auxiliary machinery room to light-off the power generator.

With the generator purring and power flowing, I stopped in the radio room and lit off the HF set and made a few off air checks. Once that was completed, I grabbed supplies from the medical locker and hurried topside through the forward hatch. Boats was my first concern. I dropped a roll of duct tape, several large battle dressings, splints, and ibuprofen on the deck beside him.

"You need any help with these or can you and Manuel manage?" I asked, plainly in a hurry.

"We're good. See if you can get us moving toward home." Boats grimaced through the pain. "Sons'a'bitches fucked my boat up! They're gonna fuckin' pay . . ." I didn't take the time to reply. We all felt the same.

My immediate concern was contacting the fortress. I frowned in distress when I discovered the long wire antenna lying on the starboard side, main deck. *"Thank God it's in one piece!"* Was my immediate reaction. The coaxial cable feed leading to the antenna was severed about eight feet from the connector. That was a bit of good luck. All I had to do was make up both ends of the cable with new connectors and then screw them together and hoist the antenna as far up the main mast as I could. I scurried to the radio room and gathered supplies I needed to repair the antenna. I met Jorge in the passageway on my way topside. He struggled with the spare mainsail but informed me he didn't need any help. I told him Boats had some mild painkillers if he needed them, and to wrap his burns in gauze then ace bandages before rigging the main.

He acknowledged with a loud, "Aye!" before I went topside trailing an extension cord tied with an underwriter's knot through a belt loop.

I hastily made up the cable ends, checked them for shorts with a digital pocket ohmmeter, connected the two ends, and looked around for a means to hoist the antenna up the mast. Jorge had the main sail rigged with a makeshift boom traveler stretched between the aft, port and starboard lifelines. He took two and a half turns around the starboard, mainsheet winch and started ratcheting the main sail into trim.

I yelled at Jorge, "We got helm?" He gave me thumbs up. "I'll grab the wheel and get us moving!" I raced to the helm, spun the wheel to starboard, and watched the main mast as the sail started to fill. The mast wobbled a bit and shuttered. The mizzenmast groaned and protested as the side stays started bearing a load. *Derdrake's* bow swung and she started moving! I glanced at the Lowrance Elite-5M Baja GPS display and breathed a sigh of relief as it started tracking. I set the autopilot so we were taking the wind two points off the port bow. I ran aft through the salon and yelled as I came out on deck. "Help me get this fuckin' antenna up the main mast! We're on autopilot and will be good until one of us can get to the helm!"

"What you want me to do with this yellowfin we have hooked up?" Jorge shot back. One fishing rod was still bouncing around like Jack Sparrow's sword during a boarding fight.

"Fuck it! We need comms right now!" I yelled back and motioned wildly for him to come and help. Jorge raced forward and pointed to a halyard that ran from the port side stay to the main mast spreader. He tied a bowline through the eye on the end of the antenna and we hoisted it most of the way to the spreader. "Cleat that off good! I'm going to see if we have comms!" I shouted over my shoulder and raced for the radio room making sure not to trip over piles of debris littering the deck.

I dialed in an international emergency frequency, keyed the mic and then thought better of it. The Mexican Navy, Armada de Mexico, would be monitoring this frequency but so would the ship that our attackers came from.

I switched to a memorized ten-meter frequency and keyed the mic. "CQ, CQ, CQ. This is SGS-390 over." Nothing! Not even static greeted me. I tried several more times with no answer. Power out, VSWR (Voltage Standing Wave Ratio), and reflected power all looked good but the modulation meter didn't even quiver. We were transmitting but not modulating! I quickly connected the CW key (continuous wave), broke out the Morse code book, took a deep breath, and sent, "S.O.S. *Derdrake*." I sent that three times followed by our GPS coordinates. I would have Boats or Manuel repeat that every half hour. I hoped to God Hawaii or Safe Haven received our

39

message. Right now, I needed to get us hidden in the mist and our radar signature masked by Isla Guadalupe. I was bone tired and my arm hurt like hell. I thought four or five hours had passed since Boats and I were arguing about who was the better fisherman. I glanced at the GPS; we were making 4.356 knots and it was 1147.

"I just cut the yellowfin lose. If you don't have anything for me to do I'll try to start the diesel." Manuel looked dejected, a bit at odds, and in pain from an obviously broken left wrist.

"Give me a hand; we need to get the Skipper up here and keep him awake. I'm sure he has a concussion. We need to get some defenses in place and need to make sure we are not taking on water! But, first, we need to drop off half our speed and get as close to the shore as we can." I was thinking, in overdrive. *"I need to get close to shore and creep north. That will make us hard to spot on radar . . . I need to rig a forestay on the mainmast and possibly set a jib to give us some speed if the diesel could not be started. I need to set defenses and need to keep sending SOS! Crap! I don't have enough hands . . ."*

Chapter 9
DISCOVERY

Jorge entered the salon from below decks. "Don't bother trying the diesel. That RPG round we took aft near the waterline ripped the salt-water intake right off the manifold. We've been taking on water but the bilge pumps almost kept up. I drove a DC, (damage control), plug into the hole and we should be completely de-watered in half an hour. I found this laying on the deck . . . It must have fallen out of the overhead. I have no idea what it is. Any ideas Mr. Kensey?"

Jorge handed me a black box, light in weight, about the size of a pack of cigarettes with an antenna attached to one end and a minuscule winking green LED.

"Son of a bitch. GPS tracker." My first thought was to throw it over board! I just finished reading a spy novel, "Operation Mince Meat," and that gave me some ideas about trying to deceive our attackers. I was certain they were looking for flotsam, a sign of our demise, and searching south of Isla Guadalupe. The GPS tracker probably could not transmit through our steel hull after being dislodged from the overhead and sitting on the deck plates, but it certainly was broadcasting our position now.

****

Crewman Jenkins, aboard the one-hundred nine foot tuna clipper *Andiamo,* a lumbering relic of the old fleet, poked his head out the door of his navigation station and yelled into the bridge. "Captain Richmond! Captain Richmond! I'm receiving a weak, but unmistakable signal from the transponder aboard ***Derdrake!***"

Captain Richmond, a tall, lean, tanned, stern, American barked, "Where the fuck are they?"

"They appear to be near the Southern tip of Isla Guadalupe about fifty miles away." Jenkins knew what was coming next and grimaced.

"God damn it! Give me their course, speed, and position." Captain Richmond screeched while advancing throttles to full speed. *Andiamo,* happy at five knots, protested mightily. She struggled and shook and slowly gained speed to please the caustic Captain. She did not know or care that the Captain's puppeteers would skin him alive if he failed. Captain Richmond was mighty displeased about abandoning the search for his three zodiacs and strike-force but sinking **Derdrake** and making sure, no one survived was his primary goal. That shouldn't be too tough he thought. *"I still have a seven man crew, a couple of RPGs and half a dozen AK47s. They don't stand a chance!* Jenkins! Give me that fuckin' course and speed now or I'll drop you where you sit!"

Jenkins, completely cowed, replied. "Captain, I don't have exact figures; the signal is weak and fades in and out. **Derdrake** appears dead in the water right off the coast. She'll probably round the southern tip of the island and make a bee line for her home port." He hoped that would get Richmond off his ass.

"Useless piece of shit boat! It'll take us three hours to get there!" Richmond banged his fist down on the binnacle. "Come take the helm Jenkins and I don't pay you to fuckin' think! I have shit to do before we finish this job."

"Aye aye sir!" Jenkins did not dare say he just lost the transponder signal.

****

"Jorge, find something to barely keep this afloat, a chunk of that burned spar on the fo'c'sle would be perfect, and set it adrift." I was plotting to buy us some time but had to think it through. *"We were sailing north at about two knots. Visibility was down to under one eight of a mile. The current was southerly at about 4 knots . . . the wind was on-shore at about 7 knots. We should be around the northern tip of the island before 'they' whoever 'they' are discover the GPS transponder. If the transponder antenna dips in and out of the water as it rides the waves that will make it even more difficult to find and buys us more time . . ."* It was worth a shot.

Jorge wrapped a section of burned, splintered spar, with some ragged, half-melted, sail Mylar, cleverly tangled the GPS transponder in it, and then set the whole package afloat off the fantail. Manuel and I helped Bill to the salon and Boats, with the aid of a crutch made from the back and legs of a teak deck chair, hobbled in and sat beside him. I told Jorge to scrounge something to make a forestay and jury-rig a jib. Manuel was looking for something to saw gun ports in our beautiful mahogany coach works. It broke my heart but had to be done. I planned for Boats to handle the Barrett .50 cal and Manuel could probably handle an M-16. I would use his FN-FAL and Jorge would be on the fo'c'sle with the M-60. I staged our two remaining Stingers aft and the four LAWS forward.

The salon clock chimed five bells, (1430), and we were as prepared as we could be. Manuel found a battery powered Sawzall, cut cross-shaped gun ports along the port and starboard coach works and scrounged hard salami, cheese, French bread, apples, and hard-boiled eggs from the galley. I asked Boats to take the helm and keep us as close to shore as he dared. The side scan sonar gave us a good degree of confidence that we would not end up on the rocks of Isla Guadalupe! I trimmed the mainsail and we slowly gained speed.

Jorge and I wolfed down some food and guzzled a quart of Perrier. On our way to the fo'c'sle, Bill motioned me over to him.

"What can I do Kensey? What shape are we in?" Bill spoke in a slightly slurred voice.

"Were not sinking or taking on water. That fuckin' GPS transponder is gone but we are still up shit creek! Diesel is dead. We are eighty or more hours from the Fortress and comms are anyone's guess. You and Boats can key our SOS every half hour and hope we are transmitting. We are going to run for it when it gets dark. That's the good news . . . You certainly have a concussion and probably a fractured skull. You will have to man an M-16 in a firefight. That's the bad news. . ."

Chapter 10
CONTACT

Manfred knocked gently on the library door and entered. "Excuse me Mum . . . do you know anything about these things?"

Joyce Masters put the finishing touches on her hand written letter; she looked up and answered with mischief in her voice. "It's a c-o-m-p-u-t-e-r Manfred, an iPad from the looks of it."

"Yes Mum I do believe it is an iPad. It belongs to Mister Kensey. He left it in his room and it keeps talking. Do you know how to turn it off?"

Joyce shook her head no. Both gave the iPad a suspicious look when it chimed followed by Holly from the BBC television series "Red Dwarf" speaking. "You have mail from the Cat, Lister."

Joyce looked a bit puzzled, scowled, and said, "I don't know how to shut it off. Who do you suppose Lister and the Cat are? Mister Kensey likes a good mystery I'll bet they have something to do with the novel he is thinking about writing." Manfred handed the iPad to Joyce and started to retreat from the library as only an English butler can.

"Wait Manfred! Take this to the communications building. Engineers are there working on equipment. They'll know how to shut the iPad off."

"Yes Mum." Manfred extracted a fine gold watch, secured to his waistcoat with a beautifully segmented gold chain, from his pocket, and checked the time. "I will be back in time for four o'clock tea Mum. It shouldn't take me more than fifteen minutes to get there and back."

Manfred chose a jeep and drove to the radio hut using the rough, bumpy, goat trail, short cut. He loved being 'out of character' and still sported a slight grin when he entered the communications hut. "Excuse me sir. Can you help with this iPad? It is rather obnoxious and I can't seem to shut it off . . ."

The iPad chimed followed by a message from Holly. "You have mail from the Cat, Lister!"

"That, Sir, is what I mean." Manfred handed the iPad to Nolan.

"Far out Man! That's Holly from the Red Dwarf. I've gotta get that app." Nolan, a thickening, gangly man with a shock of white hair wearing khaki pants and long sleeved denim shirt with his name embroidered above the single breast pocket, blurted out as he reached for the iPad. "Let's see what we have here . . . Manfred is it?"

"Yes sir. This belongs to Mister Kensey so be careful with it." Manfred cautiously handed the iPad to Nolan.

"All you gotta do is press this button, tap 'Mail' with your finger and viola." Instead of the standard mail app opening up, a sound file whispered from the tiny speakers. Nolan looked puzzled then listened intently. "Hey Cole come over here. You're a ham radio guy. You keep up on your Morse code?"

"Sure, you never forget useless shit like that!" Cole approached, stood beside Nolan and Manfred, held his hand up for silence, and listened intently. "Whoa! Whoever's sending this isn't very good on the key." Cole listened more closely to catch the sloppy code transmission. "Shit! That's S.O.S from the *Derdrake*! The next set is a letter followed by a series of numbers . . . lat and long I'll bet."

"Damn! I must notify Miss Masters immediately! She isn't anywhere near a radio repeater and won't answer the phone. I must be on my way. Would you please inform Jesus on the public address system, he's in charge of security." Manfred drove like Sterling Moss, logging airtime, all the way back to the hacienda. He drove right up to the front door, left the engine running, and sprinted to the library. When the library door burst open, Joyce jumped up from behind her desk; she was startled and completely surprised.

"We just received an S.O.S. from the *Derdrake* Mum!" Manfred blurted out.

****

On the bridge of the ***Andiamo,*** Captain Richmond asked with unusual calm and consideration, "You see anything on radar Jenkins?"

"No ship Sir . . . The cliffs and ground clutter pretty well obscure everything else." Jenkins had been on the helm for three hours and really need to make a head call!

"Piece of crap radar! How about the GPS signal? That any fuckin' better?" This, the Captain spat out more in character.

Jenkins gave some serious thought to his answer. He dreaded this moment for the past hour and a half. That kept his mind off his over-full bladder. "The signal is better and I get a hit every seven or eight minutes. *Derdrake* appears to be stationary in that cove about fifteen miles dead ahead. She's probably anchored trying to make repairs, Sir."

"That Masters is one ballsy son of a bitch! There's one entrance to that cove through the shoal water, and it's tighter than a virgin. Call me in half an hour Jenkins. I'll take us to within half a mile. You'll have to take the utility boat in the rest of the way. I'll send the engineer and one deck hand with you. You got any problems with that?"

"No sir, but I do have to take a leak real bad! Could you have someone relieve me on the helm?" Jenkins was in genuine distress.

"Get the fuck off my bridge and quit whining'! I relieve you, but make damn sure you're ready to take care of *Derdrake* and her crew!" Jenkins didn't hesitate; he was off the bridge in less than ten seconds flat.

****

The Fortress was in a bit of turmoil; Jesus, out of breath, galloped down the hall and skidded to a halt just inside the library door. "I got here as fast as I could Mam!" Joyce acknowledged him and sat back down behind her desk. She fished out a bright white sheet of monogrammed stationary from a side drawer and started writing furiously.

The note, written in a neat hand, was completed in less than two minutes. Joyce stood and reached across the desk with it in hand. "Jesus, take this to the communications building and have Nolan or Cole contact the mainland authorities. Hurry!"

Jesus scurried back down the hall, jumped into the still idling jeep, and raced toward the communications building.

Joyce turned to Manfred. "Please try and raise the mainland on the satellite telephone. Contact our man, Tejo in Cabo. Tell him

what's happened and have him get the Federales involved in an immediate rescue."
Jesus stopped abruptly outside the communications hut door. He entered the building and demanded immediate attention using a loud, commanding voice. "Mister Cole, Mister Nolan, please, drop what you are doing; I have instructions from Miss Masters. Get on the radio and transmit *Derdrake's* last coordinates on Mexican Maritime emergency frequencies. Miss Masters wants you to keep broadcasting until someone responds. She wants rescue boats on the way! Cole, you need to stay glued to Mr. Kensey's iPad and contact the house on the landline the moment you hear anything."
"Hold up a minute Nolan!" Cole interrupted, considered the situation and then hurriedly continued his thoughts. "The SOS was relayed from a place in Seattle called '*The Safe Haven Radio Room*', by an automatic system Mr. Kensey set up. I am in contact with them and a HAM station in Hawaii. They may or may not be able to hear us aboard the *Derdrake*. The SOS and coordinates come in every half hour like clockwork but they do not acknowledge any of our transmissions. They are traveling north at about six knots. Jesus, I'm a cynic, but they may be transmitting CW in the middle of the ten-meter band because that's the only communications they have or they don't want someone to know where they are and what direction they are traveling. We may want to hold off on transmitting their position until we think this through." Cole looked skeptical and sounded worried.

****

Derdrake's mizzenmast groaned noticeably as the breeze freshened. "We're looking ok Bill. The fog is lifting and we're making good speed. We rounded the north end of the island about ten minutes ago. We'll hug the coast for another half hour or so and then run like hell for the Fortress!" I didn't think I was being overly optimistic; we were in better shape than a few hours ago.
Jorge and I rigged a forestay and jib that we jerry-rigged from the mizzen staysail. It was over-large; more like a jenny than a jib. Our speed settled out at a good six knots and I thought that would increase once we got away from the lee of Isla Guadalupe and set the sails wing-and-wing.

Bill, still under the weather, started to reassert his authority. "Bob, I'm XO, (Executive Officer, second in charge), until we're out of this mess. Let's get some chow, and, you and Jorge and Manuel need to get some sleep. Boats and I can manage for a couple of hours. We can set the autopilot once we turn and run for the Fortress. It will be dark soon and the only way we will know if someone is on our ass is when they start shootin' at us or we are lucky enough to see the phosphorescence they kick up by being in a hurry! We will be ready if or when they come!" That was a long speech even for a one-hundred percent Bill Masters. He was on the mend.

****

Captain Richmond was alone on the bridge of the ***Andiamo,*** and a red hair away from rage. "You've got to be shitting me!"

"No Sir. We are just inside the breakwater and the ***Derdrake*** is not here. My portable tracker has a strong signal about two-hundred yards ahead." Jenkins was puzzled and the two crewmembers with him shook their head knowing life aboard ***Andiamo*** was going to be rough from here on out.

"Bastards are fuckin' with us! Get your asses back here right now or I'm leaving you!"

With Captain Richmond so irate, Jenkins was tempted to beach the utility boat and take his chances scaling the cliffs of Isla Guadalupe.

Chapter 11
A SPECIAL FRIEND IS CONTACTED

The initial flurry of activity was long past. The Fortress adopted a heightened security footing; most everything was buttoned down according to preordained plans. The two intervening hours between receiving an unexpected SOS and now were well spent setting rescue plans in motion.

Joyce Masters' initial reaction was to immediately notify the world of her son's plight and GPS coordinates. Jesus convinced her otherwise. Now she wasn't so sure: it didn't feel like a rescue was in motion. She fully expected to hear from her son before now.

She thought back two hours and relived her conversation with Jesus. *"Mam, I think it much wiser if we do not broadcast the **Derdrake's** position. Tejo will be discreet and he has contacts who work with the Federales in Cabo and the Armada De Mexico in La Paz. He is at the airport office and I should be in contact with him shortly."* She vividly recalled Jesus holding the satellite phone and striking the redial button every few seconds. He appeared nervous but Bill put him in charge of Fortress security in Miguel's absence because he could think clearly and decisively in situations like this. She recalled the relief she felt when Tejo finally answered. She eagerly listened to the one-sided conversation hoping her fears would be assuaged.

****

The rain in Cabo San Lucas was relentless. Tejo ran between hangers with a make shift bumbershoot fashioned from today's newspaper held ineffectively over his head. His cell phone buzzed and vibrated but he ignored it; Carlos, the guard at the office door, just informed him that the phone in his office was ringing and that trumped everything else. Tejo scrambled into his office, fumbled with his keys, and then opened the desk drawer housing the 'red phone'. He stood in a widening puddle of dripping rainwater and

51

shivered slightly but not from the cold or sodden clothing; he knew this secure phone only rang for one reason, and this was the second time in a week!

Tejo grabbed the receiver, keyed in his security code, and then held his breath and waited for the clicking and whirring of the secure connection to complete.

"Tejo! This is Jesus at the hacienda. We just received an SOS from the *Derdrake* and need you to contact the Federales and initiate some immediate action!"

"A la chingata!" Tejo replied, "I will contact our compadres. What happened? Where is *Derdrake*? How are Boats and Mr. Masters? Do we need the Armada De Mexico and Federales or just a couple of pescabarcos (fishing boats)?"

"Protocolo 'dos' estáensulugar. (Protocol two is in effect.) Only call on a secure line! At the moment, all we know is that Mr. Masters sent out an SOS and GPS coordinates. Knowing how bad we pissed the Cartels off, I think the Federales and Armada De Mexico are needed! Copy down these coordinates. Do not, I repeat, *DO NOT*, pass them on to anyone you are not one hundred percent sure of! I'll keep you informed as we learn more. Keep close to a secure phone! Is that understood?" Jesus ended the conversation with stern emphasis.

"Si Jesus!" Tejo understood only too well that secrecy was paramount. When the connection was broken, he removed a well-used Rolodex from the desk drawer containing the 'red phone'. He thumbed through it stopping on the number he sought. His party picked up on the second ring.

"Ola, Este es el Capitán Rouales. ¿Cómo le puedo ayudar?" {Hello this is Captain Rouales. How may I help?} Juan sounded preoccupied. If he was entertaining one of his many senoritas, he was not going to be happy.

Tejo took a deep breath. "This is Tejo. English por favor. Please go secure. I will initiate." Several seconds of whirring and clicking signaled a secure connection. "I need you at the airport office immediately. We have a serious problem!"

"Si. Give me ten minutes. Can you tell me what this is about?" Tejo knew Juan would ask and he had a ready answer.

"We received an SOS from our Padrone near Isla Guadalupe! We probably need your navy friend." With that, he hung up, looked through the rolodex, and jotted down a few more numbers and waited.

Captain Juan Rouales, a member of the Mexican Home Land Security force, was a trusted friend and Fortress retainer. If anybody could get the Federales involved, it was Juan. True to his word, he arrived at Tejo's hanger office in nine minutes.

Captain Juan Rouales flew into the office with his cell phone glued to his ear speaking rapid, excited, Spanish. "Lo pasoahora y le devuelva la llamada con información actualizada. {I'll pass that on right now and call you back with updated information} English por favor: you are now on speakerphone. Can you give Señor Tejo an update?"

"Señor Tejo, I am Contralmirante Olmos with Armada De Mexico, We have a patrol boat, PC-331 in the area. She is about seven hours from Isla Guadalupe. We will intercept *Derdrake* and render assistance. Is there anything specific you can tell me to help locate her?"

Tejo hesitated a second, "She is unable to talk to us but sends her GPS coordinates every thirty minutes in Morse code." Tejo read off *Derdrake's* last position and the frequency to receive her SOS." You can talk to us on that frequency too. For security reasons, it is best not to use standard emergency channels. We fear *Derdrake* was attacked but do not know for certain. Your assistance is deeply appreciated!"

"Thank you Señor Tejo. Do you have a secure phone number where I can reach you?" It was reassuring to have Rear Admiral Olmos involved.

Tejo repeated his number twice then added as an afterthought. " Sir. I am monitoring the HF frequency I gave to you. It is better if I keep informed that way. It keeps the chatter down to minimum and is one less thing you have to worry about."

"Very well, Señor Tejo. Our patrol boat has been notified and is making best speed to intercept *Derdrake*. We will dispatch a helo from Ensenada at first light to aid in the search." Juan's cell phone went dead signaling Rear Admiral Olmos broke the connection.

****

Each agonizing minute that ticked by waiting for news of her son loosened Joyce Masters' resolve to keep his whereabouts secret.

When the phone finally rang and Tejo reported the Navy was involved her anxiety eased but nothing seemed changed. She still had no idea about the condition of her son or the *Derdrake*. She felt it was time to increase the number of people involved in the rescue, but was hesitant to countermand Jesus.

The landline jingled. Jesus picked it up, listened intently, and then abruptly hung up. "Mam, Cole reported he was contacted on the radio just after the last SOS transmission from the *Derdrake*. Patrol Boat PC-331 expects to intercept her in about eight hours. All we can do is wait. I'll be in the radio hut if you need me."

"Jesus, are you absolutely certain we shouldn't inform our friends on the mainland? I'm sure they can help." Joyce was determined to get as much help as she could.

"Mam, we cannot be sure the information wouldn't fall into wrong hands. I am certain we are doing the correct thing. Right now I need to be in the radio hut in case Señor Masters sends more than SOS and coordinates." Joyce nodded in acquiescence and allowed Jesus to beat a hasty retreat.

****

Captain Richmond paced *Andiamo's* wheelhouse trying to concentrate. Jenkins and two crewmen returned from their fruitless search of the cove and were back aboard. *Andiamo* was headed south along the island's west coast, and would turn east in half an hour. If he guessed correctly, he would see the *Derdrake* on radar within the next two hours. If not, she was probably hove-to near the north end of Isla Guadalupe. He would have to devise an alternate plan of action for that eventuality. The increased chatter from the HF scanner made it difficult to concentrate and formulate a plan 'B'. He was annoyed and miffed. His options for destroying the *Derdrake* were sinking rapidly along with the setting sun.

Chapter 12

MEETING OF THE MINDS

"*God* damn it, shut that radio off Jenkins! I can't think with all that fuckin' noise. Captain Richmond thought, *"I know where you are going. I will cut you off and sink you in the open waters between here and Fortress! If you are hiding like the coward you are, I'll find you and sink you where you lie. Kensey, you are a dead man. I will see to it!"* Captain Richmond knew he had the advantage of time on his side. He could run down the ***Derdrake*** no matter where she was. The loss of his attack team worried him, but he did not think the ***Derdrake*** and crew was in any shape to put up much of a fight.

****

It was quiet aboard ***Derdrake*** and most of us were in good spirits. Jorge rigged a whisker pole to keep the jib running wing-and-wing. The mizzenmast groaned under the strain and the main mast protested mightily. ***Derdrake*** slowly picked up speed and her jerry-rigged sails billowed in a steady breeze.

"We're looking pretty good, Bob." Boats was on the helm checking our course. "Autopilot is set. We're running a little over eight knots. If this breeze holds, we'll make the one hundred seventy miles to Fortress in about twenty hours. Let's hope whoever attacked us left the area!" Boats was in pain from a nasty bullet furrow plowed down his left thigh, but super glue and duct tape, butterfly-bandages stopped the bleeding. He hobbled around but was okay on the helm and could handle the Barrett from a sitting position in a firefight.

"Yeah . . . let's hope we're alone out here!" I paused and looked at our plot myself. There was a lot of ocean between Fortress and us. We were going to need food and rest to get there in one piece. "This isn't as good as your burned eggs, but it'll fill the void." I handed Boats, Bill, and Manuel brown bags of battle-rats (battle

rations): ham and cheese roll-ups, boiled eggs, an apple, and one frosty San Magoo.
"Fucking Twidget. Beer's great but a hot meal would be nice!" Boats was hurting but couldn't let a dig go by.
"Now children . . . Be nice! We have enough trouble. And why aren't you wearing an apron Bob?" Bill interjected. It was good to see him back in the game and in good humor.
I laughed and answered, "Couldn't find that pink number Boats likes so much." It was time to get back to serious business. "Jorge is going to catnap on the fo'c'sle with the M-60 and LAWS. I'll catnap in the cockpit with the FN-FAL and a pair of Stingers. Bill, you, Boats and Manuel set up a watch rotation for the helm. There's no moon tonight so a hunter will be on top of us before we see them unless someone screws up and shows lights. Bill . . . what are your thoughts on shooting first or trying to warn someone off with the VHF radio?"
"If they are lit up with running lights we'll warn them off. If they are dark and dirty they killed three of us and fucked up my boat with no warning so we will sink them the same way!" Manuel and Boats nodded in agreement, and Bill about summed up Jorge and my sentiments exactly . . .
There is one good thing about an annoying, painful, wound: when you move or roll over you instantly wake up. I dozed off several times. Each power nap ended with a vivid reminder of our last encounter with hostile forces. We were tired and beat up; I hoped everyone else was catnapping and not sound asleep. I checked the time. My watch glowed back 0106 in vivid green. *"Time to get some coffee and check on everyone."* I half mumbled to myself.
I eased my way through the salon. The helm was bathed in a soft, dim, red glow from a single desk lamp, and I wondered if my chronometer was wrong. Boats was on watch . . . Again? "Are we there yet?" I said more in passing than needing to know our position.
"No but we are fifty miles closer. Have a nice snooze Sleeping Beauty?" Boats was sarcastically informing me that *he* was keeping close watch.
"Fuck no Hop-a-long. Want some mud?" I knew it was tough for Boats to get down to the galley. I thought I'd cut him a break. "I'll check on Jorge and be right back." I tiptoed to the galley not wanting to wake Bill or Manuel.

I stepped out on the fo'c'sle through the forward hatch and handed Jorge a cup of steaming coffee. "Everything okay? It's darker than the inside of a goat tonight. I hope no one runs over us!"

"Si. It's been six hours and I haven't had to adjust the sails. I hope this breeze keeps up all night. You feel like you're in the crosshairs?" Jorge sounded a bit rattled.

"Yes, my senses are tingling . . . If we're going to get hit I think it will be before day break." I sounded more confident than I felt. "Look for any lights. You can see a cigarette flare for five miles at sea. I'm going to get some coffee for Boats then I'll be back in the cockpit" I retraced my steps back through the galley to the salon and helm.

"'Bout time you got back. I was close to dying of thirst. Been gettin' garbled audio over the VHF. Someone is trying to contact us. Don't know who, but I sure hope they're friendly and not the fuckin' yahoos that shot us up!" Before I could answer Boats, the VHF set blared static and a distorted voice transmission. Both coffees sloshed to the deck when I instinctively lunged for the radio mic.

"Baque hacia el este no identificado, identifíquese. Esto es Armada de México patrulla barco *PC-331*" {"Unidentified eastbound vessle, identify yourself. This is Armada de Mexico **Patrol Boat PC-331.**"}

Everyone was instantly awake. Boats grabbed the mic. He paused, looked at Bill and then me. Bill shook his head *'no'*, pointed to the Barrett, and picked up his M-16. Manuel was already in firing position. I scrambled aft, double checked the magazine on the FN-FAL, released the safety, and reaffirmed the position of my Stinger missiles. I heard the reassuring metallic clink of the M-60 being loaded and locked.

The radio crackled back to life. "Buque hacia el este no identificado, identifíquese. Esto es Armada de Mexico patrulla barco PC-331. Usted está en un curso de colisión con una más lento buque viaja el sur-este. Inmediatamente cambiar de rumbo." {"Unidentified eastbound vessel, identify yourself. This is Armada de Mexico **Patrol Boat PC-331**. You are on a collision course with a slower vessel traveling southeast. Immediately change course."}

That altered the situation. I set the safety, put my rifle down, and scrambled for the radio. Boats was already on the air. "Pan-pan.

Pan-pan. Pan-pan *Patrol Boat PC-331*. English por favor. This is sailing schooner *Derdrake* requesting immediate assistance."

Patrol Boat PC-331, twenty-five miles south and east of the *Derdrake*, immediately came to flank speed. Captain Hernandez scrutinized the radar repeater. He had been monitoring the SOS from *Derdrake* and tracking the disabled schooner on radar from ninety kilometers away. He could see a ship on radar traveling east rapidly approaching *Derdrake*. The unidentified ship would close the four miles separating them in under half an hour. "Sailing schooner *Derdrake*, this is *Patrol Boat PC-331* maintain course and speed. We are here in answer to your SOS." Captain Hernandez quickly shifted to Spanish, "No identificado este limitado recipiente, inmediatamente el curso del cambio o participarán. Reconoce." {"Unidentified east bound vessel, change course immediately or we will engage you. Acknowledge."}

****

Captain Richmond on *Andiamo* had to respond and respond fast. He knew he could not engage *Derdrake* or *Patrol Boat PC-331*. That would be suicide! He heard the pan-pan and that left only one option. "*Patrol Boat PC-331*, English por favor. This is tuna clipper *Andiamo* out of Ensenada. We are experiencing main generator problems but are able to render assistance if needed." Jenkins, his back to the captain, smirked while Captain Richmond retransmitted his message.

"*Andiamo, Andiamo,* this is *Patrol Boat PC-331*. We acknowledge your transmission and course change. No assistance is required. What is your destination?"

Captain Richmond had to think fast. "This is ship's master Richmond of the *Andiamo*. We are experiencing main generator problems and require repairs. We were enroute to San Diego, California. Over."

"Very well. Stand clear of this area. Make port at Punta San Carlos for repairs. I will notify port authorities of your difficulties. *PC-331* out."

"Shit . .piss. . . FUCK!" Richmond was walking in tight circles, hands clasped behind his back and glowing brighter than Rudolf's nose on Christmas Eve. "Jenkins you have the con. I'll be on the fo'c'sle. Set course for… fuckin' Punta San Carlos."

The captain scurried out the bridge hatch. That was a good thing since Jenkins was having difficulty containing his mirth. He reveled in his Captain's discomfort. In less than two minutes he could hear Richmond yelling on the fo'c'sle. "No goddamn it! I told you morons to throw the fuckers over the side! The whole fuckin' Mexican Navy will inspect this boat in Punta San Carlos!" Not only did Richmond have to deep-six all the expensive weapons but he had to sabotage the generator.

Jenkins smiled when he set a new course and thought comforting thoughts, *"I'll never have to sail with this asshole again!"*

Richmond made one last trip to the bridge before disappearing to his cabin. He was somewhat subdued. "Jenkins, set our speed at five knots. Do not disturb me. I have to draft a report for the Paymaster about this piece of shit operation. You'll have to back me on the details. Hope to hell it is accepted." Captain Richmond retreated quietly mumbling to himself. *"Kensey, you sorry motherfucker! I will meet you again somewhere, sometime, and when I do . . ."*

CHAPTER 13
RESCUE

Regulars of Safe Haven seated around the back, rear table were engaged in a late hour poker duel. Subconsciously, everyone had an ear on the AR-5 speakers behind the bar even though the poker table action switched from half-hearted to intense. *Derdrake* missed transmitting her 0130 SOS and that heightened everyone's worry about Bob Kensey's fate.

Harry exited the *Radio Room*, dropped three quarters into the Wurlitzer on his way by, and took up position behind Burt. The gravelly voice of Kenny Rogers singing "The Gambler" drifted over the poker table.

Black Cloud looked dejectedly at his last blue chip when Burt wickedly grinned and raised him twenty dollars. A nasty looking Colt Python magically appeared in his left hand. With black, steely, eyes glued on Burt, he flipped the cylinder open and pushed a Texasten out of the safe-chamber. "See your sorry twenty and raise you ninety." Black Cloud pushed the last blue chip into the pot and carefully laid the Python on the table beside him.

Burt's piercing blue eyes never wavered. He pushed his eight blue chips into the pot, then unstrapped his Mickey Mouse Timex and dropped it on top. "Call . . ."

Gunny took up station behind Black Cloud. Other than worry over the *Derdrake* not sending an 0130 SOS, this was the most interesting event happening at the Safe Haven.

"Read em' and weep. . ." Black Cloud slowly drug a hole card to the edge of the table, grabbed its edge and slipped it under the second then turned a pair of teepees face up. Matched with the pair of black eights and queen of hearts, up-cards, it looked like he would be able to fuel *Dead Eye* for the return trip to Hansville.

A spaghetti-western tune replaced Kenny Rogers on the Wurlitzer; Burt frowned and flipped over a one-eyed-jack. He slowly drew the last hole card to the edge of the table, picked it up and gave it a mournful look, slowly shook his head, and then dropped the eight of hearts on the table. He picked up Steam-Boat-Willie from the stack of chips and strapped him back on his wrist.

"In the real service, 'trips' beats a dead-mans' hand any day. Looks like you'll be paddling that scow home" Burt's eyes twinkled; he slowly and deliberately raked in the two hundred eighty seven dollar pot.

Black Cloud stared daggers across the table and that prompted Burt to tweak the ground pounder a little more. "Wanna play Ingin' poker for that Python, dogface?"

Before Black Cloud could answer, the AR-5s came alive with a static riddled voice. "Amos de Casa, amos de Casa. Este es el barco de patrulla PC-331; estamos junto a la Derdrake. ¿Copia?" {"Casa Masters, Casa Masters. This is **Patrol Boat** *PC-331*; we are alongside the *Derdrake*. Do you copy?"} No one really understood Spanish but *Derdrake* came through loud and clear. The poker battle was instantly forgotten; everyone immediately left the poker table and gathered at the bar.

"*PC-331*, *PC-331* this is Casa Masters. English por favor. We copy you five-by-five. Over." No one noticed the bar door silently, slide open or the well-dressed man in his mid fifties enter The Haven.

"Casa Masters, We will escort the *Derdrake* to port at Isla Cedros. She is severely damaged but under way with sail and we should arrive about 1300. My deepest condolences, two crew are missing and one deceased." Gunny threw his bar towel across The Haven and noticed a stranger seated at the table nearest the bar. *PC-331* continued her litany of despair. "Señor Masters, Clark, Manuel Gonzales, and Kensey are aboard receiving first aid. They will be transported to the Casa Masters by helo at first light. Señor Jorge Gonzales has burns but will stay with the schooner until she docks. *PC-331*, out."

Harry rushed to the radio room and picked up the mic. "CQ, CQ, CQ, This is Safe Haven. Do you copy? Over."

Black Cloud, one ear on the AR-5, intently watched the stranger in the mirror behind the bar. He slowly and deliberately drifted away from the group and approached him. A neat man with a blue striped tie was seated at the small round bar table. One hand was in his raincoat pocket and the other on the table palm down.

Black Cloud could see the edges of a business card protruding from under his fingertips.

Cole Thomas keyed his mic. "Safe Haven we copy you five-by-five. Over." The radio conversation crackled from the AR-5. Gunny stood in the doorway to the radio room and gave a chopping signal while pointing to the speaker.

The stranger slid his calling card across the table. Black Cloud picked it up; his steely eyes boring into the stranger. The business card was plain white adorned with an embossed chess piece, a knight, on one side, and an email address centered in understated black print: jb@paladin.net.

Before Black Cloud could speak, the stranger did. "Master Chief Kensey speaks highly of you Mike. I see he is down in Baja. Tell Harry to transmit this . . ." He flipped his calling card over and wrote: **JB sending medical team to Casa. Will arrive in six hours.**

"I may have a job for you. We'll talk soon . . ." With a nod of his head, Jim Billings slipped from the Safe Haven as unobtrusively as he entered.

Chapter 14

THE FORTRESS

Gunny and Burt moved into the radio room to hear the conversation with Fortress. Both looked puzzled. Harry had reverted to a bazaar, abbreviated, lingo in his angst over Kensey's well being. "What's the word on Kensey? Is he *'a-f-u'*? {all fucked up} How about the schooner, is it *'s-s-f'*? {still fuckin' floatin'} Any idea about the *'f-a-h'*{fuckin assholes} who did this? WTFO?"

Static crackled from the speakers and Harry adjusted the frequency to receive a clear signal. "I only know one blue-water Coastie that talked like that . . . Am I modulating with BMC Markham? Sorry I can't fill you in on any details yet."

Black Cloud squeezed into the radio room and unceremoniously dropped Jim Billings' business card face up on the small desk. Harry was in the middle of an interesting conversation with Cole Thomas on Isla Cedros laced with Falcon Codes and strange acronyms. *"FalconOne!* Yeah . . . I'm the same Harry Markham you relieved on the nine-oh-nine boat. *'Falcon One-oh-four'*? What's up with Baja?"

Atmospherics were near perfect and very little static came over the air now. "I'm dialing in some interesting Comm-gear and fixin' some *'Falcon one-two-four'* stuff for the Masters' down here. What are you doing in Seattle? The cervesa is great down here but could you send me some decent coffee? Seattle's Best would be nice!" Harry gave Black Cloud a 'WTFO' look.

"This, I'm sure, is from Gman." Black Cloud flipped the calling card over and pointed to the message with some urgency and very little good humor. "Transmit this verbatim!"

Harry didn't hesitate. He knew when Mike was kidding and when he was not. "Cole this just, literally, walked in the door. Copy it exactly." Harry looked to Mike who nodded in approval. "JB sending medical team to Casa. Will arrive in six hours. End of message. You should probably give that to the someone in charge . . . immediately!"

"Jesus, our head of security . . ., now, is listening. He just informed the Hacienda. What about that coffee?" Harry thought the coffee down there must really suck or Cole was being security conscious. Either way it was time to sign off.

"Send us a couple cases of Modelo Especial *f-f-s* {fine-fuckin'-suds} and I'll ship you five pounds of Starbucks Americano in drip grind." Harry drove a hard bargain.

"Ten Roger! I'll be here another ten days so make it quick! Casa Masters over and out."

"I'll *f-g-i*{fuckin' get it} later today. Safe Haven, over and out!"

The entire crew crowded into the radio room. There wasn't much else anyone could do here. Frank flipped Jim Billings' calling card over and studied the design curious about its meaning.

Harry ventured the first guess. "If that was Gman he is probably a chess master . . ."

Black Cloud did not comment but Burt nodded in agreement.

Gunny lit off his iPad and Googled Paladin. Forty Nine Million hits showed up. The most prominent was the twelve knights who were champions of Charlemagne. "That has to be it . . . Gman has a sense of humor after all. Guys I'm gonna turn the lights out. It's late. Anyone wants to crash here is more than welcome to." Gunny shut down the iPad and turned off the lights, and left the radio on and the volume low.

****

Fortress tension slackened with the rescue of **Derdrake** but Jesus was still anxious and most of all, weary. He was responsible for everyone's security. The cryptic message from Seattle weighed heavily on his mind. He immediately called the hacienda and delivered the message but followed it up with a visit to Señora Masters. She assured him a friendly plane would be landing within seven hours and it would carry a medical team. Jesus accepted that but thought, *"I'll not drop my guard just the same..."*

A sleek, dark gray, nearly black, **Gulf Stream G-550** with no markings touched down at 0827. Jesus drove the follow-me jeep and guided the ominous looking jet to a parking spot in front of the big hanger. The only communications with the jet was ten minutes earlier when they informed Fortress that they would touch down at 0827, they needed accommodations for two, and a place to park the Gulf Stream inside a hanger.

When the engines completely shut down a man and woman descended the accommodation ladder. The pilot remained aboard and made sure yellow-gear was correctly attached to the Gulf Stream. It would be pushed into the hanger as requested. Jesus jumped out of the jeep and greeted the pair.

"Buenos días, I am Jesus Martinez. Señors Masters, Kensey, Clark, and Manuel arrived about half-an-hour ago. I'll take you to them."

Doctor Phillip Madison extended his hand. "Buenos dias! I'm Doctor Madison and this is Nurse Sibley. She is our x-ray technician and triage nurse. Our pilot will stay with the plane."

A prim, very attractive, dark haired woman accepted Jesus' outstretched hand. Jesus was drawn in by her soft brown eyes and easy Southern Drawl. "Jesús buena mañana. Esun placer conocerte. *{Good Morning Jesus. It is a pleasure to meet you. }* I'm sorry but that is the extent of my Spanish . . . Could you have someone unload my x-ray equipment and medical supplies and take them to the patients?"

"Si señorita." Jesus spoke rapid Spanish into the microphone attached to his dark blue, uniform shirt. "The equipment and supplies will arrive at the hacienda shortly after us. Are you ready to see your patients?" Jesus ushered them into the jeep and opted for the kinder, gentler route to the hacienda.

Doctor Phillip Madison, or just Doc as his former patients dubbed him, could not help but wonder what the **Goat Locker** crew got themselves into this time. The seven-minute drive to the hacienda gave him time to reflect back on **'The Raid'** and the last time he patched these characters up. At least this time when he was hustled out of bed at 0130 and stuffed into an airplane he ended up pretty much in his back yard and not half way around the world! *"I'll get even with Gman one of these days . . . Maybe sending Nurse Sibley with me is his way saying thanks . . ."* Those thoughts ended with the jeep coming to an abrupt stop near the hacienda's front door.

Manfred stood in the doorway and greeted the new comers. "Welcome to Casa Masters." The English accent surprised Nurse

Sibley. Nothing ever surprised Doc when on assignment from Gman. "Allow me to escort you to the patients. Señora Joyce Masters is anxious to see you"

Manfred led Doc and Nurse Sibley to the great room. It was transformed in to a hospital ward of sorts. Most of the furniture had been pushed against the walls and four hospital beds dominated the center of the room. The flexibility and inventiveness of the Masters impressed Doc.

"Doc Madison! Good to see you made it home from the IO. What the f… flamin' hell you doin' here, and who is nurse Cratchit? We gotta stop meeting like this!" Boats yelled across the room.

"I was ordered here to sew you decrepit old bums up . . . Sanchez* didn't give you braggin' scars so you could do it all over again! What's the matter with you old farts? War is a young man's game! And this isn't Nurse Cratchit, it is, to you derelicts, Miss Sibley, Lieutenant Commander Sibley, nurse and Radiologist." Doc was in rare form and all smiles. "How come you're not in pink, Boatsie?"

I was happy to see Doc Madison. He only spent a few short hours aboard **Scrap Dealer** but became part of the **Goat Locker** crew. "Damn! No one told us you were arriving. Good to see you Doc. Could you tend to Masters and Manuel first? Boats' flamin' blood pressure seems to be a bit elevated and my f…fargin' scratch can wait."

"Christ Master Chief . . . How are ya? I'll get right on it." Doc Madison replied. "I need the x-ray machine. You seen it Kensey?" Doc knew I didn't know an x-ray machine from a dinner plate. He was making a point: I was not in charge here.

Jesus arrived with air shipping crates and boxes just in time to save me from more of Doc's not so subtle satire. "Señor. Where do you want these machines?"

"Put them right over there." Doc Madison pointed to Bill and Manuel. "That is, if Boatsie doesn't mind. Miss Sibley shall we get started?"

"Yes Sir." She said in a long, soft, southern drawl.

Joyce, sitting in the chair next to her sons' sick bed, felt she had to say something. "Thank you for coming Doctor Madison. I understand you are here on Mr. Kensey's behalf. We really appreciate it. Bill said he banged his head on the galley stove. I think

It may be a little more severe than that . . ." Señora Joyce was worried and grateful simultaneously.

"Jeez Mom! Doc Madison cut his teeth on battle field triage." Bill interrupted, "He knows what's serious and what's merely a 'cool scar'.

"The x-rays will tell us what we need to know Madam." The Doctor said as he rolled the machine into place. "Miss Sibley, you're on."

Miss Sibley's speech wasn't in any hurry but her actions were. She deftly maneuvered the X-ray machine into place and casually answered with a Southern Drawl that would put a smile on Preachers' face. "Yasss Surrrr."

Boats couldn't keep his eyes off LCDR Sibley. That was enough to keep the imagination going, but Doc Madison patching us up, again, left ample room for conjecture. I couldn't help but think. *"Gman knows a hell of a lot about what's going on down here. Is he keeping tabs on me? WTFO!"*

I watched Doc and the lovely Nurse Sibley x-ray Masters then Manuel. Nurse Sibley asked for a large pan of water and rummaged around in the medical supplies. She came up with one of those plaster casts you just soak in water then set Manuel's broken wrist.

Doc held a conference with Bill and Señora Masters loud enough for us all to hear. "Bill, you have two hair line fractures and some swelling. That spells concussion. I'm calling it mild but that is not cause to jump up and do handsprings. You will have spells of double vision and nausea for a while, but that should be gone in a few days to a week. Take it easy for at least two weeks! You'll have to wear a collar for the whiplash but, luckily, none of your vertebrae are damaged." Joyce Masters breathed a audible sigh of relief. Doc continued. "Manuel isn't as lucky. His wrist is severely fractured. We're numbing it right now and will set it and put a cast on. He should see an orthopedic surgeon in a week or so just to be on the safe side."

Bill sounded relieved. "Thanks Doc. We'll see Manuel gets to a specialist and I'll take it easy. I'm pretty sure I won't be doing any sailing for a while."

Nurse Sibley carefully cut the duct-tape, butterfly bandages away from a nasty groove plowed in Boats' left thigh from an angry NATO 7.62 round. Every other one or so she glared at me. Boats

69

didn't flinch and his eyes never left her face. She addressed Boats in her magical drawl. "Was José aboard? This looks like his work. You have a name other than Boatsie?"

Before he could answer, Doc stepped to his bedside. "Nice shade of pink. Matches that apron you're so proud of Boats." Doc Madison was really enjoying himself. "If you keep this up you'll be able to play tic-tac-toe on these scars! Ah . . . too bad your ass wasn't shot up; I could have made you twins with Sweet Cheeks*!"

Boats rolled his eyes, clearly embarrassed and agitated. "Everyone's a fuckin' comedian." And added quickly, "Pardon my French!" He furtively stared into Miss Sibleys' languid brown eyes.

Doc Madison chuckled and began the process of properly stitching Boats up. Miss Sibley simply smiled and assisted. When the patchwork quilt was finished, Doc crossed the room and approached my bedside. Nurse Sibley followed with a deliberate, exaggerated swish to her hips.

"Good to see you again Doc! The surroundings are a site better than last time. How the hell did you get roped into this trip?" I was worried and a bit curious about the government keeping tabs on my whereabouts, but pleased I would not have to explain a bullet wound to border agents

Nurse Sibley removed the bandage and closely examined my wound while Doc explained how he ended up at my bedside. "Our friend Jim was in Seattle on business and stopped at your favorite pub to say howdy. He heard you were in a bit of trouble and asked Nurse Sibley and I if we would come lend a hand." Doc and I both knew Jim would not 'drop into' a waterfront pub on a whim. That piqued my interest; and I thought. *"Some sort of game is afoot."*

"Why . . . Mister Kensey, this little ol' wound is nothing more than a neat little hole. You should teach your friend Boatsie," She turned and emphasized 'Boatsie', while flashing a heart-stopping smile in his direction. ". . . to dodge bullets!" Boats' fading pink tinge instantly went to bright crimson.

"Ah don't worry about Boats, Miss Sibley; he'll be fine as long as he doesn't lose his hearing aid or eye-glasses." I said that over loud and earned myself a stern look from Señora Masters and smiles form Manuel and Bill. I decided teasing Boats would have to wait for a less crowded venue.

Doc got back to the business at hand. "Where is Jorge? I understand he was a little beat up too."

That reminded me there were still serious matters to attend to. "He's still on the schooner. Should be here in a few hours. He suffered some second and third degree burns but insisted on sailing the schooner back to port. One or two sailors on *PC-331*, the patrol boat that found us, had sailing experience but could not handle anything the size of the ***Derdrake***. Even beat up with jerry-rigged sails she was making better than eight knots but could only be towed at four. I expect Jorge will be glad to see you."

Before Doc could confirm he would be here when Jorge arrived one hell of a commotion broke out at the front door and continued down the hallway to the great room. It sounded like Julietta. She was berating Manfred in loud, rapid, Spanish. "Señor Kensey! Debo verlo. Voy a verlo ahora mismo!" *{"Mr. Kensey! I must see him. I will see him right now!"}*

I caught the 'Kensey' part and hoped Julietta was not here to make good on her promise from our last meeting a few days ago. Señora Masters hurried to the door and calmed Julietta who was gesturing in my direction, half sobbing, and half pleading.

This was the moment I had been dreading. Joyce escorted Julietta to me and I started making my sincere apology. "Señorita . . . I am so sorry that . . ." I didn't get a chance to finish.

She interrupted and switched from Spanish to very stern English, "Señor Kensey, promise me that you will avenge my brother! Promise me that those sons of dogs will pay! Do not let my husband seek revenge alone."

That took me completely by surprise. Nurse Sibley and Doc Madison had unobtrusively returned to Boats' bedside. I looked directly into distraught, tear filled eyes, and I promised to find who attacked us, killed her brother, and Fredrico and Eduardo, and make them pay in blood. She nodded her head, took a deep breath, turned on her heels, and went directly to Manuel's bedside. She was still agitated but was speaking softly and occasionally gesturing in my direction.

That was a relief: I thought Julietta would blame me for Manuel's injuries. Their conversation faded into the background and I retreated into my own thoughts. *"Glad Black Cloud didn't fuck with*

Billings! What was Gman doing at The Haven? If he sends 'The Game is Afoot', I'll shoot myself and save . . . whoever, the trouble . . ."

Chapter 15
REST AND RECOVERY

The morning was trying and tiring. Doc and Nurse Sibley completed their last rounds and sat down to enjoy afternoon tea with Joyce Masters. I checked with Bill; he and I planned to meet *Derdrake* when she moored. We saw her damage from the decks of *PC-331* and had a birds-eye view when we flew over her on the helo ride back here. She was not the same beautiful three-masted schooner that made a spectacular debut eight days ago . . .

Manuel insisted on joining us. He was worried about his brother. We three were walking-wounded and a little outing wouldn't hurt our recovery, but Doc insisted that Boats stay behind. Nurse Sibley agreed with Doc as long as we merely observed but did not participate. Boats grumbled and moaned about not being at the pier when *his* ship came in but agreed to stay at the hacienda; I thought he gave in much too quickly.

Jorge maneuvered *Derdrake* alongside the pier with a tattered and reefed main. *PC-331* stood off about fifty yards in case she needed a nudge into her berth. *Derdrake's* shiny black sides were scarred and pitted. A good-sized dent at the water line and burned blistered paint from the stern to amidships along the port side garnered a gasp from Joyce Masters. A splintered stump stood where the foremast should be and the deck and half the coachwork was fire and soot blackened. No glass survived and the coachwork was riddled with small arms bullet scars. Gun port crosses cut in the salon bulkheads stood out in stark contrast to the peaceful intention of *Derdrake's* existence.

"Holy shit Kensey! This looks more beat up than *Goat Locker* following **'The Raid'**! How did any of you survive?" Doc Madison looked revolted and sounded incredulous.

Nurse Sibley took a long lingering measure of Bill and me and spoke before I could answer Doc's breathless question. "I thought you old duffers were exaggerating . . . It appears the little skirmish

73

you described was a pitched battle! I hope someone pays for doing this. I can only imagine how beautiful ***Derdrake*** was . . . What *didn't* Doctor Madison tell me about the last time he patched you guys up?" I addressed Doc and avoided Nurse Sibley's probing question. "We were lucky. If this was a wooden or fiberglass ship none of us would have survived. Still, we lost three good men. Tomorrow's memorial service will barely honor them . . ." And Miss Sibley, "Someone is going to pay for this!"

"Goddamn right they are! Nobody kills my friends and fucks my boat up like that and gets away with it!" Boats bellowed from the golf cart he managed to commandeer. That startled us. Everyone was so focused on ***Derdrake*** that nobody heard him approach.

"Tone it down Boatsie! You're not supposed to be here; you'll burst your stitches if you carry on so." Nurse Sibley batted her eyelashes while scolding the reddening Boats in a perfect Scarlet O'Hara voice.

A subdued and toned down Boats nodded and said, 'Beg your pardon Miss Sibley, but a sneak attack, three good men killed, and a destroyed ***Derdrake*** just pisses me off!"

The solemn crowd gathered at the gangplank said no more. Security personnel carefully carried Miguel's body from the devastated schooner. Boats cleared the way with his golf cart while Jorge, Bill, and I followed behind leading the sad procession of mourners. Heads were bowed and hats removed as we proceeded to the truck parked nearby. Julietta and Selena, tears flowing freely, stood holding hands and watched intently while Miguel was gently laid on a large flowered reef in the truck bed. Bill told the driver to proceed and we stood in silence until they cleared the pier.

Mamma Maria and Selena were fluttering around Jorge like a couple of mother hens when Doc Madison and Nurse Sibley approached.

"Mamma! Selena! Give Doc Madison some room!" They grudgingly backed off a bit as Jorge greeted Doc. "It seems like just yesterday when you gave me a flight physical . . . You didn't have to wait for me. I've got a few minor burns. You know a good shipwright? Our beautiful schooner needs more help than me."

Doc Madison ushered Jorge, Selena, Julietta, and Mamma Maria to the pier office with Nurse Sibley following behind. He would tend to Jorge's burns inside, out of the sun. I watched, somewhat amused as first Selena then Julietta glanced back at Miss Sibley. I didn't have much time to think about that: a spry man in his late fifties carrying what appeared to be my iPad approached.

"Mr. Kensey, I'm Cole, Cole Thomas." He extended his right hand and I eagerly grasped and shook it. "I believe this is your iPad."

Before he could continue, I spoke. "Yes it is. Thanks for deciphering our SOS! That saved our asses and the *Derdrake*. If there is anything I can do for you don't hesitate to ask!"

Bill interrupted, "That goes double for me!"

"I didn't do much Mr. Masters. Manfred asked me to make Mr. Kensey's iPad quit beeping. That slick app he has is what saved you . . . Where did you get that app Mr. Kensey? I can't find anything like it." Cole Thomas struck me as a humble, competent, technician. I thought he might be ex-military.

We'd discussed Cole's role in the rescue with Joyce Masters and most of the staff throughout the morning while waiting for the *Derdrake*. No one said much other than he was an engineer working on communications equipment at the Fortress.

"A friend in Redmond, don't let that word get out, coded that app for me. You strike me as ex-military Cole. What branch did you serve in?" I thought I'd ask and satisfy my curiosity.

"Coast Guard Mr. Kensey. I sailed with Boatswain Harry Markham for a while on the *Campbell*. Sure was surprised to hear him on the radio in Seattle! Joined when I was twenty, served twenty-five years, and retired as an ET Chief. I've been running my own communications repair and installation company for the past fourteen years." Cole sounded sure of himself and now I knew why Bill hired him to install and repair equipment here at the Fortress.

"Consider yourself part of the family here Cole. We would appreciate your attendance at tomorrow's memorial service. Thanks again for being on the ball and helping us get home!" Bill about said it all.

"I will be there." Cole said in a somber voice as he handed me my iPad. "Right now I need to finish installation and testing of the new secure satellite communications equipment." Bill nodded and Cole executed an about face and quickly strode toward the communications building.

After Cole left there wasn't much to do. Milling about, the awkward silence, and everyone gawking at the bullet riddled,

75

scorched, schooner was a bit much for me. I told Boats to slide over and got into the golf cart's driver seat and grumbled, "I'm going back to the hacienda..."

"Ok Master Chief." was his only comment before we drove the long way back in utter silence.

Chapter 16
Funerals and Reports

The memorial service for Eduardo and Fredrico was a somber affair attended by friends and family. It was a simple service honoring their lives and accomplishments. They would be missed. Bill, Boats, and I kept to ourselves and did not attend the gathering following the service. All of us, Bill especially, felt guilty about not searching for their remains. I blamed myself solely. It was my decision to get clear of the area when command of *Derdrake* passed to me. It may have been the best plan of action but that didn't make me feel any better, and I certainly was not looking forward to Miguel's funeral day after tomorrow.

We received a message from Admiral Olmos early in the evening. An air and sea grid search starting at our last logged position turned up some charred debris from *Derdrake* but no bodies or zodiacs. Admiral Olmos said they would search until dark before calling it quits. He would be in attendance for Miguel's funeral and asked if there was any amplifying information we could add to the incident reports we made while aboard *PC-331*.

Bill, Boats, Jorge, Manuel, and I sipped brandy in the library and rehashed the attack trying to find some detail that would help Admiral Olmos pin the blame squarely on someone. It was nearly midnight when we called it a day. Actually, Julietta and Selena put an end to our meeting when they reclaimed their husbands and turned in for the night. We each made a few notes to add to our report of events but the radar contact Boats logged the night before the attack was the only bit of information that could be of any possible use in figuring out who attacked us.

The funeral for Miguel was well attended. Miguel was laid to rest in the Masters' private cemetery in a simple ceremony on a bright sunny day. Bill insisted that I stand graveside with the family. I felt awkward and out of place. I nearly managed to fade into the crowd behind us, but Julietta grabbed my hand, squeezed it tightly, and would not let go until I dropped a rose and hand full of earth onto her cousin's coffin.

Mamma Maria spent two days preparing for the reception following Miguel's funeral. That was not the only bright spot throughout three days of mourning our dead. There was another considerable improvement; we were back in our own rooms, and I finally got a decent night's sleep: I didn't have to listen to Boats snore all night!

Other things were returning to normal. Boats sneaked off right after the services. He was supposed to be bedridden, but every time Nurse Sibley or Doc wanted to change his dressing they had to chase him down. This afternoon was the last straw; they found him aboard *Derdrake* supervising a painting party. He flatly stated that no ship of his was going back to the builders looking like shit! Nurse Sibley read him the riot act about being the worse patient ever, and told him to take it easy or Playgirl would be his next nurse in attendance. Boats quietly acquiesced and said he would return to the hacienda and funeral reception with her.

The three kids Boats managed to hire for his party were disappointed until Miss Sibley told them that Boats would pay them double what he promised if they put things away. That smoothed things over and Boats seemed happy to be in Nurse Sibley's company.

The subdued wake began breaking up early in the evening. I suspiciously watched Manfred approach Boats, Manuel, and Jorge; they drifted toward the library and Manfred approached me.

"Mr. Kensey, Mr. Masters, and Admiral Olmos are in the library and would like you to join them." It was time to get back to the harsh realities of the attack, memorials, and today's funeral . . .

I was the last to enter the library. Bill hoisted a snifter of brandy when I entered; I nodded an affirmative. Bill poured a generous dram of *1973 Fine Bordeaux* into a Waterford snifter and motioned for me to have a seat.

Admiral Olmos started speaking in his heavily accented English. "First, gentlemen, Bill, Boats, and especially you Mr. Kensey, I do not blame anyone other than the attackers for what happened to my brother Miguel. It saddens me deeply, and I am disappointed that Fredrico and Eduardo could not be found. I understand the difficult decision you had to make to save your lives instead of searching for their remains. I read, with considerable horror Mr. Kensey's account of the last time he saw Fredrico . . . a bloody, torn, rag-doll tangled in the lifelines. Doctor Madison assures me you have all been screened for PTSD. We have all been close to death, and rest assured gentlemen, I will be doing everything I can to avenge my brother and your friends." Admiral Olmos paused. We sat looking at the floor slowly swirling our brandy; we all felt inadequate to speak.

Admiral Olmos broke the pregnant silence and continued. "Enough said. Let me bring you up to date on our efforts to find out who attacked you. We thoroughly searched Isla Guadalupe. We found no evidence of a ground force camped there. The ***Andiamo*** was the only ship close enough to your position to be involved. She made port at Punta San Carlos yesterday. We tore her apart! The only weapons aboard were two Very-pistols, a 12 gauge shotgun, an '03 Springfield, and the Captain's personal Smith and Wesson, forty-four caliber, Russian. Her main generator was burned and in pieces. We examined her GPS and Deck Log. Both showed her too far south and west of the attack to take part. I don't believe that for a second! I will keep an eye on the ***Andiamo***, her crew, and especially Captain Richmond from now on. I looked over the notes you all wrote. Until we can identify the radar contact Mr. Clark logged, and the one Miguel reported, there isn't much else we can do . . . officially."

Even the smallest detail could be of help finding who assaulted us. I filed the name Admiral Olmos mentioned, Captain Richmond of the ***Andiamo***, away for further research, and then cleared my throat and hesitantly spoke. "Admiral Olmos, I am terribly sorry your brother did not survive the attack. I deeply regret not spending the time to search for Eduardo and Fredrico. That was my decision and mine alone. I know you forgave me but that doesn't assuage the guilt I feel. It will be hard to move on but I guess I must . . ."

I swirled the last of the brandy in the snifter, downed it, and then continued. "The attack was a complete surprise. Three zodiacs came screaming out of the fog and launched an RPG attack and strafed us with automatic small arms fire before we even knew they were hostile. Those three zodiacs did not get all the way out there on their own. Either the radar contact Miguel reported thirty-five miles east of us was the mother ship or someone set up a land based camp on Isla Guadalupe. Boats logged one other ship in the area and that was about twelve hours before the attack. *Andiamo* may well be our poltroon but from what you say, Admiral, it would be hard to prove." That pretty much completed my report as matter of fact as I could make it.

Boats took up the narrative. "I want to say how sorry I am Admiral . . . And Bob, we all made that decision . . . I had a good look at the pirates through the riflescope on the Barrett. I shot two and sank their zodiac. Both were Latino. One man was down on the second zodiac but the other was definitely Latino. Jorge tore the boat up with the M-60 and I think Kensey dispatched the driver. The third zodiac had one man standing, he was black, and I squeezed off one round before Kensey fired the Stinger. Nothing was left after that. The only other thing I noticed was all three motors were gray Yamaha, ninety horse, four strokes. If they were bought recently they might be traceable." Boats paused then turned to Manuel. "Anything you can add?"

"I too wish to express my deepest condolences Admiral Olmos." Manuel answered in his heavy accent. "Miguel and I were very close. I will miss him terribly." After a short pause, he continued, "I did not notice anything that stands out. I think we were set upon by professionals, Mercs perhaps. The timing, the location, and the attack was well planned. The first RPG was concentrated on our communications, radar, and sails. The second RPG was intended to sink us. Thank God for our steel hull! They used concentrated suppressing fire until they got out of casual small arms range, about two hundred fifty yards, and then spun around to watch us burn and sink. Boats got their attention with the Barrett and Kensey had them ducking with the FAL. Once Jorge got the M-60 in operation, the sole survivor tried to retreat. They had a plan and stuck to it. I don't think you need to look for day laborers or field hands. We were targeted . . . plain and simple."

Jorge continued the narrative in the identical passion and manner of his brother. "I could see that smug bastard just standing there expecting us to roll over and sink. I got the M-60 into action and that changed his mind! My hands and arms were burned from pushing and throwing burning rigging and sails over the side: that made handling the M-60 difficult. We could have saved a stinger if my aim was better. Our ship was still burning in places, My Padrone was injured, and three of us were dead; revenge was all I could think of! I apologize for not paying more attention." He spoke with passion and bitterness.

Masters looked at Jorge with affection reserved for brothers. "You needn't apologize Jorge. None of us thought about much other than survival."

A light rap on the door cut Bill off in mid sentence. I expected Manfred to enter with refreshments. Cole Thomas entered. The silence could be cut with a knife. Cole, clearly uncomfortable, with all eyes on him, began to speak. "Excuse the intrusion; Boats asked Nolan and me to download and analyze navigation, communication, and radar data from the *Derdrake*. This is it. I think this data has some clues to help unravel what happened and who did it. When we first identified your SOS, the signal was fading in and out. I set the Fortress receiver to record all transmissions fifteen-mega-hertz either side of the *Derdrake's* frequency. We just reviewed that tape. This bit of chatter sounds like it may be of use." Cole handed Bill a fat manila envelope with a single sheet on top. Bill quickly read the transcript and handed it to Admiral Olmos with raised eyebrows and no comment.

Admiral Olmos read out loud:

> "**4/4/12 0530: North Star this is Tuna Belle. Fish in the water.**
>
> **4/4/12 1730: North Star this is Tuna Belle. We have a hole in the net.**
>
> **4/5/12 0145: North Star Tuna Belle. Ordered into port.**
>
> **5/5/12 0150: Tuna Belle North Star. Comply.**"

Admiral Olmos, deep in thought, nodded and then dropped the transcript on Bill's desk. "Interesting. I'll have our signals team look into this. Do you have extra copies?"

He looked directly at Cole who nodded an affirmative and then added, "Yes sir; Jesus delivered all the information to your pilot."

Admiral Olmos tugged on a thick gold chain adorning his vest. A fine Hamilton railroad pocket watch appeared, he checked the time. "I can't add anything more. We will follow the movements of the *Andiamo* and Captain Richmond and the company he works for. Right now I must take my leave; my helo is waiting. Thank you, Bill, for taking care of my brother. And . . . thank you Mr. Kensey, Mr. Clark, Jorge and Manuel for being good friends to him." Admiral Olmos was clearly choked up and on the verge of shedding a tear as he hastily departed the library.

Bill poured a healthy dram of brandy in a fresh snifter and handed it to Cole. "Thanks! That was quick thinking."

Cole accepted the brandy clearly embarrassed with the attention and a bit shy. He took a sip of brandy to deflect the spotlight, but I pressed the obvious question. "Before we break up for the evening and that will be shortly because Doc and Nurse Sibley will be making final rounds in a few minutes, did anything else catch your attention? Any idea who or where those transmissions came from?"

"No Mr. Kensey"

"Call me Bob" I interrupted.

Cole continued." Bob, I . . . now that I think of it. Both North Star and Tuna Belle were transmitting on single-side-band. Tuna Belle came in undistorted but North Star didn't. North Star sounded like . . . the frequency drift you get from long distant transmissions. Once you listen to the tape, you will recognize it immediately. That's all I can think of. Oh! Boats Markham sent me some 'Seattle's Best' from the Haven. It should be here tomorrow. Come down to the shack and I'll play the tape and brew you a great cupper!"

"A cupper? I knew a couple of beautiful young woman from England, back in the sixties, who talked like that. . . You spend time in England?" I was fishing for information and everyone frowned at the effort.

"Cupper . . .smupper; what the fuck, Twidget! I gotta get back to my room before Nurse Sibley puts that fuckin' goat in my bed!" Boats blanched drained his snifter, pulled the door open, and hurried toward his room.

"FMTT! Boats is afraid of Playgirl? Never thought I'd see the day, but it is time for Doc to make his last rounds before leaving." Bill placed the transcript into the manila folder and handed it to me with a wink and said, "Won't be sorry to see Doc leave but Nurse Sibley . . . Hummmm. Good night gentlemen"

That ended the meeting. I walked Cole to the front door before facing the displeasure of Nurse Sibley and Doc Madison for not taking it easy. "Cole, I'll be down to the shack to listen to those tapes some time tomorrow afternoon, but I want to be sure there's decent coffee down there before I walk all that way! Call me when it arrives"

"Ten-Roger Master Chief! I'll be looking forward to that." Cole executed a perfect about face and marched off toward the airstrip and communications shack.

I returned to my room. I was weary and my arm ached. Painkillers were wearing off. Everyone was tired. Miguel's funeral this afternoon seemed to take the wind out of all our sails. I left my door open hoping Doc would see me first. He had requested that all of us stay in one place tonight. He wanted to make one final check before he and Nurse Sibley left early the next morning.

Nurse Sibley was attending to Manuel across the passageway from me. Julietta, hurrying down the hall, caught my attention. She entered the room speaking rapid Spanish to Manuel. He looked a bit cowed and made no comment. Julietta unceremoniously scooted Nurse Sibley aside and pointedly switched to English. "I will tend to my husband!"

"Si Señora. May I assist you operating this x-ray machine?" Nurse Sibley's sarcasm did not escape Manuel; he visually rolled his eyes to the ceiling fully expecting WWIII to break out.

Julietta, hands on hips, quickly and curtly answered. "Ser rápido sobre el!" {"Be quick about it!"}

Nurse Sibley didn't change her demeanor or tone but I thought she was enjoying herself when she said, "If you are thinking about having bambinos please step back while I take this picture." I didn't catch Julietta's reply but it was in Spanish and Manuel turned bright red.

Nurse Sibley's last duty was taking Manuel's vitals. When that was finished, she spoke to Julietta more than to Manuel. "Presión arterial un poco... pero todo lo demás parece aceptable." {"Blood pressure's up a bit . . . but everything else seems ok."}

Nurse Sibley wheeled the x-ray machine out into the hall while pulling the vitals tree behind her. Julietta rapidly, just short of slammed, closed the door behind her. Nurse Sibley parked the x-ray machine and came in to check my wound and vitals.

"Julietta seems a bit agitated or perhaps her green-eyed-monster is showing." I teased when Nurse Sibley approached my bed.

She was smiling and humming but nonetheless answered in her soft, slow southern drawl, "I am used to it. Now Mister Kensey, lay down, it is time to take your vitals and please wipe that smirk off your face."

I assumed my most serious look and mimicking Manfred's best English accent and continued where I left off. "Why Miss Sibley I do believe you are enjoying this"

Before she could answer, Doc walked in absently scanning notes scrawled in an illegible doctor's hand. "I just read Mr. Masters' x-rays and his concussion is clearing up nicely. Rest and headache meds for the next week should do it. As for the rest of you, Mr. Kensey, you should take it real easy. You old farts don't spring back as quickly as you used to. You and Boats still both have slight limps from your last outing. Regardless y'all should be your ornery selves within the next week or so. Nurse would you check Mr. Masters' vitals when you are finished here? I'll just pop across the hall and check on Manuel."

"Before you go Doc I have a favor to ask. Would you hand deliver this to our mutual friend?" I handed him the manila envelope. He gave it a skeptical look, hefted it, studied it a second, and then nodded his head in agreement.

Once Doc was safely behind Manuel and Julietta's closed door, Nurse Sibley resumed her humming through a crooked little smile. Quite out of the blue she asked, "Bye the way, is Mister Masters married or is he seeing someone special?"

That completely took me by surprise, "No, I don't think so. He knows a lot of women stateside but I don't think he's involved with anyone in particular. Why? You interested?"

She thought a moment, never averted her gaze, took on an air of mystery, and with a twinkle in her eyes answered matter-of-factly. "I just might be." I had to strain to hear her husky whisper. Her cheeks suddenly reddened; she turned away quickly and started securing her equipment. "Please, could you make this our secret?"

"I am a bit surprised, but I certainly can and will." She wheeled her equipment toward the door and I could not suppress a chuckle; her fading scarlet tinge intensified.

CHAPTER 17
A SURPRISING FAREWELL

Captain Richmond was in a foul mood. It was early, 0630, and men describing themselves only as 'Federal Agents' were even now checking every nook and cranny aboard *Andiamo*. Uniformed men did the same thing a day earlier. This did not feel right and he wanted to be away from here and back in the relative safety near his employer. At the last moment, he thought it prudent to take Jenkins along in case he said something he should not. That might not go over well with the Paymaster but he did not dare contact him with all the added interest in *Andiamo*.

A new ship's master showed up at sunrise this morning. Richmond did not think much of him and pegged him as a yes-man. *"Let that sniveling, butt-kisser, deal with it."* He thought standing there in the armpit of the world, impatiently waiting for Jenkins.

Jenkins was not in much of a hurry. He stood talking to the Second Mate at the end of the gangway. "Get the fuckin' lead out Jenkins. We have a plane to catch and it won't wait on us." Richmond was out of patience and bellowed the order.

The sooner he left this shit hole, Puerto San Carlos, the happier he would be. Missing the plane was the least of his worries. He was still alive but that might not be permanent if he made one wrong step in explaining why *Derdrake* was still afloat, most of her crew was still alive, and one complete tactical team was not. Paymaster seemed to accept his abbreviated phone report and asked very few questions but that probably had to do with security concerns. The real test would come during their one-on-one meeting this afternoon in Cabo.

****

I opted to walk to the airstrip; Doc and Nurse Sibley planned to leave at 0900. I needed the exercise. I never thought I'd miss my wet, windy, rainy, cold, gray Seattle morning walk to Starbucks for a piping hot grande cup of clover brewed coffee but walking this dusty path in eighty degree morning heat made me think twice about that. I was two thirds of the way there when the hanger doors opened and the black Gulf Stream 550 rolled out onto the tarmac. That got me to thinking, *"I should have hitched a ride then returned to Seattle! Too late now."*

I could see two jeeps from the hacienda making their way down the paved road. Sure as shit, a golf cart followed far enough behind them so as not to be noticed. Boats! He was ordered to stay in bed, his leg wound was seeping blood from yesterday's activities, but that wasn't stopping him from seeing Nurse Sibley off! I stepped the pace up from a leisurely walk to a brisk march. That got my heart rate up; it didn't forty years ago . . .

I arrived shortly before the two jeeps. Bill drove one with Nurse Sibley and Doc riding along. Selena drove the second with Jorge and Manuel; Julietta was noticeably missing. Boats squeaked to a stop beside the jeeps sporting a face splitting smile. "Didn't think I'd miss our last date did you Nurse Sibley?"

"You'll be sleeping with Playgirl tonight Boatsie. I'm jealous!" Nurse Sibley flashed Boats a big smile followed by a seductive wink. I think she was glad to see us all together and in good spirits before leaving Isla Cedros and its most hospitable hacienda.

I was glad Doc arrived when he did and patched us up. His being here suggested Gman had something in the wind but I could not put my finger on whatever *'it'* was. *"Gman didn't just happened to be in Seattle at the Safe Haven at just the right time to send Doc and Nurse Sibley to patch us up."* I had my reservations and would definitely keep an ear to the ground.

Regardless of the intrigue, I needed to say my goodbyes. "Well Doc, can't say I enjoyed your visit but I do appreciate all of the work you and . . . What is the lovely Miss Sibley's first name? I seem to have forgotten."

"Commander or Nurse. You know that Bob." Doc was enjoying himself and couldn't help but notice Boats cock his head to his good ear and lean forward to the point of falling over.

"Sí, Bob todos lo sabemos!" {"Yes, Bob we all know that!"} Selena politely pointed that out while squeezing Jorge's hand hard enough to make him wince. She looked Manuel square in the eye then flashed a crooked smile at Bill. He was amused, and I thought I might have been here too long: I understood what Selena said and what she didn't exactly say in words.

I extended my hand and shook Doc's vigorously. "I'd love to buy you a San Magoo and just visit for a change." The yellow start cart was in place and I saw the pilot give the wind-it-up signal. "Say hi to Jim for me and tell him not to call me; I'll call him!" Doc chuckled and started for the plane.

Nurse Sibley completely surprised me. She stepped up, gave me a big hug, and whispered in my ear. "It's our secret, but not for long." Boats stood there with a hangdog look waiting for his hug.

The Gulf Stream's engines whined to life. Nurse Sibley nodded to me and walked straight over to Bill. They stood there gazing into each other's eyes. Like two magnets, they drew together and embraced in a passionate lingering kiss. I do not know who was more surprised, Bill or Boats. Doc either missed the tender moment or chose to ignore it; he has half way up the boarding ladder. Nurse Sibley disengaged and walked backward until their hands slowly slipped apart. She turned abruptly and dashed for the boarding ladder. Once at the top, she turned, waived, and blew us all a farewell kiss.

"Good bye Caroline. . ." I was not sure Bill knew he uttered that but I knew I was the only one close enough to hear.

Chapter 18

A SPECIAL SUMMONS

The Cessna Caravan Amphibian flew low over the breakwater, circled once and then set down in the choppy water and motored to a skilled mooring next to the last finger pier of the Gran Peninsula Boat Yard. Captain Richmond was explicitly instructed to be here no later than 0700. Paymaster was notoriously as punctual as he was tough and humorless. It was no surprise when they cleared the breakwater and then turned south at 0710. He and Jenkins were the only passengers in the ten-seat cabin and that made the ex-captain of *Andiamo* nervous.

Nearly two hours and ten fingernails later, Richmond tried to calm his butterflies; the Cessna banked into its final approach. This would be his first face to face meeting with the man he only knew as Paymaster but whom he referred to as 'PMS' in private conversations. He assumed they would land at the Cabo San Lucas commercial airport but they bypassed Cabo's airport and proceeded to a private airstrip about ten kilometers north.

The Cessna touched down, taxied to the end of the runway, and then stopped. The pilot turned to Richmond and Jenkins and gestured for them to get out. "Este es el final de la línea. Un coche le recogerá poco" {"This is the end of the line. A car will pick you up shortly."} Richmond and Jenkins exited and stood in the harsh sun nervously watching the Cessna turn around, rev its engine, and take off.

"What the fuck Skipper? I don't like this at all. There isn't a person anywhere near here!" Jenkins sounded nervous and scared.

Richmond was about to answer but a jeep exiting the tree line cut him short. It crossed the runway and stopped next to them. The driver spoke in rapid Spanish. "Conseguir, la hacienda esmenos de un kilómetro. Deberíamos estar allí en unos minutos." {"Get in; the hacienda is less than a kilometer. We should be there in a few minutes."}

89

"English. Por Favor." was about all Richmond could think of to say. "Get the fuck in. I ain't got all day!" The driver's disdain for these two Gringos clearly showed.

They drove down a dusty road that ended at a massive gate set into a wrought iron fence with pillars that appeared to be adobe but were actually made of reinforced concrete. The gate noiselessly and effortlessly opened with a remote control operated by the driver. Two minutes later, they pulled up to wide front doors leading into a beautiful hacienda. The driver pointed an ominous finger at Richmond. "Come with me." He stabbed his index finger in Jenkins's general direction and barked. "You fuckin' stay put!"

Richmond followed his driver into an office just off the foyer. The driver knocked on a richly carved, mahogany, double door before opening it. Richmond entered; he left deep footprints in the soft red carpet as he marched toward Paymaster's desk with false bravado. The surroundings were definitely upscale from the shithole he just left.

Paymaster, sitting behind his huge bakote desk, looked a lot like the cartoon character Charlie Brown. His head was big and almost round. Small wire frame, granny-glasses hung precariously close to the end of his pug nose. He was dressed in appropriate garb for a ranch hand: plaid shirt, faded Levi jeans, and expensive eel-skin cowboy boots. This did not come close to the buttoned-down, no nonsense businessman Richmond expected.

Paymaster pointed to a red leather chair. Before Richmond could sit, Paymaster began chiding him in a heavy accent that Richmond thought could be Russian. "I assumed a man of your experience could handle a schooner full of *old men*. It is a good thing you are required for another job or you would be feeding the crabs along with five of my men! Your next assignment will be more difficult than sinking one small schooner full of old farts!" Paymaster's sarcasm was not misconstrued.

Paymaster glared at Richmond over the top of his small round spectacles. "Convince me it wasn't your incompetence that caused your miserable failure. And what the fuck is the idea of bringing Jenkins? I didn't tell you to do that!"

The dreaded moment was here, Richmond stuttered; near panic washed over him! "I . . . I followed the plan precisely. That schooner should have sunk. She was burning and our team reported 'mission accomplished' that was their last transmission. I searched for the team at the rendezvous as well as around the contingency point. I . . . I still do not know what happened to them. I set a plan in motion to intercept ***Derdrake*** in case she was still afloat and making for Isla Cedros. I came within four miles of them when the Armada De Mexico interceded and ordered us to Puerto San Carlos. I devised a conceivable plan to explain our presence, executed it, and then proceeded to port. I … I can't prove any of what I say. I threw all electronics, including cell phones, laptops, iPads, iPods, or anything else the crew had that could pin our location down, overboard. I wiped all the hard drives on the navigation gear and input false courses, speeds, and GPS locations. And . . . Jenkins was the only one privy to communications with North Star. I didn't want him left alone with all the Federales swarming over ***Andiamo***. I'm sorry. I failed but I did all I could . . ."

"I know what you did and didn't do. That is the very reason you are not buried and will do this next job without any fuck ups! You understand?" Paymaster was as humorless as ever. He frowned deeply and shuffled some papers waiting for Richmond' answer.

"Yes sir." Richmond's nervousness subsided and he listened intently. He did not want to miss one detail.

"Find and procure a fairly large, modern cargo ship. *I* will hire the crew. Keep Jenkins with you as first mate. Outfit the ship for trans-pacific cargo hauling. Can you handle that Captain Richmond?"

"Yes sir but it may take a few months." Paymaster addressing him as 'Captain Richmond' brought a great deal of relief and he reflected inward for a second. *"Thank God I'm alive, employed, and still on the inside. Jenkins! I'll have to watch him."*

"You have four months maximum. Keep me informed of your progress through normal channels. You will receive further instructions periodically. Your credentials, ID, passport, and lines of credit are established." He handed Richmond a hefty, sealed, manila envelope with some stern advice. "And one more thing, a cat has nine lives; you don't!"

Paymaster paused long enough for that to sink in before giving Captain Richmond his orders. "We are finished for now. Feo, my driver, will take you to a cabaña in Cabo. You will use that as your office. Don't let me down." Paymaster's implied threat did not fall on deaf ears.

"Thank you sir." Richmond turned on his heel and hurried from Paymaster's lair.

Feo was stationed outside the office. He pointed to the large double doors and then fell in behind Captain Richmond. Jenkins sat in the jeep parked outside the hacienda; sweat rolling down his face and neck. Captain Richmond took the shotgun seat without a word. Feo started the jeep and casually drove to the gate and then out onto the same dirt road they arrived on.

"I take you to cabaña. You have car there." With that said Feo accelerated to well over seventy.

Captain Richmond closed his eyes, exhaled a deep sigh of relief, and started planning his next move.

****

Cole Thomas rang the hacienda and left a message with Manfred: Coffee's cooked. When Manfred delivered the message I thanked him and started on my second trek of the day to the airfield. The magic aroma of fresh brewed coffee filled the air near the communications hut that we called the 'shack'. I entered and shouted, "Cole, Nolan, is that coffee brewed up for me?"

Cole zigzagged his way through scattered equipment and cables and handed me a large mug filled with steaming, black coffee, "This is Seattle's Best, Master Chief, direct from Seattle. It cost me dearly but it's well worth it!"

I took the mug and stared at it. Memories flooded back. A ***Pegasus*** class hydrofoil in full flight adorned one side and ***Goat Locker*** in bold black, gilt edged, letters the other.

"That arrived in the package with the coffee. This was inside the mug." Cole handed me a small envelope addressed in a delicate, recognizable, hand.

"*Oh . . . Oh*" I thought. I stepped a little aside and opened the lavender, scented envelope with my K-bar. The short reminder read: Roses are red, violets are too. This note is lavender, but I'm really blue. Call! It was signed in a girlish hand with a small heart dotting the 'i' in Lois.

"I assume Chief Markham sent the mug, but who sent the note? That's one cool looking ship. You stationed aboard her?" Cole looked to be enamored with the hydrofoil emblazoned on my new coffee mug.

"Yeah, I'm sure Harry sent the mug. I served aboard the *Hercules* for a while and commanded another on a special op. . . . Coffee sure is good." I was just a bit at loss for words at the moment.

Nolan bailed me out. "I know the Navy is fucked up, but they actually named a ship *Goat Locker*?"

"No. *Goat Locker* came later. It's inside-baseball stuff. The crew in Seattle have anything else to say?" My mind drifted back to the note safely hidden away in my shirt pocket now that the subject was firmly changed.

"Yes" Cole piped up. "I've been on the Hallicrafters with **The Haven** crew. They said get well soon and send details of *Derdrake's* maiden voyage . . . And, Oh . . . Ah . . . someone named Smith wanted me to pass this on to you. Verbatim: Gman has a job for Black Cloud."

"That's odd . . . That all Smith said? Nothing else?" I figured I'd better get on the iPad later and see if Mike was still at the Haven. I could not clear my mind of one nagging thought. *"Black Cloud and Gman in the same sentence spells trouble!"*

"Nope, that was it." Cole drug me back to the present.

"Let's review those radio transmission recordings you told Admiral Olmos about. Pour me another cup of joe and I'll tell you about flyin' a boat!" That helped clear my persistent trepidation surrounding Black Cloud and Gman.

I spent the next few hours listening to radio transmissions recorded before, during, and after someone tried to sink the *Derdrake.* The single-side-band distortion Cole described was very noticeable in the transmissions from North Star. I would bet Tuna Belle was the mother ship, and the . . . Ah *Andiamo* and Captain Richmond, I recalled, was the only ship in the area. I would certainly find Captain Richmond some day. I would vigorously question him at that time!

I asked Cole if anything else piqued his curiosity. He said other than North Star and Tuna Belle nothing had. Manfred called from the hacienda to inform me dinner would be ready when I arrived if I left the shack now and hurried back. I asked Cole to monitor radio transmissions for more messages from Tuna Belle or North Star. Before I left, I asked him to set up a monitor program to record broadcast TV for any mentions of *Derdrake*, *Andiamo*, Richmond, Tuna Belle and North Star and anything else he could think of linking newscasts to the attack on us.

The walk back to the hacienda gave me time to ponder what Gman, Black Cloud, North Star, Tuna Belle, and the attack on the *Derdrake* had in common or more importantly what it all had to do with me! I drew a blank; I got nothing but a headache.

The next week passed quickly. A daily regimen of light exercises in the gym, half an hour doing laps in the pool followed by a brisk walk, usually ending at the shack, had me feeling pretty good. My arm was still sore but even it was coming along nicely. This was Bill's routine and neither of us would give up while the other was alongside. Boats paced us in the gym and pool but lifted weights when we strolled off to tour the airfield and surrounding facilities. He usually drove the golf cart, and joined us in the shack for our daily BS session with Cole and Nolan over a pot of Seattle's Best.

Derdrake was as patched up and as spiffy looking as Boats could make her. He finalized arrangements to have her towed north for repairs and refitting at Marine Group Boat Works in Chula Vista, California. That would work out well. The boat yard was located just behind Wal-Mart so we could put our ever-increasing Spanish vocabulary to good use.

Late afternoons mostly found Bill in the library writing. He said he was writing a book based on a bunch of old goats making mincemeat out of drug cartels in foreign lands. I almost believed him but I do not know many people writing novels on expensive stationary with a Mont Blanc fountain pen. I deduced he was writing Nurse Sibly. In this day of Skype, Face Book, Twitter, Face Time, email, and cell phones it was refreshing to see someone using ". . .ink stains dried upon a line . . ." That reminded me. " *Shit . . . I still hadn't called or written Lois.*"

I opened the iPad but before I could even bring mail up Manfred rang and said dinner would be served in ten minutes. When I hung up someone knocked on my door. "Grand Central Station come on in!"

Bill, much to my surprise, opened my door. "There's a *Goat Locker* meeting in the library right now!"

"Sure, what's up?" I asked while shutting the iPad down and tossing it onto my bed.

"I'll tell you in the library." With that he wheeled about and trotted toward the library.

I hurriedly followed. Jorge, Boats, and Manuel were already present when Bill, with me on his heels, entered. Boats poured two generous brandies in snifters and handed one to Bill and one to me. He raised his glass and offered a toast. "Here's to the crew of the best ship ever built, *Goat Locker*!"

"That goes without saying but why the gathering?" I amended the toast and held my snifter out for a refill.

"Bob," Bill started and then paused, "I've been in contact with Gman more than I let on. He was supposed to come down here and surprise you on the pier when we got back from our shakedown cruise. When things got out of hand that fell through. He added a few goodies to the Fortress, we all know about them, but he never said much about why. Boats, Jorge, Manuel, and I just thought he was trying to make amends for *Goat Locker*. About a month ago he said he had a surprise but wanted us all together when he spilled the beans. I figured that would be pay back of some sort for all the goodies. Well . . . about twenty minutes ago, this came in over secure comms:

    To: *Goat Locker* Captain and crew

    From: **JB**

    Subject: Summons

    1. **Report to Descanso, CA, Goats On A Roof Restaurant**

    2. **Arrive NLT 1600, 15 April**

"That's it?" I asked curious and somewhat incredulous at the same time. "Summoned? What the fuck? Did he say who else was going to be there besides José and us? Summoned . . .?"

"Yeah, summoned is a strange choice of words but you know Gman: if it isn't cryptic it isn't Gman." Bill appeared just as puzzled as the rest of us.

"Chingata! Julietta will not like this one bit. I think we should not tell her or Selena." Jorge looked right at his brother who was nodding like a bobble-head doll.

"Today is the 13th. Doesn't give us much time. How are we getting there?" I was trying to think ahead.

"That has all been sorted. Jorge and Manuel are taking the helo to San Diego for factory retrofits and maintenance. You, Boats, and I are going by Lear Jet. It too is due for annual maintenance. We leave day after tomorrow in the morning. Car rental and lodging reservations have been or soon will be made. I guess we will just have to play it by ear. We can speculate until we are blue in the face, but trying to figure out what Gman is up to is like spitting in the wind. We will just have to wait."

Manfred rapped on door, opened it, and announced, "Dinner is served sirs."

"This meeting of the *Goat Locker* is adjourned." I drained the last of my 97 Monte Sabotino, Gran Riserva Superiori, a fine Grappa if ever there was one, and followed Manfred to the dining room but could not shut my mind off. *"The game is afoot . . . First Black Cloud, now a summons from Gman . . . What next? I'll have think about it later . . ."* I did not want to miss one of Mamma Maria's meals trying to figure things out; they could be few and far between after tomorrow.

CHAPTER 19
MISSION FOR BLACK CLOUD

Friday, April 13th greeted Seattle with cold, wind driven, spring rain. Bumbershoot weather kept the unadventurous at home all day, but this evening saw the Safe Haven alive with regulars. Tonight was 'New Brew Night' featuring Dick's Golden Ale from a custom brewery in Centralia.

Burt and Harry were talking to Hawaii on the Hallicrafters; they were bartering. Hawaii was getting the better end of the trade: three pounds of Seattle's Best 'dark and intense' plus a pound of Tully's 'compadre blend' for two pounds of chocolate covered macadamia nuts.

Earlier Black Cloud did a decent job, decent for him, of mooring *Dead Eye*. No new repairs to the dock were needed, but *Dead Eye's* paint would have to be touched up. Twenty knots of wind, four knots of tidal current and sideways rain made mooring the single screw, Nordic Tug 37 tricky. Gunny cut Mike a break and gave him a 'can of puke' (Bush Bavarian beer) on the house for not damaging his dock. "Thanks. You didn't shake this fucker up, did you?" was Black Cloud's only comment before wandering off to circulate among the regulars and chat up Lenni, the new bar maid.

A three handed poker game was in progress along with a double-deck pinochle game, three cribbage matches, and a game of acey-ducy. Gunny had the bar polished to a fine sheen, but continued to buff the mahogany surface in case he missed a spot. Black Cloud looked on impatiently and finally crushed the empty Bush Bavarian can against his forehead with a resounding 'thunk!' to get Gunny's attention. "Can you stop spit-shinin' the bar long enough to get me another brew? One of those Dick's Golden Ales and put it on Kensey's tab. Is he still fuckin' around down south? When's he comin' back? We're supposed to be chasing Springers on the Willamette next week."

"Don't keep tabs on Kensey except to keep the riffraff filter working on his condo. You're sleeping on *Dead Eye* tonight I expect . . ." Mike noted that Gunny had his eyes on a new comer entering the bar.

Jim Billings paused a second gathering his thoughts and cataloguing everyone in the bar. So far, today was a hard fought success. Negotiations with Boeing nearly failed. Jim's knowledge of the long forgotten Supermar prototype saved the day. If this late night meeting was successful two legs of the milking stool would be in place. With a course of action set firmly in his mind, Jim proceeded to the bar, sidled up to Mike, and dropped his calling card face up on the bar.

"Master Chief Kensey says your scow is interesting and I should take a tour some day. I see you forgot to put fenders out. This might be a good time to take care of that, and my tour."

"Hear anything new from Kensey down south Mr. Billings?" Everyone knew there was trouble down there and Gunny suspected Gman had amplifying information.

"No. Not really. They had a little bit of trouble. The *Derdrake* got shot up and they lost three crew, but they made it back to Isla Cedros ok. I can add a few details later but right now Mike needs to take care of those fenders. Wouldn't want to damage your dock!" Gunny just nodded. He knew there were too many people in the Haven for Gman to talk openly.

"Make that two ales and a double shot of Pinch to go, and put them on Kensey's tab . . ." Gunny nodded again and filled Mike's order.

Harry and Burt waited until Black Cloud and Gman left the bar before exiting the radio room. They carried on a low, animated conversation with Gunny behind the bar. Gunny just shook his head 'no'. The only discernible conversation heard was, "Wait . . ."

Black Cloud surveyed *Dead Eye*: she had three odd sized fenders, one blue and two white, secured strategically around the port side with granny knots. Gman shrugged his shoulders and patiently sipped his scotch in the abbreviated custom salon.

The rain that subsided to a drizzle earlier flooded down in a torrent now that Black Cloud was alone on deck without foul weather gear. He sloshed in to the salon and scooped up a Dick's

Golden Ale. "Gman . . . right?" he did not wait for an answer. "You here about that little job you mentioned a few days ago?"

"Kensey was right. This is a very interesting, sea worthy, boat. You interested in doing a little fishing in Alaska?" Black Cloud, always up for a fishing trip, was skeptical. Alaska in April could be brutal.

"May be . . . what else do you have in mind?" There had to more than chasing Chinook at stake.

"I need you for an important, special task. I need someone nondescript and you about fit the bill perfectly. Your training and Desert Storm deployments uniquely qualify you for this job. You interested?" Jim went on when Mike acknowledged with a nod of his head. "I did my home work. If you complete this job the IRS will forget who you are."

Black Cloud drained his ale and opened another; he pondered the positives before answering. "I need a passport. I'll have to navigate the Inside Passage this time of year. That means anchoring and fueling in Canada. What's this job pay and where is it *'exactly'* in Alaska?" He paused a second then jokingly continued. "Who do I have to kill?"

"Ah, we'll discuss logistics in a moment, but a successful mission leaves the target 'winged' but living. Period!" Gman gave Black Cloud a moment to ponder that point.

"If I aim at someone, he dies. Period." Black Cloud emphasized *'period'* mocking Gman but continued, "I do not miss. End of story."

"I know, and that is exactly why I'm hiring you. It's worth a quarter million for you to leave us a scared-rabbit; it's worth shit if the dumb bunny dies . . ." Gman struck a chord that was hard to ignore.

After a long pause, and several sips of beer, Mike answered, "Who is the target and where will I find him?"

"He is a real dick-head: Richard Kopf. He operates out of a compound on Pennock Island just south of Ketchikan." Gman studied Black Cloud closely looking for signs that he might back out.

"Ketchikan! That's one fuck of a long way from here! If I'm goin' that far I'm gonna do some fishing." Mike was already calculating ***Dead Eye's*** range, fuel, and provision requirements for a trip that far.

"You bet, and that is another reason I'm recruiting you. There will be salmon fishermen all over the area starting the last week in April. You in? Yes or no?" Bill was not going to disclose details until Mike made a firm commitment.

"Yes, me and Varmint are in." Black Cloud was grinning from ear to ear.

"Whoa! You go alone!" Gman made that clear.

"Yeah, sure. Varmint is my fish-dog, an Alsatian."

"All right, this is how we will proceed. First: *Dead Eye* needs a face lift. Take her to Sea Marine in Port Townsend between 2100 and 2130 tomorrow. She'll be moored in a covered drydock, repainted, renamed *Springer*, and reregistered out of Scappoose, Oregon. Radar, Sonar, autopilot, and GPS will be updated and integrated. You will get a new HF transmitter/receiver, and her diesel will be tuned and any repairs needed will be made. Two seventy-gallon auxiliary fuel tanks will be added and she'll get a new 'silent' screw. Ok so far? Mike nodded understanding but felt a bit overwhelmed; Bill continued. "Second: You *'will not'* set foot in the boat yard until you pick the *Springer* up. Check into the Swan Hotel, the 'dockside cottage' is reserved for you. All operational details will be waiting in the cottage's safe. You will reclaim *Springer* between 0330 and 0430 on the twentieth and immediately depart for Ketchikan. And finally, you will find a Barrett in .338 Lapua Magnum already aboard. Make what bullets you'll need from components you can buy at any sporting goods store. Before you load your rifle wipe down all bullets. Leave no clues that can be traced back to you or me." Gman paused so all the information could soak in.

"Jeez . . . All that and a quarter million too? What's the catch?" Black Cloud's demeanor progressed from astonishment to skeptical. This was just too good to be true.

"No catch, just absolute requirements." Jim handed the puzzled Black Cloud a satellite phone. "My number is programmed in. Call me immediately after, the very second, the job is done. Pitch the phone, special equipment, left over ammo and your rifle over the side when you are in the clear. Fish all you want after that and return if and when you want. Any questions?"

"Fuckin' 'A', but not about the mission. I'm *'in'* on one condition: What happened to my friend Kensey?" Black Cloud was adamant; Bill could plainly see that.

"They were attacked off Isla Guadalupe. The **Derdrake** was shot up and suffered several RPG attacks. Three men died and Kensey, and his friends, Masters, Clark, and the Gonzalez brothers were wounded. They are on the mend now; I've seen to that." Gman thought about this last piece of information and decided Black Cloud could be trusted. "The operation you are on is vital to finding out who attacked them.*"*

"Shit, I get it. Can I kill the fuckin' dick head after you have no use for him?" Skepticism now shifted to determination and revenge.

"Yes . . ." Gman opened the salon hatch and disappeared into the drizzle. He thought to himself, *"God I hope I chose the right person."*

Chapter 20
PREPARATION

Down time felt good. Tomorrow would be busy. I looked forward to seeing José and his new restaurant: **Goats On A Roof**. I was adding the finishing touches to a long overdue email to Lois explaining, with as little detail as possible, my activities over the past two weeks. I included my itinerary for the next few days including my expected date of return to Seattle.

Roses are red violets not so much.

I'm really sorry I haven't kept in touch.

Love Bob.

There that did it. I rubbed my itching wound, thought better of it, tapped 'send' and shut the iPad down. I managed to remove one shoe in preparation for bed before Manfred knocked on my door, cracked it open, poked his head in, and announced, "Master Kensey; Master Masters and Master Clark are in the Library enjoying a nightcap and would enjoy your company. Master Cole will arrive shortly." I thanked him, put my shoe back on, and then made my way to the Library.

Half a bottle of Glenfiddich, 21 year, single malt, sat on Bill's desk. He motioned to the ice bucket and neatly arranged and polished Waterford tumblers on the sideboard. "Help yourself. This is nearly as good as Laphroaig!"

I poured a healthy, neat, shot and sampled it with approval. Manfred ushered Cole into the Library and announced, "Master Cole has arrived."

"Glad you could make it, Cole. Would you like a shot of a good single malt scotch?" Bill said while pouring a very generous libation into a tumbler for Cole. "I'll be gone for a few days. I know you were supposed to be out of here four days ago and I'm glad you

103

could stay on and do some extra work. How is the job going? And do you have any idea how much longer you think the extra work we discussed earlier will take?" Bill made this sound more like a planning session than a get together.

Cole shuffled through a sheaf of loose papers. "Well . . . High Frequency send and receive are up and running. Secure landline is up and running. Broadcast and satellite TV are up and running. We just got the encrypted satellite communications array installed but the rest of the equipment isn't scheduled for delivery for about . . ." Cole scrutinized a few papers and then continued. "Looks like two weeks. Nolan and I cobbled a limited capability together that can be used in a pinch."

Cole sipped his drink then continued. "Good Scotch! You know, Bob asked me to monitor radio and TV broadcast channels for any news about us or the attack on *Derdrake*." He shot me a quick look. "One network, Televisa, mentioned several acts of piracy occurred off the Baja coast and at least one near the Panama Canal. TV Azteca, another Baja network, reported heightened Federal activity down south at Puerto San Carlos. Mexico Distrito Federal, XEIMT Channel 23, reported the Schooner *Derdrake* was attacked and three crew killed. CNN picked up the story and added drug cartel activity was suspected. They speculated the Melendez Cartel was to blame. That particular Cartel operates from Tijuana to the boarder of Ecuador."

Cole shuffled a few more papers. "The piracy subject turns up quite regularly on late night talk radio. Most of it is anecdotal . . . Ah, yesterday Glenn Beck broached the subject bouncing off the CNN report. He reported the Melendez Cartel is a growing threat to US trade and security. They appear to center their operations in and around the Panama Canal. They may be using the Canal as a highway to ship drugs to the East Coast. This bit was of particular interest; they prefer old but well armed tuna clippers as their drug running ships. . ." Cole paused to take another sip.

"Fuckin' *Andiamo!*" I blurted out.

"I'll bet my bottom dollar Admiral Olmos floated our name out there. Fuckin' *Andiamo* is my guess too." Boats nodded in agreement.

We sat in silence digesting Cole's report. The CNN report was sketchy but did mention us. My thoughts wandered a different path.

Too many things didn't add up and needed answering. *"Was **Andiamo** a Melendez Cartel drug runner? Was the **Derdrake** mentioned to smoke them out? Was our summons to Descanso part of this? Normally a private yacht being attacked in foreign waters did not get the attention of DEA. Nope, things did not add up. . ."*

Bill broke the silence and my reverie. "Thanks Cole. I appreciate the update and information." Cole finished his scotch and Bill drained his. "I'll give you a ride back to the shack. We need to discuss the increasing scope and duration of your work."

"Great. Thanks. I'm at odds when we finish up here. Not much going on this time of year."

Bill turned back to me and Boats before he and Cole departed. "See you all in the morning. Breakfast is at 0700 and we leave at 0900 on the dot. We will be landing at Brown Field in San Diego. Immigration and Customs are already taken care of."

Boats and I talked for a while trying to piece everything together. We decided Descanso would answer a lot of our questions. It was time to turn in . . .

CHAPTER 21
REUNION

Our Lear Jet landed at Brown Field southeast of San Diego. I could see Tijuana, Mexico just across the Otay Mesa Freeway that runs along the landing strip. We taxied into a hanger owned by a close friend of the Masters' family. Bill told me they flew in and out of here quite a bit. Regular supply runs to the Fortress were made from here every month or so. An ICE agent boarded our jet, and cleared us through customs and emigration before we deplaned.

We waited a few moments until a minivan entered the hanger and glided to a stop next to us. We were treated to a soft female voice when the side-door slid open. "It is so nice to see you Mister Masters; your stagecoach awaits your orders."

"On to Descanso Ava; we have been ordered to a banquet!"

"Good to see you beautiful! You busy tonight?" Boats butted in with a wink and big smile.

"Yeah . . . got to wash my hair and later I have a date with a Cholla. Who's the handsome devil you brought along? A blind date for me?"

"Bob Kensey," Masters said. "He's more irascible than handsome and certainly not blind . . . yet!"

Ava turned in her seat and shook my hand when I entered the van. "Hi Bob. Welcome to San Diego! Ever been here?"

Boats, always quick to help, piped up before I had a chance to answer. "He was here about *fifty* years ago when he was in the Navy and we spent a few days here last year."

"He moves pretty well for an octogenarian. Saved your decrepit ass last year and again three weeks ago!" Bill laughed as he slid into the shotgun seat. "Ava is our *'Man Friday'* here in San Diego. Keeping the hacienda supplied and running would be difficult without her."

107

We exited Brown Field and sped south on the South Bay Expressway. Ava said this eastern route would keep us well clear of metropolitan traffic.

No one had much to say until we turned off State Route 125 and onto I-8 east. "Cat got your tongue Bob?" Boats was thoroughly enjoying my apparent loss for words. I thought his speaking up now might be payback for the hug Nurse Sibley gave me a few weeks back.

I was not exactly speechless but Ava, a striking woman in her mid fifties, or maybe mid forties, captured my attention. Her long auburn hair was pulled back into a ponytail secured with a turquoise scrunchy. Her attire seemed a bit out of place for such an important cog in the Fortress administration. She wore a faded pink and gray, plaid, flannel shirt, tight Wrangler blue jeans, and what I thought might be Tony Lama Madera Cherokee cowboy boots.

"No Boatsie! I'm thinking about what possessed Californians' to build a toll road; it's totally out of character."

"It's great if you are traveling to Spring Valley, El Cajon, Santee or like us, out past Alpine and on into the back country, Boatsie . . . Boatsie, I like that!" Boats reddened with the attention from Ava. He glared at me but I was not paying attention; my attention was fixed on Ava's unwavering gaze in the rear view mirror.

We turned onto State Route 79, Ava said we would be at **Goats On A Roof** in a few minutes and then added, "Whatever possessed Mr. Sanchez to build a five star restaurant way out in Descanso?" That question was addressed directly to me.

Bill quickly answered for me. "Bob scared the crap out of him the last time we were together and he wanted to get as far from him as he could!"

That garnered a big smile from Boats, and he jumped right in. "You two scared the crap out of me and I'm still here. I think José, Mr. Sanchez, wanted to forget all of us. Does he know we are coming for dinner?"

"We'll know that if your pink apron is flying from the yard arm, Boatsie!" It was time I got into the game. "Really, Ava, it is as much a mystery as his '**Goats On A Roof**' theme. I expect we'll find the answers when we get there."

Ava's eyes twinkled mischief in the rearview mirror. "Boatsie, you like pink aprons?"

Bill and I both burst in to laughter. Ava looked puzzled but flashed Boats a smile and wink. "I hate that f . . . farggin apron! The last time I saw it, it was wrapped around a bottle of Laphroaig single malt scotch and better damn well be the last time I see it! I don't like anything f . . . . friggin' pink. Ah . . . except that fine plaid shirt you're wearing Ava."

Our laughter subsided until Ava pointed to the yardarm flagpole display at the edge of José's parking lot. Bill and I both rolled out of the van, doubled over laughing. The club burgee flapped in the breeze. It was clearly a goat wearing a bright pink apron adorned with crossed anchors. Seven more fluttered about the yardarm. One was missing . . .

Ava pointed to one in particular, turned to Boats, flashed a smile and asked the grumbling, grimacing Boats. "What's the story behind the Sweet Cheeks Flag?"

"Hummm . . . A guy named Bishop got his ass in a sling and José had to sew him up. You'll have to ask José about the rest."

Bill and I regained our composure and stood admiring José's handy work. His restaurant was set in a wooded patch and was dug into a craggy hill that steeply rose several hundred feet. The landscape made as natural a goat habitat as you could find this side of Basque country near Winnemucca, Nevada. The photos I'd seen didn't do it justice. Eight goats peacefully grazed on what should be the restaurant's roof. One goat wore a navy blue blanket trimmed in gold and decorated with a gold fouled anchor topped by two stars.

"Good looking goat." I thought.

Boats, Ava, and Bill started for the main entrance. Before I could follow, a pickup truck, horn honking, hauling a U-Haul trailer, pulled off the highway and into the parking lot.

Bill motioned for Ava to continue on. He and Boats turned back toward me and started for the truck and trailer. This was definitely one of those '*WTFO*' moments. Boats did his best limp-shuffle-run clearly wanting to be the first to the truck. Jorge stepped out of the cab and gave Boats a hurry-up hand wave.

"Give me a hand, Boats. Manuel is nursing his broken wrist for all it's worth." Jorge beamed while Manuel untangled himself from the seat belt and joined the other two.

Boats, Manuel, and Jorge slipped around the back of the U-Haul while Bill took up position beside me. "What the hell's in . . . .?"

Before I could finish my sentence, Boats' loud, brassy voice filled the parking lot. "Peee-eue! What's that stinkin, fuckin' goat doin' here? Every time you take her anywhere she shits all over everything. Get her out of there and close that fuckin' door before I pass out! What the fuck . . . is this pick on Boats week?" Boats was pointing behind us and shaking his head in disbelief.

Bill and I turned around in time to see José, wearing a bright pink apron, smiling from ear to ear, double-timing it toward us.

Ava, and a women who looked a lot like Mamma Maria's twin, emerged from an adjacent building that was still under construction; it would be a well-proportioned hacienda when completed. José had emailed me about his twenty-room convention center and conference room and I was a bit jealous that Ava got the first grand tour.

José was bubbly and excited but still managed to feign mock concern about the Chinese-fire-drill taking place in his parking lot. "Bill, Master Chief, it's great to see you. What's all the commotion in my parking lot? Hey! Jorge, Manuel, Boats glad you could make it. What's in the trailer?"

"From the sounds of Boats' bellowing, my guess is Playgirl." José gave me a curious look and followed us to the back of the trailer.

Bill answered José's question in a voice reminiscent of an official at a ribbon cutting ceremony. "We noticed your menagerie is one goat short of a herd. Jorge and Manuel decided to correct that problem."

In the excitement, no one noticed Ava and her escort thirty feet away watching in silence mixed with some disbelief and extreme curiosity.

Jorge and Manuel laid into a long lead rope trying to coax Playgirl out of the trailer. The, overpowering, noxious, stench did not seem to bother her. Boats just stood there, arms folded, with a malicious grin on his face. The trailer blocked his view of the new hacienda.

Playgirl finally came down the loading ramp, half sliding, protesting mightily and shitting up a storm. She was decked out with pink ribbons and a blindingly pink blanket decorated with crossed anchors on each side.

"Congratulations José! You are the proud owner of the finest specimen of stinkin', fuckin' goat God ever put on this green earth! Take this mangy-assed shit-machine to her new billet!" Boats reached back to his hip pocket were his 9mm usually resided and gave a deep sigh. Two of José's staffers took charge of Playgirl before Boats could scrounge up a firearm.

"Why mister Boatsie! That's no way to talk to a perfectly lovely goat and certainly no way to carry on with women in attendance. "Ava was electric with tomfoolery and all smiles.

She and her new acquaintance sauntered toward our group giggling and pointing first at Boats, then the flagpole, and finally at Playgirl. This was starting out to be one interesting banquet. I was glad I was here!

"Sorry Ava! Mam! But you didn't have to spend three hours in a hot helo with that damn obnoxious, stinkin', f.....friggin', goat!" That was as good an apology as anyone was getting from Boats today.

"Hey Boats you're glowin' brighter than the blanket on Playgirl. Why is she named Playgirl? I hope she behaves around my rams. Oh guys . . . this is Carmen. She is my Head Chef and business partner. Let's get out of the sun."

We started toward the restaurant with José chattering non-stop all the way. I couldn't get a word in edgewise; I wanted to ask who arranged all this. "Damn! It's good to see you all again! Boats you still limping? I thought that little scratch would have healed by now, and I see Manuel has a new cast and Bob you seem to still favor that right arm.Thought I patched up the left. Oh shit! It was your leg. Think I'm getting old. You guys getting too old to sail a little boat for a few days? How was the maiden voyage of the **Derdrake**? Damn! It's good to see you all again!"

Before anyone of us could begin to answer José, the front door to **Goats On A Roof** flew open Three familiar guys came rushing at us. "Master Chief! How the fuck are you?" A slightly less rotund, nattily dressed, Lieutenant Commander McHale from the old TV show 'McHale's Navy,' look-alike, John Henry 'Greasey' Bishop, led the pack with outstretched hands.

José stopped chattering long enough to tell us a few friends arrived about an hour ago. That gave me an opening to express my surprise. I was especially taken aback to see Marcie, John's daughter, standing in the doorway with a tall blond, Nordic looking woman.

"Check *'you'* out." I said, "All dressed up in a tailored suit! That a Brooks Brothers? You're lookin' good, Sweet Cheeks! Sweet Jesus! who are those clowns behind you?" I grasped an outstretched hand.

A tall African American, wearing a starched, white, preacher's collar, Joseph 'Preacher' Meechum stepped around Sweet Cheeks, gave me a big hug, and whispered in my ear, "God bless you. It is so very good to be with the ***Goat Locker*** crew again!"

Before I could tell Preacher how glad I was to see him, a precise, clipped, accented, voice broke in. "Wie gehts, Herr Skipper. Es ist so gut, Sie zu sehen!" Fritz Heinrich Schmidt, standing at full attention, grasped my hand and shook it so hard I thought it would dislocate from the shoulder!

With the exception of Simon 'Sparks' Radisson, the entire crew of ***Goat Locker*** was standing in the **Goats On A Roof** parking lot.

Sweet Cheeks saw me looking around and asked, "You lookin' for Sparks? He ain't gonna be here. His new wife won't let him out of the house! I think he told her about our last get together. Getting shot at by fuckin' Pir. . ." Sweet Cheeks evidently spotted Ava and Carmen, stopped in mid sentence, and then continued. "Who are the lovely ladies?"

José, still a bit overwhelmed, introduced Carmen "Sorry guys! This is my Head Chef."

Bill waded in with, "And the lovely cowgirl is my associate Ava." He addressed Ava explaining who everyone was. "Ava, I sailed with these feather merchants last year. It's a shame Sparks couldn't make it. Our entire crew would be here if he made it to this get together."

"Mein Got! Ve ist not der Fedder Merchant! Ve ist . . !" Fritz read my expression precisely and continued. "Ve ist very goot sailors frau Ava und Carmen.

"Hey! Let's get inside and get this party started. Marcie and her friend look a little bit lost. Who's Marcie's friend Sweet

Cheeks?" Explaining **'The Raid'** wasn't going to happen so I changed the subject.

"Helga ist mein liebchen." Fritz solved that mystery and left us all shaking our heads. Today was full of surprises indeed.

We entered the restaurant as a group. Marcie gave me a big hug and thanked me profusely. Helga stood a little aside. She appeared as stand-offish and brusque as Fritz.

Some pieces to the puzzle were still missing. I talked to José but became silent when we approached an oversized oak plank door made from what appeared to be an old cargo hatch. Large, bold hammered brass letters pronounced, *'Goat Locker'*, while blood-red lettering below pronounced, *'knock before entering'*.

Ava, auburn ponytail swinging, grasped the heavy, anchor, doorknocker and rapped it twice then pushed the door open and entered. We, the *Goat Locker* crew, just stood there in silence and awe marveling at the work a beaming José put in to this lounge.

We entered a room decorated in a distinct maritime theme. The back bar was not the typical mirror. It was a mural signed by Mark Trubisky. It was titled, "Float Like A Butterfly; Sting Like A Bee!" Seven Pegasus class hydrofoil ships were prominent. They were engaged in single-close action against a superior naval force. One had to look very closely in the background to see a lone, ghost white, PHM hydrofoil, engaging shore targets and taking heavy fire. That was *Goat Locker*; she was number eight.

José was bubbling. "I had to scramble to get things ready for this reunion. Gman insisted on it being today. The mural was just finished yesterday. Lets' grab a San Magoo and get this party started!"

We pushed into the room. Everyone just sort of stopped to look around. The maritime theme was cleverly integrated with the restaurant's main attraction. Hung at various places were poster sized drawings of Hydrofoil PHMs. Each had goats prominently displayed. One cut-away showed the 76mm Magazine with an old black goat wearing a white collar and a blanket adorned with crossed cannons instructing two kids how to load and shoot. Another showed just the tattooed south end of a goat firing a 20mm on the fantail during an intense fire fight.

Several more scenes from the raid were depicted but five of us gathered around a zebra wood plaque in the center of the room. The

113

obverse and reverse of mementos surrounded by pure gold were realistically portrayed in high relief. A ships clock hung above and a brass plate proudly proclaimed: **Goat Locker**. One hell of a ship! I fiddled with the medallion in my pocket. I removed it and gently set it on the table. Four more followed in short order . . .

Ava, Helga, Marcie, and Carmen had Preacher and Sweet Cheeks surrounded in front of the tattooed goat poster. Sweet Cheeks glowed like a port side running light so I surmised he was forced to explain how he earned his moniker.

I barked an order. "Preacher! Sweet Cheeks! Front and center! Present your credentials!" They both looked relieved and hurried in our direction. Carmen surrounded the chicks with her ample wings and gently maneuvered them in the general direction of the kitchen.

José signaled to the bartender. Preacher and Sweet Cheeks placed their medals with ours. Everyone's attention was focused on the meaning of those tokens. Each of us was deep in thought. I was transported back to the Indian Ocean, (IO), and fighting for our lives . . .

José broke the mood and pointed to the back bar; he could not contain himself. "Let's drink to the best damn ship and crew that ever introduced pirates to Davy Jones' Locker!"

"I'll drink to that!" Jim Billings, Gman, was striding toward us with a tray full of highball glasses and what could only be a bottle of Laphroaig single malt scotch wrapped in a faded, blood stained, pink apron . . .

Chapter 22
THE GATHERING

"Don't just stand there; everyone take a seat." Gman beamed and squirmed a bit in his signature buttoned down, pin striped, suit and blue and white striped tie. "Boats, you do the honors and pour."

Boats reluctantly accepted the pink package and grumbled, "That better be Laphorig or I'm gonna strangle you with this pink-mother-fucker! Then I'm gonna burn it."

When the eye rolling, ribbing, backslapping, and good-natured laughing subsided each of our tumblers contained four fingers of fine single malt scotch; conversation came to a standstill and Gman proposed a toast. "To the finest bunch of over the hill old farts and to one hell of a ship they sailed and fought: *Goat Locker*! May she live again." Glasses clinked and we drank in silence.

I was deep in thought stuck on a reoccurring theme. *"Oh, oh . . . Jim's up to something."* Sweet Cheeks was uncommonly quiet; Preacher, Jorge, and Manuel sort of stared at one another; Boats stepped a little closer to Gman and clearly started to say something; Fritz assumed a calculating pose and José accomplished a slow, deliberate survey of his lounge. I thought I detected a far-away look in his eyes.

Bill was the first to speak; he voiced what we all caught in Gman's toast. "May she live again? Was that a slip of the tongue Jim?"

"Not exactly but I see the women are returning from their tour of the kitchen. Let's eat; José's been cooking for two days and I put a mountain of San Magoo on ice. I want to catch up on what all of you have been up to since our last meeting." Jim was in his *'what I have to say is for privileged ears only'* mode. Everyone recognized it and understood its meaning.

Ava swished up to the table, winked at Boats, and feigned intense interest in a breathless, excited voice. "Boatsie! Is that your infamous pink apron on the table? Don't you know how to use a washing machine? I could help you with that if you're not busy later this evening."

That broke the tension and some of my apprehension subsided. I knew something was definitely afoot; I hoped it was not another pirate chasing game half way around the world.

We sat, and the staff began serving mounds of five-star Mexican food. After a few minutes the sea stories started along with: Do you remember . . . What the fuck happened at . . . Who are you with now . . . How is this or that doing . . . and the inevitable, no shit, that really happened?

Each of us was several San Magoos into forgetting where we were. The wait staff worked in slow motion. They hung on snippets of enlightening, amusing, and sometimes gory conversations. The Laphroaig was long gone and I noticed an intense silence from the women sitting at one end of the pushed together tables. Ava pushed her chair back from the table, leaned toward me, and asked, "Can you tell me what this is all about? What was **'The Raid'**? What is or was *Goat Locker* and *Scrap Dealer*? Why was *Derdrake* named after you and why was it attacked?" She stared more than gazed at me and screwed her face into a petulant, demanding scowl.

All eyes turned to us. Ava was a bit tipsy and her speech bordered on loud; that, alone, attracted everyone's attention. Carman, Helga, and the wait staff waited in anticipation for the all-encompassing sea-story about **'The Raid'** and attack on the *Derdrake* to began. Marcie looked excited; she anticipated finding out how her dad earned the nickname, 'Sweet Cheeks'.

"What would Nick Charles do?" flashed through my mind. *"Walk Asta was all I could think of and that wouldn't work here!"* I decided it was payback time. "Jim, are we still subject to life in prison for telling sea stories from half way around the world?"

Boats, Fritz, and Preacher broke into big smiles; José just rolled his eyes and shook his head from side to side. Gman was silent. I finally got one over on him.

Bill bailed him out. "Checkmate! We've had some interesting adventures together and we will write a book about them some day. Let's just say Master Chief Kensey led us out of a ticklish situation and deserved some recognition. That's why I named our schooner after him.

We ran into some pirates off Isla Guadalupe on our maiden voyage. Master Chief Kensey got us out of that situation alive even though we lost three good men. It may take a while before I feel comfortable talking about the gory details. I can't speak for the others but I'll bet they feel the same. Sorry to disappoint you ladies . . . Jim can you add anything?" Ava looked placated but not entirely satisfied.

"No. Not really. I can say that this group of curmudgeons did a fantastic service for their country and each of them would all be highly decorated if they were still part of the active Navy. You will get details but you will have to wait for the book, I'd title it '*Goat Locker Strikes!*', and it would be a best seller. Just wait . . ." It was evident that Bill was finished. Little conversations broke out all around the table and Gman wagged his finger at me but he was smiling.

Jim held a barely audible conversation with José and Bill. José summoned the wait staff and they began clearing the odds and ends left over from tonight's festivities.

Bill wandered to the ladies end of the table clearly on a mission. "Ladies, It appears this is going to be an all nighter. José arranged accommodations for everyone in the Viejas Casino Resort down the street. The staff will shuttle you there when they've finished here."

He sidled up to Ava and in a lowered voice gave her separate instructions. "We are going to talk about and discuss things your lawyer self doesn't want to know. We will make our way to the hotel later . . . much later. I'll see you in the morning and I'm sure I'll have some specific directons for you then."

Ava was not happy. She really wanted to hear firsthand about the adventures of this motley crew of old sailors but she learned long ago that once Bill gave instructions they were to be followed. "Come on ladies let's leave this den of sea-stories and try our luck at the casino. Jose, this was the best banquet ever! We will be holding all our seminars and shindigs right here from now on." She stood up to a chorus of wolf whistles from Greasey and Fritz.

"Good night Boatsie, see you later. Bring that apron; I'll wash it for you!" Ava was definitely being impish. She leaned over and whispered in my ear, "I'll see you later."

Before I could think up a suitable quip John, the headwaiter, announced he was ready to drive the ladies to the Viejas. I was not sure if I was relieved or disappointed.

Jim wandered to the bar, picked up a tray of small crystal snifters and a bottle of Hennessy Cognac Paradis. He distributed snifters all around while talking. "Gentlemen let's get to why we are here. First, though, I'd really like to know what happened on the *Derdrake's* maiden voyage. I think that attack and what I have to discuss are related."

Bill, Manuel, and Jorge turned to me giving me the go-ahead to relate what happened. I thought about it for a few moments then decided to give a brief report. "We shook the schooner down for three days then set up to fish off Isla Guadalupe. Three zodiacs, with five or six men, attacked out of the fog with no warning. They hit us with RPGs that took out our sails, communications, and engine. They made two strafing runs then laid off about three hundred yards taking pot shots watching us burn and waiting for us to sink . . . Stupid fuckers thought we'd roll over and give up! My FN-FAL kept them ducking but Boats, Jorge and Manuel took two zodiacs out with the Barrett, and M-60. The lone survivor turned to run but I ruined his day with a Stinger." I paused for another sip of Cognac.

Boats was eager to continue the saga. "Bastards fucked up my boat bad! We limped north with makeshift sails. Kensey jerry-rigged communications and we made a run for the Fortress. Dick heads had a GPS tracker stashed aboard. When Manuel found it Kensey used it as a decoy. If I ever catch those fuckers I'll feed them my beautiful mahogany coach work one splinter at a time!" Boats slammed an empty San Magoo bottle down on the table his anger visibly boiling.

"Take it easy Boats . . . We *'will'* find them." Bill took over the narrative. "We rounded Isla Guadalupe and ran for the Fortress. We were sending S.O.S. but didn't think anyone heard. About two in the morning the bridge-to-bridge started squawking. (VHF radio) We prepared for another fire-fight."

Manuel, uncharacteristically, interrupted. "Sure was glad the Mexican Navy showed up instead of the assholes that attacked us!"

"How the fuck did they get there?" That was a typical Sweet Cheeks question. Jorge continued where his brother left off.

"Bob's makeshift antenna and SOS saved our asses! There was another boat in the vicinity, the ***Andiamo***, an old style tuna clipper, that I think had something to do with the attack."

Gman nodded and took over the conversation. "I got involved about that time. I was in Seattle working on a little something. Mind if I take over." Gman got a unanimous nod and started filling in some details. "The Mexican authorities believed ***Andiamo,*** and more importantly her Master, Captain Richmond was involved. The Mexican authorities tore that ship apart, twice! She was clean, entirely too clean. The US and Mexico are monitoring her movements and will for some time to come, but she has a new Master and is actually fishing for tuna. Captain Richmond gave us the slip. I expect to locate him when a little operation I have going up North finishes." Jim took a sip of cognac.

"Oh, oh!" I thought. *"Black Cloud! I'll have to see if I can contact him when we are finished here."*

"The rest of this is going to take a while. Let's make a quick head call." Chairs scooted away from the table and most made for the head, (restroom), while carrying on conversations and answering questions.

I was deep in thought and decided to wait until the milling herd vacated the head. I could not help but think, *"What could the attack on **Derdrake**, Gman's summons and Black Cloud possibly have in common?"*

Chapter 23
NORTH TO ALASKA

Mike, not all that patient a person, put the finishing five wraps of forty-pound-test monofilament fishing line around the shank of a number-six hook. He usually just bought mooching-rigs but forgot to pick them up at Cabalas. *"Where's that fuckin' Kensey when I need him?"* ran through his mind as the bumper knot he just painstakingly finished unraveled when a bit of strain was applied to the hook. "Fuck it! I'll buy some in Ketchikan." Mike informed Varmint who just cocked an ear and eyed the remnants of the other ten or so attempts lying on the floor.

Mike placed the hooks and leader into a plastic zip lock bag and tossed them in the shit-can. He picked up a good-sized stack of documents that was the contents of the room safe and browsed through them. His passport, Oregon State driver license, international credit/debit card, and new Umpqua Bank statement were already neatly stacked in a separate pile beside five-thousand dollars in well used twenty and one-hundred dollar bills. Mike laid the Inside Passage charts, tide and current tables, and satellite photos aside and concentrated on the dossier of one 'Richard Kopf'.

Forty five minutes passed in a wink. A deep growl and nudge by Varmint performing his, *'take me for a walk or I'll piss all over the floor'* dance put an end to his concentration.

"Midnight! Fuckin' midnight and you want to go for a walk?" Mike would pick **Dead Eye**, now, **Springer,** up in four hours and did not look forward to Varmint sniffing around for half an hour just to find the perfect place to pee.

"Its' raining cats and dogs! Can't you just use the toilet like everyone else?" Mike grumbled while putting his rain gear on; Varmint danced at the door not paying a bit of attention to Mike's carping.

"Jesus! Now what?" The dragging cuff on his rain pants was repaired but a bright red heart was embroidered on the right cheek of the ass. "Kensey . . . fuckin' Kensey . . ." Mike remembered leaving his rain gear in the Havens' radio room a few months back and Bob said he'd fix them. "Fixed 'em he did. Varmint, you got my permission to bite his ass next time we see him!" Varmint paid no attention but his dance was now accentuated with a growl and whine.

Fifteen-after-midnight was probably too late for a normal person needing to awake in less than three hours to think about sleep but Mike could fall asleep anywhere, anytime, and wake precisely when he needed to. Ten seconds, ten minutes, ten hours, it mattered not. A soaking wet Varmint lay crosswise on the queen-sized bed snoring gently. Mike made one last sweep of the room and checked to make sure nothing was left in the safe. Everything was ready to roll. He checked the oversized wheelie suitcase for the umpteenth time and made certain his Barrett, model 98B, 338 Lapua magnum, sniper rifle and ten rounds of custom-made ammunition were secure.

"Push over Varmint or you're sleepin' in the rain." Varmint did not budge but emitted a cloud of gas that could have been caught and painted green! "Don't fuckin' beg for pickled eggs and beer ever again!" Mike beat a hasty retreat to the chez near the air conditioning/heating unit, turned the fan to high, and then threw a blanket over his head and drifted off to sleep.

It was good to be back aboard *Dead Eye* now renamed *Springer*. Her diesel purred like a kitten. Outwardly, except for the color scheme, she seemed the same but vibrated like a high-strung quarter horse. Several thick packets of instructions laid on the portside navigation table one deck below and would have to be reviewed when time permitted. Every system was upgraded to Raymarine G series. Radar showed no nearby traffic and a concise plot showed the way to *Springer's* first Canadian stop. A note flashed: Customs cleared with CANPASS but notify customs at first port of entry north of Nanaimo. "Fuckin' cool Varmint! Where's your life jacket?" Varmint paid little attention and continued sniffing his way around this familiar but changed boat.

Four hours passed without incident. Transit of the Rosario Strait through the San Juan Islands was a cinch with the new radar integrated with GPS. An annoying, insistent alarm squawked from the edge speakers on the plasma display. *"What the fuck? Gotta read those operating instructions."* Mike thought as he idly mashed buttons until a message stating 'collision possible' and a graphic depicting a dangerous CPA, (closest point of approach), showed on the screen.

"I can see the fuckin' Tsawwassen Ferry you dip stick . . . Shut up already!" Varmint growled and came to alert with Mike's raised voice. The attention getting squawk and flashing alert disappeared when Mike changed course and advanced the throttle bringing *Springer* up to twenty-two knots.

"Hot damn Varmint; that's cool! The new screw and tuned engine work good!" Mike throttled back to fifteen knots and mashed the button labeled '*auto pilot*'.

Fair Winds, Schooner Cove Marina answered up on the first bridge-to-bridge call Mike made before entering Nanoose Bay. The transit from Port Townsend, Washington took a mere ten hours and forty-three minutes. With the exception of the last hour, the Strait of Georgia was calm and pleasant. Varmint had a bit of trouble in six-foot rollers but soon found his sea legs. Everything on *Springer* was working well and Mike had plenty of time to familiarize himself with the electronic gizmos and improvements.

He had his instructions from the marina office; he would moor port-side-to at the long, empty, finger pier. Mike idled *Springer* down to a crawl wondering if someone warned the marina about his close-quarters maneuvering skills. *Springer* all but stopped; Mike checked set and drift, and then eased into the pier making a perfect approach. Screeching seagull cries and deep, angry barking filled the silence. A flock of angry gulls wheeled in tight circles around a determined, barking, Varmint. Two young boys stopped fifty feet down the pier coiled mooring lines dangling from hesitant hands. Mike gave three short blasts on the silent dog whistle; that was Varmint's 'return to me' signal. He leapt back aboard tail wagging 'mission accomplished'.

"Good job dude! Don't want any more web-footed crap machines fuckin' up our fly-bridge bimini!" Guarding Springer and keeping all seagulls and ducks away was Varmint's first-mate duty and he took it seriously.

Two gangly teenage boys closely watched by an ever-vigilant Varmint, made *Springer* fast to the pier while Mike set out fenders fore and aft. The taller boy, a lanky, geek-looking, red head wearing thick black glasses meekly approached the open wheelhouse hatch.

"Skipper if you'll follow me I'll take you to the marina office. Dan, the owner, said you are already checked in and customs was notified of your arrival. Nice dog. What's his name?"

"Varmint and he doesn't much like anyone. I'd stay clear of the boat if I were you. I'll be with you in a second." Mike was on assignment and on guard. It was unlikely anyone here would snoop around *Springer* let alone board her but there was no sense taking chances.

Mike leapt onto the dock and landed squarely on the neatly flemished bitter end of a mooring line. It rolled out from under his foot; he slipped and fell on his butt landing in a fresh patch of white, gooey, seagull shit. "I hate fuckin' seagulls! What are you two lookin' at?" Mike picked himself up and started down the pier.

"Can I hose that off for you Skipper?" The smaller dark haired lad in yellow rain gear asked with a snicker.

It occurred to Mike the pink heart embroidered on his foul-weather pants must be noticed by the two deck hands. *"Kensey! I will get even."* ran through his mind before answering. "Yeah. Thanks."

Fair Winds, Schooner Cove Marina was a nice sized resort catering to pleasure cruisers transiting the Inside Passage looking for adventure, and local fishing boats, sail boats, and cruisers. It was a good hike to the marina office. The rain was pelting down at an acute angle and the wind felt like it increased to near gale force. *"Might have to spend a day or so here . . ."* crossed Mikes' mind as he entered the marina office.

Mike casually entered the marina office and was greeted by a weather beaten, portly, man wearing foul-weather pants, a Blue Jay ball cap, and a red and black checked flannel shirt. He stopped pecking at a keyboard and ambled from behind the office counter with hand extended. "Hi. I'm Dan. You must be Mr. Smith. Looks like you got moored up before the weather turned nasty. Welcome to Schooner Cove."

"Just call me Mike." Mike accepted Dan's firm, friendly grip and hand shake. "Weather guessers missed this little blow! Got room at the inn if I have to stay an extra day?"

"No problem this time of year." Dan Looked longingly at a wall chart showing a plethora of empty slips. "You can stay a couple of months if you want to. Clubhouse, lounge, and grill are all being renovated so you'll have to go a few miles for entertainment and meals. One of the boys can give you a lift, give me a shout on channel 69, (Canadian VHF pleasure boat channel), and I'll arrange that for you. I recommend the Rocking Horse Inn. You'll have to get a cab back."

"Thanks, I'll think about it. You got diesel?" Mike could run two more days before refueling was necessary but keeping the tanks topped-off was always a good idea.

Dan didn't hesitate; this was a common query. "Yeah. A fueling barge comes around in an hour or so. How many liters do you need?"

"Crap! I don't know, about 130 US gallons. What's the cost?" Mike did not do metric conversions all that well.

"Cost is around a dollar forty-one, Canadian, a liter and you'll need about five hundred liters . . ." Dan did not show a glimmer of a question. Everyone cruising these waters needed fuel and all could pay the going price. That was explicitly understood for someone soloing on a Nordic Tug 37.

"Cool. Have them stop by. I'll be waiting." With that said Mike turned about and retraced his path to *Springer*.

Varmint greeted him with that *'what's for dinner'* look and crossed legs. "Don't give me that shit! Use the port or starboard side scupper. I had them specially made for you. And it's chips, (Brit french-fries), eggs, and beer for dinner. After last night, you get Alpo!"

Springer rocked gently in protected water of the pre-dawn harbor. A chilly breeze and gray mist was all that remained from last night's blow. Mike started the engine room ventilation blower as Varmint scratched on the port side hatch to be let back in out of the drizzle. Breakfast, a couple of toasted English-muffins and peanut butter, was finished half an hour ago and the galley made ship-shape and ready for sea. "Well Varmint, let's get out of here. We want to be past Ripple Rock and the Seymour Narrows before the tide gets to running. Might even stop at the Browns Bay Marina floating restaurant for lunch if you behave yourself."

Mike brought the diesel to life and cocked an ear listening to it tick-over. "Sounds better than ever and seems to be running about twelve gallons an hour!" Varmint stared with indifference. If goodies were not mentioned he just was not all that interested.

125

Mike swung the helm hard to starboard and engaged the screw in reverse. The bow swung away from the pier nicely but abruptly stopped. Varmint did a little jig momentarily losing his balance; a half-full cup of coffee sloshed off the small chart table and into Mike's lap. "Fuckin' mooring lines!" Bright red streaked the Eastern sky. Mike unsecured the aft mooring lines and *Springer* finally swung her bow into the Strait of Georgia and continued north.

CHAPTER 24
INSIDE PASSAGE

Schooner Cove receded astern. Radar, sonar, and GPS all tracked nicely. Running with the wind gently kissing the fantail made for easy and boring cruising in the Georgia Strait. Mike's thoughts drifted. He recalled a sea story told by one of the old duffers who hung out at the Safe Haven. *"I guess maybe that BS about coming up here from Steilacoom, Washington in an eighteen-foot Glasspar boat might be true. Hell, I could manage this mill pond in a row boat."*

Ripple Rock and the Seymour Narrows were notorious boat killers; that prompted Mike to study current flows and pencil notes on his chart showing ebb tides running north and flood tides running south. This was going to be a piece of cake. He would enter the discovery Passage just at slack tide and run all the way to Kelsey Bay Marina on the ebb.

"Ok Varmint. Here we go. Ripple Rock, what's left of it, is just off the starboard side." Mike was talking to an uninterested party.

"You want me to read any more "Call of the Wild"? You better get interested in some history. Captain George Vancouver sailed through here and said this is one of the vilest stretches of water in the world." Varmint opened one eye for a second then drifted back to sleep.

Springer crabbed sideways in a thirty-foot maelstrom that opened on her port side. Varmint jumped to his feet, hackles bristling, and suspiciously eyeballed a log sporting fifty or so cormorants sliding down the starboard side. Mike idly checked the GPS and verified they were still on course.

"I'll have to watch for that shit!" Mike did not added a turn to ***Springer's*** screw, (increased propeller RPM), but GPS reported speed increased to twenty-two knots.

"We'll be at the Narrows Floating Restaurant in Brown's Bay in no time. Think I'll stop for a decent meal. You want a fillet?" Varmint didn't move a muscle. "Ok . . . It's Alpo for you!"

Mike idly unhooked the VHF radio's mic, verified he was transmitting at peak power on channel sixty-nine and keyed the transmit button.

"Browns Bay Marina, Browns Bay Marina, this is pleasure craft *Springer*." No one answered.

He tried to reach the marina twice more and all but gave up on the idea of a fine rib eye or porterhouse steak for lunch. A soft, pleasant but somewhat out-of-breath female voice filled the cabin.

"Pleasure craft *Springer*, pleasure craft *Springer*, this is the Browns Bay Marina. How may I be of service?"

"I'll be at the Marina shortly; what time does the restaurant open?"

"The floating restaurant doesn't open until the second or third week in May and there isn't anything else within walking distance. Sorry!" The disembodied voice sounded truly disappointed.

Mike thought, *"business is slow or she is bored or both."* But managed to keep disappointment from creeping into his reply. "Thanks for the info. Looks like Varmint gets Alpo again. He sure was looking forward to chomping a T-bone! *Springer* Out"

"Stop on your return voyage. We'll leave a light on and I'll save a T-bone for the varmint. Browns Bay Marina, out."

Lunch would have to wait until they cleared the Seymour Narrows and entered the Johnstone Strait. One did not navigate this vile stretch of water with ones' eyes closed or auto-helm engaged. Varmint nosed through his doggie-door and trotted down the port side to use one of his 'special scuppers'.

"That's the windward side Varmint! When will you ever learn?" Mike shook his head in bewilderment and reduced speed. He planned to stop at Kelsey Bay Marina about thirty miles further up the Inside Passage. Another two and a half hours would easily put them there by 1530.

"Perfect, that gives me time to look around Sayward. Might even be a decent bar in town." Mikes' thoughts wandered in the relative calm of the Johnstone Strait.

"Kelsey Bay Marina, Kelsey Bay Marina, this is pleasure craft *Springer*." Mike's call was answered immediately and slip and mooring requirements were arranged.

A Zodiac Solstice Sportster, a twin of the one secured behind Mike on the flying bridge, propelled by an electric motor, piloted by a pudgy middle aged women decked out in bright orange foul weather gear, met *Springer* at the Marina entrance and guided her to the assigned slip. Dee, as she called herself, tied up in the adjacent slip, hopped up onto the dock and helped Mike set fenders and tie off mooring lines. She kept a wary eye on Varmint.

"Those granny-knots hold? Nice looking dog. Does he bite?" Dee pulled a smattering of papers out from under her foul weather jacket and looked like she wanted to come aboard.

"Yes! His name is Varmint and he is attack-trained. Do you need to come aboard? I'll tie him up if you do." Mike immediately reverted to mission-mode whenever anyone wanted to board *Springer.* *"Probably just paranoia."* He thought.

"No. That's ok. You can take care of checking in at the office. My husband is minding the store and should be there for another half hour. Anything else you need, give us a shout on the VHF." That was that. Dee scurried back into her Zodiac and set course for the marina office.

Mike donned foul weather gear, protection against a steady, soaking drizzle, stepped onto the pier and gave two short puffs on the silent dog whistle. He watched Varmint quickly verify no one was left aboard *Springer,* jump onto the pier and silently catch up with him taking advantage of every scrap of cover available. Barely noticeable hand signals sent Varmint coursing ahead scouting Mikes' path.

"Can't teach an old dog new tricks but I see he hasn't forgotten any either. Hope he remembers he's just looking and not hunting!" Mike smiled wondering what Dee would do if Varmint suddenly confronted her . . .

Mike stopped just outside the marina office, signaled for Varmint to return, gave him several hand signals, and then pushed open the door. A large cowbell clanged and banged and announced Mikes' arrival into a dimly lighted, barely functional, cubbyhole of an office. Varmint followed heeling along Mikes' left side and sat when Mike came to a stop. A short, dark haired, diminutive man wearing a plaid shirt, and logger's wide, red, suspenders sat behind a cluttered desk. He was obviously startled and jumped up so fast that his reading glasses slid off the end of his Roman nose and flipped onto the desk.

"Hi . . . I'm Robert. You must be Mr. Smith. Dee said you'd be by to register." Well worn Levis and Sperry Topsiders completed Robert's ensemble.

"Those the forms I need to fill out?" Mike gestured toward the only neatly stacked papers in the office.

"Yeah. Just sign the top two; the rest are yours. Ah . . . the fuel pier opens at 4:30 in the morning if you plan on starting out early. We're expecting wind just short of gale force, and heavy rain starting around midnight. You are welcome to stay as long as you like." Robert looked and sounded nervous. Mike chalked it up to Varmint carefully watching every move he made.

"We should be fine. *Springer* handles weather really well. Any place close to get a good meal?" Mike still had his heart set on a good steak and a Bowser-bag for Varmint.

"The Cable House is six or seven kilometers down the road you can't miss it. Dee drives right by it on her way to the cannery. She can drop you off but you'll have to walk back. If you are interested give me a shout before half-five; Dee has to be at work around six." Robert scooped up his glasses and a stack of bills and gave a disdainful glance at the beeping laptop half buried on the desk.

"Thanks. I'll think about it, but it ain't exactly a great night for a walk in the rain!" Mike and Varmint wheeled as one and started back down the pier to the clang and bang of a well-agitated cowbell.

0500 arrived dark, wet, and windy. Tight quarters near the fueling pier added a splash of sail boat blue and float green to *Springer's* general paint scheme. Black Cloud was in a dark mood. The sea was churned up with white caps on top of ground swells. There would not be much rest today. The inside passage was stirred to a froth and traveling the open ocean of Queen Charlotte Sound might be tedious and for sure interesting.

"Shearwater Marina on Denny Island is our next stop. I wonder how long that will take? I hope Old Bella Bella has a decent pub! Someone stocked us with five cases of San Magoo but no real beer. Probably Kensey's doing." Mike spoke more or less to Varmint, who, as usual, completely ignored him.

CHAPTER 25
ROUGH DAY

Five hours of bouncing around kept Mike on his toes. Queen Charlotte Sound could be a 'muther' but it was comparatively calm. The short, tiring, chop of Johnstone Strait gave way to a sizeable but gentle roll in the Cook Trough, Sea Otter Valley and Goose Island Bank.

"Up and at 'em! It's time for lunch while the gettins' good!" Varmint was still curled up in a corner under the galley table and was not about to move if it was not absolutely necessary.

Mike set the auto helm, took a good look around, and then busied himself in the galley. Less than ten minutes work had a paper plate stacked with cheese and crackers, salami sandwich, and a pair of pickled eggs teetering on his lap. A fresh Keurig-brewed, Pacific Bold, cup of coffee steamed in a cup holder animated by ***Springer*** pitching into one wave after another. A sharp thud and a sledgehammer like banging reverberated down ***Springer's*** hull from bow to stern. Mike inhaled a pickled egg, throttled down, and slammed the engine into neutral. He left the paper plate on the captain's chair and rocketed below decks.

A quick but thorough stem to stern search revealed no signs of leakage. Mike throttled the engine back 'up'; no unusual vibrations or sounds followed. "We were lucky Varmint. We ran over a barely floating log; good thing it wasn't a dead head! Don't need to start takin' on water in this shit! You listening?" Varmint ignored Mike and continued nosing around making sure Mike did not miss any leaks.

"Better try long haul HF; (High frequency, radio, voice, communications) it's the only thing anyone's likely to hear out here." Mike muttered to no one in particular. Varmint was still below; Mike could hear his choke chain tinkle against the stainless steel bowl as he wolfed down lunch.

Mike dialed a memorized frequency in the ten-meter band into the brand new, Yaesu FT DX 9000, transceiver and keyed the mic. "Haven this is *Springer*. Over." Static and a bit of single-side-band distortion greeted his hail.

"CQ, CQ, CQ. Safe Haven, this is *Springer*. Any of you Feather Merchants awake at this hour? Over."

****

"Gunny you know anyone named Springer?" Harry, sipped an Elk Head, Elk Dandee Ale, while finishing up his mid-morning snack in the radio room of the Safe Haven bar on Seattle's waterfront; he connected the Hallicrafters, (HF communications transceiver), output to the AR5 speakers hanging over the bar, and turned up the volume.

Gunny, polishing the elbow smoothed mahogany bar in preparation for the soon to arrive lunch crowd, paused and then joined Harry at the HF set. "Sounds like Black Cloud . . . What the fuck? He win enough off you shallow water sailors to buy a new boat? I just got the dock repaired from his last visit. Hope he ain't comin' here! Answer up; let's see what gives."

"*Springer* this is The Safe Haven Bar and Grill in Seattle. We have you five-by-five." Gunny nodded in approval at Harry's noncommittal answer.

"Safe Haven, this is *Springer*. I'm cruising the Puget Sound and wondered if you carried any decent beer. I've been plagued with salt brine called San Magoo and need a real brew."

Harry reached up and tapped a plain white calling card adorned with an embossed chess knight. Gunny nodded in agreement. It was unsaid, but Harry was on guard about what he would say from this point on. "*Springer*, today is Micro Brew day featuring the Elk Head Brewery in Buckley. Stop at our guest dock. The first one is on the house."

"Thanks; maybe later. I'm a bit too far north to make it there today. Besides, I prefer Wingman's 'Miss-B-Haven'. I'll take a rain check. *Springer* out." Mike was dying to ask about his friend Kensey, but thought better of broaching the subject over the open air.

"HF is working just tits Varmint. That's good to know. Oh shit! Tell me you didn't snarf my pickled egg." Every silver lining had a black cloud for Mike . . .

"Where do you suppose that boat wrecking, ground pounder is? And, why would he want a Wingman micro-brew when he clearly prefers Bush Bavarian in a can over everything else?" Burt was leaning over the bar listening in. He voiced the question Gunny and Harry didn't.

"Beats the shit out of me . . ." Harry keyed the mic. (Pressed the transmit button on the microphone) "We'll catch ya in a few days. Gunny said he'd run over to the Ram and get you a special brew. That would be a Butt-Face Ale! Safe Haven, Seattle, out." Harry left the mic open, (keyed and transmitting), long enough for Black Cloud to hear the laughter in the back ground.

****

"Fuckin' Twidgits. They're worse than the Jarhead. I'll call a few buddies at Rollies. They should be able to get one over on them next time they're in Seattle!" Mike smiled thinking about the world's best practical joker and how he could easily '**get ahead**'. "Fuckin-a! I'll sic Fred on them. He probably still has some mighty fine Brown-Water-Army tricks up his sleeve. Butt-Face Ale my ass!"

The busy morning slipped into early afternoon. First Calvert then Hecate Island slid past the port side and receded astern. Rain cascaded down in torrents cutting visibility down to about two-hundred yards. Radar, sonar, and GPS all worked to keep Springer on course and away from hazards. The rain was bothersome but tolerable, and beating through a mild chop within Fitz Hugh Sound on Canada's Inside Passage was much preferable to the waves and wind in Queen Charlotte Sound.

"About three hours and we should be parked for the night. Word on the grapevine is Shearwater Marina has a very good restaurant. Maybe we'll stay an extra day and let the weather settle a bit. Varmint . . . you listening? Fuckin' Gman. I could have talked, Lenni into coming along if he didn't insist I do this alone. She would have been much better company. Besides, she certainly has enough sense not to piss into the wind!" Mike needed a night on the town. One-sided conversations with Varmint were getting old and less than satisfying.

Shearwater Marina was a modern gem in the midst of a wilderness. With the exception of the marina and associated buildings there was not much to explore. A fairly good road led to

Old Bella Bella about three kilometers away. Word was that the old fishing village was fairly rundown and a good site for rustic photography but not much else. One pub, The Bad Screw, was nestled among fairly dilapidated buildings on the waterfront; locals described it as a 'roughneck' pub that should be given a wide berth.

Chapter 26
BAD SCREW

"It'll be light in a while. Today is a training day . . ." Varmint was finishing up the last of an excellent T-bone steak Mike brought back from Fisherman's bar last night.

Mike decided to make sure both he and Varmint were on top of their game. He planned to hike to Old Bella Bella through the woods then run back to the marina on the surface road. It was a perfect day for their kind of training. A foggy, soaking mist hung just above the trees. Sunrise was nothing more than a gloomy lightning of the eastern sky. Mike squared the galley away, went over his mental checklist, and started gathering equipment and supplies for a day out.

First thing was changing Varmint's noisy choke chain collar for his VOX (voice operated transmit) unit. The VOX collar was not so much for Mike to give voice commands but its super sensitive audio pick-up allowed Mike to 'hear' what transpired near Varmint, and the GPS tracker allowed him to see where Varmint was. With that job completed and tested, Mike added items to the pack to approximate the fifty or so pounds of equipment he'd need for his up-coming mission. The last thing he checked before leaving was his Smith and Wesson XD-40 and two extra magazines. This area teemed with wildlife, especially bears! He would feel better carrying his prized possession, an original AMP 44-Auto-Mag, but it was difficult to carry concealed.

Mike slid the stainless steel sheet behind the doggie-door, set security devices, and then quickly departed ***Springer***. Varmint lay on the port side deck waiting patiently. Within ten minutes, a dripping evergreen forest surrounded Mike. He checked his back trail for telltale signs of his passing. The casual observer would never suspect his presence. He leaned against a tree, started his stopwatch, and then gave three short blasts on the silent dog whistle. Five minutes and twenty-three seconds later a wet nose nudged his dangling left hand.

137

"Getting a bit slow in your old age . . . but not much!" Mike scratched Varmint's ears for a few seconds then gave one gentle puff on the silent dog whistle. Varmint disappeared among the trees. He would 'dog' Mike's back trail until told to do differently. Mike verified Varmint was doing his job with the GPS Tracker and plotted a general course covering the two kilometers to Old Bella Bella.

It took a little over an hour to carefully zigzag one kilometer. Mike wasn't instinctively masking his trail. He had to constantly check and make sure he wasn't leaving much for anyone to follow. That burned a lot of time. A low growl from his ear-bud, (miniature receiver plugged into Mike's left ear*)*, stopped Mike in his tracks. Something or someone attracted Varmint's attention. Four short blasts on the dog whistle put Varmint on alert and told him to *'shadow'*. He would get close enough to pick up conversation on his VOX unit and wait for Mike's voice command: *'kill'*.

Mike continued along his chosen path. Within ten minutes, a distinct grunting and the sound of bark being torn from a tree trunk filled his left ear. He immediately sounded *'return'*. A bear three hundred yards behind was a worry. Within two minutes, Varmint slid silently into step beside him. Mike picked up the pace; he wanted more distance between them and the bear. He sent Varmint scouting *'ahead'* with hand signals, recalled him ten minutes later and sent him on *'orbit'* for another fifteen. Stealth training finished when they emerged from the forest on the edge of a shabby little village at 1141.

Mike stashed his pack under a pile of brush, thought about his Smith and Wesson XD-40, removed it from the small of his back, placed it in the pack, and pocketed a roll of quarters. "It's probably better to explore Old Bella Bella unarmed. You got my back Varmint? Ok . . . let's go see what this has-been berg offers."

The only sign of life entailed two fairly new pickup trucks and a Range Rover Discovery parked in front of a dumpy, weather beaten, waterfront bar. The pub sign, shaped like a boat propeller with half of one blade missing, one riddled with holes, and the other severely bent, proudly announced this was the **'Bad Screw Pub'**.

When Mike entered, five customers and the bartender gave him dismissive, disapproving, glances. With the exception of the man sitting at the bar wearing slacks, loafers, and a neatly laundered, plaid shirt, all eyes focused on Varmint. Two gruff snooker players, dressed like loggers with plaid flannel shirts, wide, red, braces buttoned into their Carhart jeans, and substantial boots laced to just below the knee, rolled their eyes, and then continued their game.

Mike left Varmint lying under a mid-room table with intentions of meandering to the bar. This was recon; for the most part, it went unnoticed. The full sized snooker table took up most of the room to Mike's left. Tables and chairs were pushed against the back wall and the wall at the end of the bar to make room for the players. To his right, several round tables, and chairs littered the eight or ten feet separating him from another wall. A stout barred and padlocked door behind the bar to the left caught Mike's eye: it was out of place in this shabby pub. He filed that information away and mentally laid out an escape route if needed.

Two grubby men, dressed in shabby woolen shirts, yellow foul weather pants and wellies, (rubber, knee high, boots), sat one table away and downwind from Varmint. They appeared to be fresh off a fishing boat. The rotund, older man spoke loudly to his younger duplicate.

"That mutt smells like a wet rug. He should be outside with the rest of the shit!" Mike was four steps away but turned at the obvious challenge.

"I'm surprised you can smell a wet rug or anything besides yourself . . . Varmint stays where he is."

The bartender, polishing half a dozen schooners with a frayed, limp bar rag, stopped what he was doing and stared at Mike. The well-dressed man Mike mentally named 'Loafers' spun halfway around on his bar stool. Mike dismissed the fishermen as blowhards and stepped to the bar to order.

He dismissed Loafers and directly addressed the barkeep. "Got any Bush Bavarian?"

"No. What's with the mutt? Eh?"

Mike ignored the question; the last thing he needed here was trouble."I'll have a Kokanee. . . and a bowl of water for my dog if you would."

"Beer's four dollars, water's, twenty-five cents, and rent on the bowl is seventy-five cents."

Mike fished six US dollars out of his pocket, laid it on the bar, picked up his British-warm bottle of Kokanee and a sloppily poured bowl of water, and then backed away. "Keep the change. Dog's name is Varmint in case you didn't hear, and he'll rip your face off in a heartbeat."

'Loafers' made eye contact with rotund and his clone, and raised his eyebrows. Mike took note.

"Those fat fish-mongers friends of yours? A word of advice: tell them not to fuck with my dog." Mike said that low enough to be heard by Loafers and the bartender but no one else. The snooker players were re-racking the balls; both stopped what they were doing. The one with a ruddy complexion, unkempt, long scraggly hair and a long jagged scar running from the right eye to the corner of his mouth whom Mike dubbed Scarface, paid close attention when Loafers spoke.

"No need to be rude mister. This is a friendly pub. . ." Before 'Loafers' could continue, a commotion broke out mid-pub.

"Whewiee! What the fuck!" One fisherman pushed away from the table holding his nose with his eyes watering.

"Pickled eggs!" Mike knew Varmint just expelled one of his excruciatingly nasty SBDs. (Silent but Deadly fart) He clutched the roll of quarters in his jacket pocket with his right hand and ordered Varmint to *'alert'* with his left.

He took two strides toward Varmint when he had to dodge a red snooker ball thrown by Scarface. Mike heard it smack resoundingly into the wall. The second ball caught him just under the breastbone and knocked the wind out of him. He doubled up and instinctively rolled under a table catching his breath. He felt more than saw a brown haze streak under the snooker table followed by a blood-curdling scream; Varmint was trained to go for the scrotum!

Someone grabbed Mike's left foot and dragged him from under the table. Black Cloud took over and delivered a pile driving kick square to someone's right knee. A bellowing, yowling, fisherman writhing on the floor in agony followed a sharp snap much like a dry twig braking. Mike scrambled up into a deep knee bend, and focused all of his attention on the younger fisherman who appeared determined to impale him with a pool cue. Black Cloud's reflexes and training kicked in; his roundhouse came from the legs and finished with the right hand, fortified by the roll of quarters, landing just under the scraggly mustache of a surprised foe. A resounding 'splat' and the sound of a crumpling body filled the barely perceptible silence.

A yip and deep bark from the snooker table got Black Cloud's attention. One logger kicked Varmint off his buddy and was trying to draw a wicked looking six-shooter. One hundred ten pounds of wolf fury crossed six feet in an instant going for the jugular. A deafening roar and a yelp of pain stopped everyone in their tracks. Black Cloud issued one order; "Heel!" that stopped Varmint's attack. He still straddled Scarface looking more like Cujo than Varmint.

Scarface was lucky, his balls were intact, but Varmint had caught his open mouth and ripped half his jaw away. Muscle and bone could be seen through the gushing blood.

"Anybody else want a piece of this?" Black Cloud was in charge. 'Loafers' and the Barkeep backed off.

"Get me a bar towel now!" Black Cloud ordered as he rushed to the fallen logger. Varmint gave up his kill position and Mike noticed singed fur, an oozing gash, and a pronounced limp. "I'll fix you up in a while buddy but right now I have to see to this dumb fuck"

Mike scooped up the revolver lying nearby, flipped open the cylinder, dumped the cartridges into his pocket, and then pitched the six-shooter to the opposite wall. He wound the bar towel around the damaged jaw as tight as he could. *"A tourniquet around this fucker's neck is what's needed! Take a shot at my dog . . . you piece of shit!"* is what he thought. He'd seen men survive worse injuries in battle. He was all business and looking for a way to disappear quickly. "You, Barkeep, hold this and keep pressure on it. This looks worse than it is. Can you get this guy to a doctor?"

"I can . . . but it will take a while. I'll have to get him on a ferry to Bella Bella across the strait." That was good news to Black Cloud.

"You ever want to fuck with strangers again make damn sure they are wimps! I'm out of here, and it is best you think about me never being here."

With that said, Black Cloud and Varmint backed out of the Bad Screw Pub and disappeared into the afternoon gloom.

CHAPTER 27
SIXTH SENSE

Varmint was bleeding and limping. Mike rubbed what felt like a fractured rib just below his breastbone on the right side. He stopped only long enough to retrieve his backpack and arm himself. About three hundred yards inside the gloomy, dripping, evergreen forest he stopped to tend to Varmint's wounds. The bullet creased his left haunch, singed a lot of fur, and left a shallow six-inch long furrow. That was minor; the right, front leg limp worried Mike more.

Superglue closed the bleeding wound. Stitches would be better but Mike still carried the scars from the last time he tried that! He manipulated all the joints in Varmint's right front leg, massaged, and probed it from paw to knee. Varmint winced a bit but did not yip or nip! The Logger's kick didn't do much damage and the leg would be good-as-new in a few days.

It would be dark in about five hours. Mike adopted a leisurely pace, after one kilometer left the trail, and stopped under a large evergreen tree with limbs dangling all the way to the ground.

"It's time for lunch and a snooze. We'll get back to *Springer* some time after dark." Varmint didn't object. He plopped down and expelled his second SBD of the day. Several small critters noisily scurried into the underbrush from downwind.

Just after sunset, Mike surveyed Shearwater Marina from the forest's edge. No flashing red and blue lights or unusual activity showed. He dug his iPhone out of the backpack to check security devices aboard *Springer*. *"Fuck! No 4G network or even cell service here. Forgot to leave wifi up and running . . . that won't happen again! Hope those hicks heeded my advice."*

"Let's do this buddy. We're either fucked or we ain't . . ."

Once aboard *Springer* Mike sighed in relief. A quick look around showed no signs that anyone had been aboard and snooped around.

"We gotta be more careful Varmint. Gman will have our ass if we fuck this up and finding who shot up my friend Kensey depends on us." Varmint hobbled below decks, nudged his bowl into the center of the passageway so Mike could see it, and then whined to let him know it was past dinnertime.

0530, an hour before sunrise, found *Springer* in Seaforth Channel on her way to Milbanke Sound. Mike planned to forgo his last scheduled stop in Prince Rupert, Canada and anchor somewhere after he crossed back into the US and southern Alaska. It would be a long day but the brawl at the Bad Screw Pub made it necessary.

The weather was deteriorating. Visibility was down to about one-half a mile with fog and a light rain. The wind wasn't up yet; that made cruising at twenty-two knots comfortable. A jet departing the local airport flew over *Springer* when she passed the north end of Campbell Island. Mike heard it, and that got him to thinking about the tussle at the Bad Screw Pub. *"What if that wasn't just a gaggle of local yahoos blowing off steam?"*

Mike's sixth sense saved him time after time during Desert Storm operations; he did not discard any foreboding thoughts lightly. Throttling down to five-knots was instinct. After a quick look around, and a moment's study of the radar display, Mike ducked below and returned with his moose and bear rifle, a Remington Model 700 XCR in .300 WinMag. He flipped the scope-caps off the Leupold Mk-4 ER /T 20x50, sighted ahead and grunted with satisfaction. His 'artillery' was ready, loaded, and three extra Kwik-Klip magazines were close by. He smiled with satisfaction while withdrawing his pride-and-joy from its web-rig hanging from the captain's chair. He jacked a round into the AMP 44 Auto Mag, set the safety, dropped the magazine, inserted a round, slid the magazine home, and then returned his close range cannon to the web-rig.

When *Springer* reduced speed, Varmint limped out from under the salon table alert and ready to fight. He watched Mike load and check weapons. That always excited him; he lived for action . . .

"I think we're ready to fend off marauding seagulls. That's the only thing out here liable to crap up our day. Go back to sleep!" Mike throttled back up to twenty-two knots his sixth sense mollified.

"Looks like it's gonna turn nasty." Mike throttled back to twelve knots and noted the temperature was down to thirty-three

degrees Fahrenheit, and snow and sleet driven by an increasing wind reduced visibility to about two-hundred yards.

Mike's navigation waypoint was ten minutes ahead according to GPS. An eighty-degree course change north would put ***Springer*** in the lee of Price Island and out of worsening weather.

The insistent beeping Mike mistakenly assumed was a waypoint warning from the GPS was in fact a contact warning from the radar. A vessel approximately three miles away just cleared the northern point of Athlone Island and was painting on the radar display. It was closing at a little over nine knots; that was a worry.

"Looks like we've got company." Mike consulted his chart and decided a boat, probably a fishing boat, from St. Johns Harbor would intercept in twenty minutes or so. *"Nasty day to go fishing. Whatever . . . Once I turn we'll never see one another."* Mike's sixth sense kicked up a notch. *"Fuck it; I'll change course now and see what happens."* Changing course dropped the closing speed to a satisfying two knots. Seven minutes later the radar contact had changed course and the closing speed increased to ten knots. Mike slithered into the web-rig, checked the Auto Mag once more, and made sure the WinMag was secure just in case he had to do some radical maneuvering. Varmint came to full alert; Mike felt pity for anyone who tried to come aboard!

"Looks like they may be fishing for us. Can't outrun 'em if they're making twenty knots in this weather. If they start shooting, you'll have to hide under the bed. Fiberglass bulkheads ain't gonna stop shit. Shit!" Black Cloud went into action.

Sniper training taught Black Cloud to look for the high ground and seek any advantage available. Following those rules, he changed course, putting ***Springer*** into a quartering sea, throttled down to five knots and set the auto-helm. The mystery boat was now eleven-hundred yards away and still closing at 10 knots.

He hurriedly 'layered-up' with a long sleeve shirt, a heavy, Oregon Ducks sweat shirt, and a North Face hooded parka. He jammed the three Kwik-Klips and a hand full of extra .300 WinMag rounds in one parka pocket and the extra .44 AutoMag magazines in the other. He jammed a woolen watch cap on his head, ordered Varmint to 'stay' below decks, scooped up his artillery piece, slung it over his shoulder, and hurried to the flying bridge. He untied and peeled back the canvas along the port side of the Zodiac jumped in

and pulled the canvas back over the port pontoon. He assumed a prone firing position with just the barrel and an inch or less of the scope peeking out from under the tarp. What happened next was entirely up to the approaching boat . . .
"*What did Kensey always say? Fire on the up roll . . .*" Springer was rolling; the approaching boat would be pitching. If this turned into a firefight, accuracy would be tough! The twenty-power Leupold scope cut through the fog and revealed a good-sized trawler bearing down on *Springer* with two armed men on the bow. It was decision time. It was possible these men were just cautious fishermen.

The trawler, an Eagle-40, slowed and approached to approximately two-hundred yards, paralleled Mike's course, and matched speed. One minute ticked by, then two. No attempt was made to contact *Springer* on the VHF radio. Mike saw fire spit from the muzzle of two rifles and heard *Springer's* portside windows shatter. He fired on the up roll and one man flew backward and disappeared behind the gunnels. The second man dropped below the gunnels and fired blindly. The fully automatic rounds were hitting Springer everywhere. The Zodiac's port pontoon deflated. That made aiming more difficult but not impossible. Mike drilled three rounds through the Eagle's gunnels below the belching rifle. Incoming fire ceased.

Mike slammed another magazine into his rifle, fired two quick rounds in the general direction of the navigation station as the trawler belched diesel smoke, and turned away trying to escape. The next two rounds demolished the radar and GPS module. Mike slammed another magazine home and fired all four rounds into the rapidly receding transom. The Eagle visibly slowed and diesel smoke stopped pouring from her stack. Mike now had time to think about his next move. He carefully used his last magazine to demolish the outboard on the towed dingy and the two communications antennas he could see on top of the trawler.

Mike crawled out from under the tarp and made a quick survey. His Zodiac was holed in two places and the radar outer covering and antenna were shattered. He checked fly-bridge controls, throttled up to ten knots, and changed course for the channel between Prince and Swindle islands.

He dreaded the thought of what numerous small arms rounds did to the salon and inside of ***Springer***. He heard a lot of bullets *'thunk'* into her during the firefight. Instead of splintered fiberglass and wood, there were a lot of pockmarks and dents along the port side salon and hull all the way to the water line. Most showed a dark gray fiber where the paint chipped away. *"I love Gman! But . . . why did he Kevlar coat Springer?"*

Mike's mind was racing. He needed to get out of here and into US waters quickly. With the exception of the Zodiac and radar, damage was superficial. Trash bags and 'duck' tape would take care of the shattered windows. That trawler, adrift with two maybe three dead aboard was the real concern. *"Was this all about a bar brawl . . . Don't think so . . . Is my mission still a go or am I going to end up in some Provincial slammer? I have to get in contact with Gman."*

Chapter 28

SPRINGER'S DILEMMA

The Eagle Trawler was a memory in the mist. Eighteen knots was a bit fast for running without radar while visibility was two-hundred yards at best but it couldn't be helped. Mike wanted to be in Laredo Channel in an hour and well away from the recent scuffle. The wind would push the shot-up trawler back toward Athlone Island but the current and tide would try to carry it out to sea. Mike hoped the bad weather would keep anyone from discovering it for several hours. Another concern was communications: cell phone reception was nonexistent and Mike was sure he destroyed all radio antennas. The chance of a satellite phone still existed, but it was possible that no one was alive to use one.

"I should contact Gman." Mike took a quick look around, throttled back to ten knots, went below to his cabin, rummaged around in his backpack, and retrieved the satellite phone Gman gave him. Back on the helm, he looked at the phone, turned it on, but decided against calling, throttled back up to twenty knots and thought about the long day ahead.

A hollow but resounding 'thunk' at ***Springer's*** bow caused her to shimmy. Three more solid deadhead hits could be heard bouncing down the hull before Mike could throttle down and slam ***Springer*** into neutral. An alarm started wailing.

"What the fuck now!" Mike yelled out of frustration. He rushed below, and threw open the engine compartment hatch. Water was gushing in at an alarming rate! Four inches of water sloshed around his ankles before Mike could get the dewatering pump working. This wasn't the first time he'd had water coming aboard ***Springer*** but it was the most inopportune. Mike waded over to the storage locker and took out a can of, (As seen on TV!), Flex Seal. Earlier this year, Kensey sent a case of the stuff to Mike as a joke. The Safe Haven crew still teased him about it. Mike thought, *"Just* *might work as a temporary fix . . . Works on a screen door used as the bottom of a row boat."*

Each time Springer rolled starboard, the two-foot crack along the port hard chine stopped gushing water. Mike took that opportunity to spray it down with Flex Seal. At first, nothing seemed to work but little by little the Flex Seal cured and less and less water came aboard. After the second can was empty, water only 'seeped' in. Mike hurried to the head, retrieved his hair dryer and an extension cord, returned below, and started heating the Flex Seal to cure it faster. One more can of Flex Seal helped by heat from the hair dryer had the crack just barely weeping. Mike estimated about half a gallon an hour would get in now. That was adequate for an emergency repair: the dewatering pump could handle that easily, but he would have to rethink his pounding open-sea plan for running to Alaskan waters today.

"I have to contact Gman now. Shit! Shit! Shit! I'm only supposed to contact him once my mission is complete then ditch the phone. I'll have to get 'him' to call me. Kensey . . . Where the fuck is Kensey?" Mike was thinking in over time. *"First things first."*

Mike studied the charts for five minutes and then laid a course for Finlayson Channel and the narrow confines of the Inside Passage. If this bad weather held, ten knots should get him to Horse Fly cove, forty miles north, with very little chance of being spotted along the way. Some of the narrow, shallow passes would be tricky without radar, but GPS and sonar should see him through.

Mike throttled down to five knots, crossed his fingers, and then proceeded to his little office niche. He fished a Morse code book out of a drawer, disconnected the remote from the HF set, connected the Code key, shut off modulation, then sat a moment to compose his thoughts. *"Gman said Kensey had an app on his iPad that copied radio traffic from the Haven during closed hours. That's what saved his ass down south. Safe Haven won't be open for another couple of hours . . . and I don't know who is listening in . . . I'll send an S.O.S. now and think about a voice message later."* Mike clumsily tapped: BC, BC, SOS, SOS, on the code key.

"That's all we can do for now Varmint." Mike sat wearily down in the captain's chair and throttled up to ten knots. A barely perceptible vibration set in. Varmint noticed it and made rounds checking every nook and cranny. .*"Fuck . . . now what? Log must*

150

have got a piece of the screw." Black Cloud just shook his head and made sure they were on course.

Horse Fly cove at Green Inlet Marine Park was tranquil compared to the past four hours. It would be very difficult to spot *Springer* from the air in the light snow and heavy overcast, and impossible to see her from the Inside Passage. This was the definition of wilderness. Mike hadn't seen so much as a light for two hours. *Springer* swung comfortably on her anchor. Mike thanked Gman once again. *Springer* was fitted with a wildcat, anchor windless, and hawse pipe that housed the anchor on the bow.

Hauling the one-hundred-twenty pound danforth anchor in by hand would be brutal work for one man. Mike smiled; he remembered Kensey having him haul **Ketch 'Em's** 60 pound sand anchor three times while fishing for fall Chinook on the Columbia River. Kensey's excuse was he couldn't get lined-up on the 'hog-line'. Black Cloud still thought Kensey was just fucking with him and vowed, then and there, to get even if he didn't respond to his SOS.

Mike checked how Springer swung on the hook, and was satisfied she hadn't slipped so much as an inch. The previous four hours of white-knuckle navigation didn't give him much time to think about contacting Safe Haven but he had a general idea of how to convey his situation without raising too many eyebrows. It was time . . . "Here goes nothin'. Gman hasn't called so Kensey probably didn't get my SOS . . . FMTT!"

"CQ, CQ, CQ, Safe Haven, Safe Haven, this is *Springer*, over." Static answered his call.

"What the fuck . . . Burt and Harry on vacation? It's 1129! Ok Varmint, let's try again."

"CQ, CQ, CQ, Safe Haven, Safe Haven, this is *Springer*, over."

Burt's bored voice, sounding completely uninterested, filled *Springer's* salon. "*Springer* this is the Haven" He paused only long enough to flip the switch connecting the AR-5 speakers behind the bar to 'on'. "You lost? You still on your way here?"

Mike could hear Johnny Horton on the Haven's Wurlitzer belting out "Spring Time in Alaska."

"You guys into shit-kickin' music now? Johnny has it right about springtime weather in Alaska, and no, I'm not lost, just hung up. I should be there pretty soon. I have a hankering for some of Gunny's world famous chipped-beef-on-toast."

Harry hurried into the radio room frowning at Mike's strange request. Gunny stopped polishing his spotless mahogany bar and listened.

"Can't wait. . . Gunny has the dock all repaired, and we have a one-hundred dollar pool on how long it will take you to screw it up."

Gunny stuck his head into the radio room and scolded Burt, "We don't serve SOS, here. That fuckin' dock-wreckin' groundpounder lose the rest of his marbles?"

"SOS . . ." Burt shut the outside speakers off and motioned for Gunny to shut the door.

Mike's voice echoed off the walls of the buttoned-up radio room. Burt quickly turned the volume down.

"Listen, I can't get a hold of Kensey. I dropped my iPhone overboard, would you call him and tell him, copy this down, white knight to QB4, that's Queen's Bishop 4 to you checker players."

"Yeah, got it: White knight to QB4. Didn't know Grunts could play chess."

"We can do a lot of things . . . even swim unlike you shallow water sailors. If Kensey can't figure this move out it's just about checkmate and a rematch may be tough."

"I can swim doughboy, and shoot straight too. I'll call Kensey for you when we get off the air. When can we expect you?" Burt asked that question in a tentative voice.

"Don't know. I'll let you know when I can get a hold of Kensey. *Springer* out."

"Ok see you soon . . . Safe Haven over and out."

Harry liberated his iPhone from his vest pocket, punched in his security code, called up contacts, located, FTCM Kensey, and launched the call. Kensey's phone rang five times and went to voice mail.

"So Burt . . . what do you suppose Black Cloud is up to?"

"Don't know Harry, but I'll bet it has to do with him." Burt tapped Gman's calling card pinned to the bulletin board; Harry nodded in agreement.

"Better keep trying Kensey 'till you get him . . ." Burt fully intended to do just that even without Harry's insistence.

Mike's teakettle, burbling on the galley stove, just started to whistle when the satellite phone on the salon table vibrated and chimed. Varmint jumped up, hackles raised, and growling deep within his chest. Mike immediately turned the galley stove's burner off, picked the phone up, punched in his code, and listened.

"Report . . . ." Came over the phone in a flat monotone.

"How many fenders and what color were they at our last meet?" Mike said quickly; he was still on high alert and security conscious.

"Three. Two white one blue all secured to the port rail with granny knots. I hold you at 52,55,28 North by 128,28,54 West. Report." The monotone voice answered.

Mike took a deep breath and began. "I had a bit of trouble at a pub, The Bad Screw, in Old Bella Bella yesterday. Varmint sent two men to the hospital and I sent one. We left this morning with no trouble and no follow on action by any authorities. . ." Mike paused to gather his thoughts.

"About 0700 this morning I was ambushed and attacked with automatic weapons in the middle of Milbanke Sound by at least three men in an Eagle-40 Trawler. There are definitely two, probably three, KIA. I left the trawler adrift with no communications, engine, or lifeboat.

My windows were shot out, the Zodiac was holed, and the radar antenna was shattered. Fifteen minutes after the attack, I hit a submerged log at high speed. Springer has a two-foot crack, amidships, at the hard chine, and a screw vibration at speeds above ten knots. I made temporary repairs but had to change course back into the Inside Passage. I can't run in rough water until the hull's repaired. I don't think I can have repairs done In Prince Rupert without too many questions being asked . . ." Mike thought that was a good summary and listened for Gman's response.

"I'll see what I can do. Your fishing trip may be cancelled. Stand by where you are until I contact you. Pass phrase for our next contact is: Kensey's Tyee. Response is: Bull shit!" The phone went dead.

Mike finished his hourly bilge check. Setting calmly at anchor, ***Springer's*** wound barely wept a quart of seawater an hour. Mike settled back into his lounge chair in the darkened salon. The only light showing was the dull blue square on the microwave oven telling him it was now 2236.

The satellite phone vibrated and chimed. Mike instantly picked it up, his night vision destroyed by the lighted screen. He scrunched his eyes up, punched in the security code, and listened.

"Kensey's Tyee."

"Bull shit!"

"I've got good news. No one checked into the hospital at Bella Bella or Waglisla. No damaged Eagle-40 trawler has shown up and no one reported one missing. It is possible you stumbled on a major drug smuggling operation. The RCMP, (Royal Canadian Mounted Police), is very interested and agreed to help. Proceed to Prince Rupert. Write this down." Gman paused.

"Roger that. Go" Mike switched on a small desk lamp that emitted a subdued red glow.

"Be off the north coast of Kaien Island one hour after sunset tomorrow. Proceed to WCMR, (Western Canada Marine Response), covered dry dock at 54,19,22.35 North by 130,18,25.76 West. Pull directly into the dry dock. Stay aboard during repairs. You will be underway by 0430 on the 26th or 27th. You will most likely be visited by RCMP Special Agent Angus McKinney. He will ask you if you've ever eaten at the Fung Lung restaurant in Scappoose. Any questions?"

Mike had no pressing questions. He repeated his instructions and verified coordinates for WCMR, all the time wondering if his mission was still a 'go'.

"Ok you're good to go. The fishing trip is still on but you owe me a bottle of fine single-malt, a Mcallan will do."

"Roger that. I'll run down to Albertsons and pick you up a case." The phone went silent and the mission was on.

CHAPTER 29
DRY DOCK SURPRISE

Today's cruise was uneventful. Slate grey skies, light winds, and occasional snow flurries gradually gave way to light fog when the sun went down. That was barely an hour ago. As directed *Springer* turned east and traversed the northern end of Kaien Island at a leisurely five knots. Mike chose a course three-quarters of a mile north of the coast and away from prying eyes. *Springer* would be nestled in the WCMR (Western Canada Marine Response Corporation.) dry dock by 2200.

With little notice and no apparent outside interest, *Springer* quietly slipped into the flooded dry dock. Mike felt a slight jolt when she nudged the blocks previously set by divers.

Mike was satisfied but still considered vigilance and caution was his best course of action. He summed the situation up and thought, *"2210, that ain't bad. I hope these Canucks don't ask too many questions."*

Eight men were present when *Springer* eased into the covered dry dock. One man, who identified himself as John, came aboard and politely asked if he could take the helm and operate the thruster to position her *'precisely'* over the docking blocks.

Fifteen minutes work had *Springer* positioned to John's satisfaction. He said a repair group would be aboard shortly, two radar technicians and one ship fitter, and Mike could retire to the Captain's suite if he so desired. Mike wasn't used to being treated like royalty or, for the most part, cordially. He decided this was not the time to ask questions. There would be time enough tomorrow.

Mike slept poorly. He was up every hour checking on work. Varmint didn't help matters. He paced and growled and was not a bit comfortable with strangers aboard. He appeared confused. He could not quite understand why *Springer* was not rolling and pitching: he thought they were still at sea . . . When he did sleep it was with one eye open and any new sound sent him pacing again. Mike finally

155

allowed Varmint half his queen-sized bed in the Captain's cabin and that seemed to calm him down.

A survey and planning team from WCMR finished their work a little after 0200. Mike paid close attention to the name badge worn by the team leader: Kurten. Mike could not make out her last name but noted she was a lovely blonde woman probably in her mid forties. She told Mike that windows, radar, and his Zodiac would be replaced by 1600. Repair of the fracture along the chine was well underway and would be completed early in the afternoon including the addition of an aluminum armor strip to reinforce the hull. Over a steaming cup of Keurig brewed hot chocolate, Kurten gave Mike a bit of bad news:

"Because of the special nature of your unusual screw," She maintained a perfectly straight face but her eyes absolutely sparkled. "Repairing the chipped blade will take some time, perhaps as much as two days."

Mike merely nodded as Kurten continued. "This black cloud does have a silver lining. The extra time will allow us to properly repair all the dings, dents, cracks, and pock-marks caused by . . . exceptionally vicious hail?" She left the question hanging. A slight frown and narrowed eyes betrayed her distaste for what she thought this boat was: a drug smuggler.

She continued before Mike could answer. "These repairs, and replacing your Zodiac, and completely changing your boat's color scheme in such a short time are not inexpensive. The full cost is guaranteed by your . . . benefactor?" That, more than anything, convinced Kurten this was part of something other than the fishing trip that she'd been led to believe.

Mike decided the truth wouldn't do, but something close was in order. The polar chill and disdain radiating from Kurten was something Mike desperately wanted to thaw. He could plainly see the evidence pointed straight to him treading on the wrong side of the law.

"I have a meeting with an RCMP special agent later today or tomorrow. They are very interested in what transpired two days ago. I ran over a deadhead, and that caused the bottom damage. On the other hand, it wasn't *'vicious hail'* that caused the rest. You probably won't believe this, but I was attacked by pirates! Until yesterday, I thought they were confined to Africa. I guess they took a liking to this beat up old tug. Who'd a thought?" Mike didn't consider the inevitable follow on questions.

"Pirates? How many were there? How *'did'* you manage to escape?" The sparkle returned to Kurten's green eyes and a smile curled the corners of her lightly glossed lips.

"Like you said, black clouds sometime have silver linings. The weather was nasty, they were in a scow, and they couldn't shoot straight. I out ran them." A sly smile crossed Mike's face.

Kurten rolled her eyes a bit and shook her head. "Thanks for the cocoa. I've got to check on the hull work. We'll hold off on the really noisy stuff until 0700. Nice meeting you; if you stay a couple of days look me up. Bring Varmint; he looks kind of cuddly." She handed Mike a shipyard business card with a hand written phone number on the back before departing.

"Orders suck! I will positively stop at Prince Rupert on the way home from fishing." Mike idly watched Kurten descend into the dry dock. He daydreamed until she disappeared beneath **Springer**.

Mike was up twice more before sunrise, Varmint once. Repairs were progressing nicely. Sanders McLean Jr., as he called himself, made final checks on the radar while Mike cooked ham and eggs for breakfast. Sanders declined breakfast but eagerly accepted another cup of Tully's French Roast coffee while chattering about the local pub he would visit for lunch. Mike saw an opening for barter.

"I'll trade you two cases of San Miguel beer for a case of Bush Bavarian. If you can't get that, Kokanee will do." Much to Mike's surprise, Sanders accepted.

"I haven't had one of those since my dad smuggled some home. He was aboard the High Endurance Cutter **Campbell** and stopped in Subic Bay, Philippines, on his way home from Vietnam. I was just a freshman in high school and me and my buddies got into it. Dad wasn't so pissed at our drunken escapades as he was at losing a case of, as he called it, San Magoo. Dad will turn seventy-nine in a few days. I'd love to return that case of San Magoo to him, with interest!"

"So you're not a Canuk? I know Coasties who served aboard **Campbell**. She is a US Coast Guard Ship." Mike was on alert.

"Oh! Talk about six-degrees-of-separation . . . Mom is from Prince Rupert and Dad loves the fishing up here. I took a sabbatical and came up here to help them out when the sequester delayed the radar program I was working on. My brother runs the WCMR electronics shop and asked me to help with this rush job. I kind of like it here. I may just stay."

That helped assuage Mike's suspicion but all he could think about was Kensey's satellite photo of *Goat Locker* riding *Scrap Dealer* with the caption "Loose Lips Sink Ships"

Morning wore on into early afternoon. Mike grew edgy. Three men replaced all the windows and then left. Mike didn't ask their names but he was suspicious about their work. The windows seemed a lot heavier than the old ones. One man would struggle while lifting the windows into place but two made an easy job of holding it while the third glazed and sealed it.   Mike retrieved Kurten's business card, added the shipyard's and her phone number to his iPhone contact list, and then called her.

She answered on the third ring in a demure, sleepy voice. "Yes . . . Is this an emergency?"

"It certainly is; I made too much lunch and need help eating it."

"Who is this?"

"Mike, Mike Smith, and his sidekick Varmint. I need to talk to you about some of the work being done on *Springer.*"

"What work? And, can it wait?"

Kurten sounded annoyed and that was the last thing Mike wanted.

"It is trivial, but why did it take three men to replace my windows? I'm really sorry to bother you but no one else is around right now." Mike tried to sound apologetic in hopes she would forgive him for waking her.

"Oh . . . Ah . . .Those . . . 'hail-proof' windows are heavy. They were a last minute order from your benefactor: Mr. Gregg Mann. I can't make it for lunch. How about a rain check? It rains three hundred days a year here . . ."

Mike was about to protest and insist on lunch when Varmint came to alert and warned him of a stranger coming aboard.

"I'm really disappointed you can't make it for lunch. We *'will'* get together. Right now, I have an official looking visitor so I'll have to let you go. My apologies for bothering you. Will I see you later?"

"Today is my day off but I will stop by this evening to QA, (Quality Assurance), check the work

Mike reluctantly ended the call deferring his attention to a large well proportioned, obviously armed, man in a business suit who stepped into the salon. He took one look at an annoyed Varmint and stopped short.

"Hello. I'm Angus McKinney. Lunch looks good. Ever eat at the Fung Lung Chinese restaurant in Scappoose, Oregon?"

"No. The place always looks abandoned so I avoid it. Bings, in St. Helens, is just down the street and a much better choice. Care for some lunch? I have plenty. Eh!" Mike saw an excellent opportunity to off load yet another San Magoo.

"Yes. It smells delicious. I just flew in from Ontario and they don't feed you on the plane anymore. What are you cooking? *'Eh'*!" Mike got the hint and noted that Angus had a sense of humor.

"BBQ Tri-tip steak, home fries, sautéed portabella mushroom, and," Mike opened the galley fridge and extracted a brew, "one of these rare and exotic pilsners from the Philippines. If you like it I'll trade you for anything locally brewed!"

"Our friend in Washington sent you twelve more cases, they're in my car. You won't run out. I may take you up on your offer. Thanks!"

Mike and Angus ate in silence. Angus kept a nervous eye on Varmint who crept closer and closer, looking fierce and unfriendly, trying to intimidate Mike or Angus out of their leftovers.

Angus broke the silence. "Your dog, Varmint I believe, caused quite a furor among cartel folks. When Jim Billings contacted us, agents were talking about a news report concerning a wolf attack in Old Bella Bella. We connected the dots when he explained your dilemma. Your actions put us on alert. We started investigating the good possibility of a major drug operation moving in up here. good possibility of a major drug operation moving in up here. If that turns out to be true, I don't think we will be able to thank you enough."

Angus dug a sheaf of papers out of his inside jacket pocket, laid them on the table and then hoisted his San Magoo and proposed a toast.

"To the wolf!"

"To Varmint! May he be as cuddly as he looks." Mike handed Varmint the last of his sandwich scooted the papers around, shuffled through them, shook his head, and then got up, grabbed two more brews from the fridge, sat them on the table and sat back down.

"I only recognize one of the assholes in the photos." Mike picked up a picture and handed it to Angus. "I named him Loafers. He was out of place and I'll bet he drove the Range Rover Discovery parked outside the Bad Screw Pub. That SUV was definitely out of place. It had Alberta plates and I remember the first three letters: MIC. Does that help any?"

"Sure does! Can you think of anything else strange or out of place? Tell me about the attack in Milbanke Sound . . ."

Mike related events in detail. With questions from Angus, it turned into a two-Magoo tale. Mike enjoyed talking to Angus and was annoyed when four ship fitters struggling with two large, custom-made propane tanks entered the salon from the rear entrance.

"What the fuck are those?" Mike asked with incredulity. "I really have no need for them."

"Sorry Sir . . . These are to fuel your new LEHR outboard. Kurten said to install them as soon as they were fabricated."

"LEHR outboard? What the fuck is that and where is it? Nothing like that came aboard."

"It's a new propane fueled outboard on your Zodiac, Sir." The ship fitter grunted that information while struggling to snake the last cylinder below.

"Oh man . . . I wonder what they did with my kicker. I've had Old Smoky forever!" Mike bought the 1979, Johnson, two-stroke kicker, new and nursed it along ever since. He wasn't happy about losing it.

Angus stood up. The meeting was over. He handed Mike a business card, shook his hand, and started to leave. He stopped and turned.

"Thanks for the detailed report and the excellent lunch! I will report our meeting to Mr. Billings and my boss in the CSIS, (Canadian Intelligence Security Service). By the way, stick to your cover story about being attacked by pirates. We will corroborate that. It is a perfect fit and should keep the locals from asking too many questions. They always get nervous when CSIS noses around. " Angus paused then asked, "Do you have any questions for me?"

Mike shook his head and answered with a simple, "No."

"I didn't think you would . . . I'll take those two cases of San Magoo. What do you want in exchange?"

Mike thought a moment. "I have a friend who likes a good brandy. A bottle of decent Canadian Brandy would be great."

Angus didn't hesitate. "I think Canadian Mist will do. I'll have a bottle delivered to you in an hour or so. Good luck fishing and . . . until two days ago I didn't think there was such a thing as a bad screw! You proved me wrong . . ." Angus crossed over to the dry dock's catwalk, turned and gave Mike a thumbs up.

"That's why they call me Black Cloud!" Mike laughed

Angus just shook his head and disappeared among the dry dock's machinery.

After Angus departed there wasn't much to do except wait for his screw to arrive. The sooner it arrived the sooner Mike and Varmint could be on their way to Ketchikan. He impatiently watched until workers completed the propane tank installation. His screw was being installed and that got Mike to wondering. *"Hummmm . . . Kurten has to eat . . . Wonder what she's doing for dinner. I have a couple of rib eyes in the freezer . . ."*

CHAPTER 30
KETCHIKAN

Springer ran like a top. The transit to Ketchikan was actually pleasant. The constant flapping of trash bags covering the windows on the run to WCMR was thankfully gone. The weather cooperated with light overcast and occasional sun breaks even though it was still a chilly thirty-seven degrees.

Mike smiled as the southern end of Pennock Island came into sight. He thought about his departure from dry dock ten hours earlier. *Springer* was afloat by 0345. John, Kurten, and surprisingly, Angus came aboard to make sure everything was in working order. All systems tested A-OK and no leaks appeared. Angus and Kurten departed at 0405 and John backed *Springer* out of dry dock and into Tuck Inlet. A small yard-tender picked him up and Mike was underway by 0415.

Kurten walked to the end of the pier, waved, blew Mike a kiss, and sadly watched *Springer* silently and unobtrusively slip into the early morning mist.

Mike watched Kurten blow him a kiss and knew he would return. He forced his thoughts to the job at hand. *"As Kensey, where the fuck is he anyway . . ., would say: The Game is Afoot! Ok, time to get my head in the game."*

Mike slowed to seven knots and ran up the east coast of Pennock Island. This would be his first look at the assignment. He slowed to five knots on approach to the GPS coordinates of his target and fought the urge to pick up his binoculars for a closer look. Mike logged the time and date: 1437, 27 April. He took a mental inventory of the site and determined his mission would be accomplished from ashore.

"Looks like we are going to spend a few days in the woods. Good thing we trained in Old Bella Bella!" Varmint awoke and padded out from his favorite spot under the salon table with *Springer's* change of speed.

"Wish I had Kurten to talk to . . . She answers back. . . I think you'll be better company in the forest though. Study that house and take notes." Mike chuckled a bit and pointed in the general direction of the Pennock Island compound.

A large, two-story structure with a wide deck that looked like it extended all the way around the house stood dead center in a small cove. It looked like all the brush and small trees were cleared for at least fifty yards on all sides. This reminded Mike of a deliberate security/killing zone. Mike made a mental determination and note. *"Oh, oh, Varmint. Bet they have guard dogs. We'll have to be careful!"*

Large picture windows looked out on the Narrows and the city of Ketchikan a mile to the northeast. A spit of land protected the compound from the south and a pier that extended at least one hundred yards into the Tongass Narrows closed off the cove's entire north end. A floatplane that looked like it could hold six passengers rested at the pier's end. An orange weather sock on a twenty-foot pole registered about ten knots of wind out of the southeast. *"I hope the wind blows from that direction most days! That puts the woods downwind of the compound . . ."*

The entire area behind the house, from the cleared area on, was heavily forested and sloped up and west to a small hillock about a quarter-mile inland. Cover was sparse in some areas where mostly naked deciduous trees prevailed. Other, more promising areas were heavily forested with evergreens. That, Mike thought, is where he would concentrate his efforts.

The compound slipped astern. Mike maintained his slow pace and consulted his notes before picking up the VHF radio mic and dialing up channel seventy-nine.

"Tongass Warden, Tongass Warden, this is pleasure craft ***Springer***."

"***Springer***, this is Tongass. What is your ETA?"

Mike was pleased the man he only knew as Charles Cooley answered his first call.

"I should be there in twenty minutes or less. Any particular place you want me to park?"

"Use the south side of the float. It has the best protection from the weather. I'll be there shortly after you tie up. Tongass out."

"Aye. ***Springer*** out."

Docking was a cinch. ***Springer*** was secured to a float at the end of a fifty-yard pier. Two white and one blue fender secured with granny knots kept her from getting chipped and dented. Mike chose two sturdy fore and aft lines and a lighter spring-line amidships to allow some movement, but not much. Mike rechecked all lines making sure they were properly secured to the float cleats with figure eight knots and three solid half hitches. He did not want to worry about ***Springer*** slipping her mooring lines while he and Varmint were hunting.

The rear door of the log house at the head of the pier opened and an overweight, rotund man in his mid forties started down the pier carrying a brown grocery bag in each hand. Varmint growled letting Mike know someone was approaching and jumped onto the float.

"At ease Varmint. This should be our contact."

Mike watched Charles approach with amusement. His boots were light gray. They stood out in stark contrast to his blue jeans, white hoodie, and black down vest sporting a bright gold badge. As he drew closer, Mike noted a large face with a prominent, reddish nose. The topper was a black, fur lined hunting cap: the type with earflaps. The flaps were up but the securing straps were sticking nearly straight out on both sides. Mike instantly thought of 'Deputy Dawg' and smiled but stifled his laughter.

"Howdy. I'm Charles Cooley, call me Huck. Good lookin' dawg." Huck's southern drawl was as thick as uncooked okra. "These were sent over for you yesterday."

Mike accepted the two paper grocery bags and peeked inside. One contained a six-pack of San Miguel; Mike frowned and looked into the other expecting the same. The second grocery bag garnered an ear-to-ear smile; it contained a six-pack of Bush Bavarian tall boys!

"Thanks! I owe whoever sent the tall boys. Here, you deserve these." Mike handed the San Miguel back to Huck. There was no doubt in Mike's mind that he was in the right place and Huck could be trusted.

"Golly, thanks! These here are *really* good . . . I hear. Ya'll need a hand with anything?"

Mike was glad for the offer. Getting the Zodiac off the top of Springer wasn't all that difficult a job but it was much easier with two people.

"Yeah. Come aboard and give me a hand getting the Zodiac in the water. I'll use it to run over to Ketchikan and maybe do a little scouting before fishing season starts.

When Mike and Huck jumped aboard *Springer,* Varmint rumbled with a deep down growl. Huck gave him a wide berth and hurried up the ladder to the Zodiac. Mike put Varmint at ease with hand signals but still wanted him alert.

"Don't mind the dog. He doesn't much like anyone."

Huck, glad to be out of reach of 'the dawg', removed the Zodiac's tarp, and stood looking wide-eyed.

"I'll be dipped in shit . . . I read about these here propane motors but ain't never seen one. This here one's a big som-bitch! 9.9 horsepower and a four-stroke to boot . . . Them two fuel cylinders are see through just like a Bic butane lighter. How's she run?"

Mike didn't have a good answer but he was just as curious.

"Beats the shit out of me. I haven't had a chance to test her out. Let's see what she'll do when we get her in the water."

Varmint stood on the bow of *Springer* and glared at Mike and Huck; they silently glided away from the pier at an alarming rate. Varmint was a fish-dog and this looked like a fishing trip to him; he did not like being left behind.

"Shazam! This fucker is silent as a whisper . . ." Deputy Dawg hung on; seventeen knots of wind and a wake were the only signs of the Zodiac's passing.

It took less than ten minutes to determine this skiff was more than a lifeboat. Mike was impressed. It was not the fastest boat on the water but it had the potential to be the stealthiest. *"Gman knows his shit! I'll bet this dark gray material is Kevlar."* Mike gave three short blasts on the silent dog whistle and eased alongside the pier. He ran the Zodiac nearly to the beach before tying up.

"That dawg don't look happy. He bite?" Huck didn't make a move to get out of the Zodiac.

"Fuckin' A! but only folks he don't like." Mike's grin was ear to ear as he put Varmint at ease with hand signals.

"His name is Varmint. Just reach up scratch his ears and mention pickled eggs. That's his safe word. You may need it if you piss him off."

Huck tentatively let Varmint sniff his outstretched hand.

"Pickled eggs!" Varmint's eyes lit up, his tail wagged and Huck felt at ease.

Mike and Huck climbed out of the Zodiac and up onto the dock. Mike started back toward **Springer** but Huck stopped him when he spoke up.

"Come on in to headquarters. Some stuff arrived by currier from my friend Jim and I got a quadrangle map of the area for you and some interesting observations. Got those fine San Miguel brews too!" Huck hefted the brown grocery bag sitting on the pier.

"Don't like that piss. Billings keeps me supplied in case my friend Kensey, the Squid, shows up. Got anything decent to drink?"

"Squid? Got mint julep fixins, Ancient Age Keeentucky bourbon, and some Wisers Canadian whiskey that ain't zacly 'brown vodka' but sure as shit ain't Jack or Jim Beam. Got some fine eggs pickled in Luuusiana hot sauce too. What the fuck is a Squid?" Huck beamed; except for the occasional hiker or boater, he didn't get all that much company.

"Squid's a Navy guy . . . Never mind." Mike and Huck entered the living quarters of the ranger station through a door with a sign that clearly said: use the door around front.

Living quarters in the Ranger Station were cozy and well used. One or two hardbound books rested atop every flat surface. The furniture wasn't exactly sparse but was scaled down and rustic in a backwoods Alaskan motif. The thing that caught Mike's eye and stopped Varmint in his tracks was the Kodiak Bear rug that completely filled the fourteen by fourteen foot living room. Its massive head glared out from one corner of the room.

"Where'd you buy this bear rug? I gotta get one for my friend Kensey!"

"Buy it? I shot that bar! Felt bad about it too. Brownie, I call him Brownie, was doing his civic duty, but got too close to town. When I split him open he had part of a red sneaker, a bar-bell, (bear-bell), and an Obama lapel pin in his gut . . ." Huck pointed to an impressive looking bolt action rifle nestled in a pair of moose antlers hanging on one wall.

"Shot him with that thar Rigby 416. It was my Pappy's and his Pappy's before him. Ya'll need something like that if ya'll want to hunt around here!"

Varmint growled a bit, padded to the center of the room, plopped himself down and dozed off.

"Hope I don't run into any of those fuckers in the woods! I've got a .300 Win Mag with me but that might even be a little light for something the size of Brownie . . .What ya got for me?" Mike was anxious to get started.

Huck cleared a small pile of books from the counter separating the living room from the kitchen. "Be back in a minute. I've got your stuff in the safe."

Mike walked over to the only wall not hung with artwork or hunting trophies and gazed through a good-sized one-way window into the ranger station foyer. It was a smallish room hung with maps and notices. A writing podium was stuck in one corner and various forms occupied half a dozen pigeonholes above it. *"Doesn't seem to be much to this ranger station. I wonder how Huck finagled this job? He seems to know Gman pretty well . . ."*

Mike didn't have a chance to think about his question. Huck came back with an armful of maps and other papers. He spread papers and satellite photos out on the counter, opened a cabinet near his knee, brought out two tumblers and a half empty bottle of Ancient Age bourbon, poured two fingers in each tumbler and said, "Let's light this fire!"

Mike studied the photos and Huck started a running commentary. "Mr. Star . . . I still don't know zakly who he is other than a *'POI'* (Person of Interest), runs a quiet operation. He keeps to himself *'but'* every Tuesday for the past six months a floatplane comes to visit. He flies out early Wednesday morning and returns sometime Friday. Jim asked me to keep an eye on him a couple of weeks ago. He flies right over the station before sunup on Tuesdays and Wednesdays and wakes me up! I thought about takin' a pot shot at him but haven't so far."

Mike interrupted, "You do any hiking in the woods? How tough will it be for me and Varmint to get toooo. . . about here?" Mike pointed to a spot on a satellite photo in dense trees behind the compound.

"Not too bad. It's a little swampy in spots but if you follow this here ridge," Huck spread a quadrangle map out and traced a contour. "Shouldn't take more'n a couple hours."

"Looks good . . ." How about getting down to the west coast of the island from there?"

"Same-o, same-o. No problem. It's all downhill too." Huck traced the route with his index finger. "Nope! Don't see no problems with that. Take less than two hours."

"Hummm . . . Today's Friday. Varmint and I might do some hikin' and campin' before fishin' season opens. What's the weather like for the next few days?"

"Take sterno! It'll be either raining a little, a lot or anything betwixt. Findin' dry camp- fire wood will be a test of your injun-u-te! Wind should be light and out of the southeast or northwest. It ain't ideal but not all that bad. Ya'll really fixin' t' go campin'? Most folks don't start that 'till around Juuuly or there 'bouts." Huck was skeptical, he reached up and scratched the back of his head for emphasis.

Mike drained the last of his bourbon. "Jim Billings wants this job done . . . expeditiously. How do you know Jim anyway?"

Huck stalled giving him time to think before answering. "I was in law enforcement in Key West fur a spell. I worked with Jim on some drug related shit and later helped him and the navy weed out some bad apples involved with a drug cartel. 'Bout a year ago he asked me to come up here and help him finish up an operation. I jumped at the offer." Huck gestured with a sweeping motion, "Gives me time to catch up on my readin'!"

"The fuckin' 'Raid' Kensey won't talk much about . . . The recent ambush on **Derdrake** that no one will talk about at all! That fuckin' Gman is one fine chess player . . ."* The pieces were coming together and Mike was more determined than ever to succeed.

Mike held out his empty tumbler. Huck filled it half full and renewed his.

"What else do you have for me? I need to get started ."

Chapter 31

TANGLED MESS

"O337! If Huck doesn't take that fucker out I'm going to!" Mike wasn't amused and Varmint was up and pacing. The neighbor's floatplane roared by on its final approach.

Yesterday was the last day of hiking, training, and preliminary scouting. Mike had a plausible attack and exit plan worked out. His mission would be accomplished from atop a large Sitka Spruce tree eight-hundred-eighty yards from the weather sock at the end of Mr. Star's pier. Today, later today, would be spent getting all trolling and spey fishing, (Two handed fly casting with an exceptionally long pole), gear in order and ready for opening day tomorrow. Mike needed to establish a viable cover and he thought a week's fishing should do the trick. Varmint pranced around nosing everything; he was ready for some serious fishing.

"Crap . . . I still need some salmon leaders unless you want to try your paw at tying a few." Varmint wasn't impressed. "Guess that's a 'no'. I'll have to run the Zodiac into Ketchikan later."

Tongass Trading Company on Dock Street was crowded. A cruise ship was in Ketchikan for the day and tourists clogged every section except the fly-fishing area. The purveyor, a real spey-fishing enthusiast, was trying to talk Mike out of modifying his G. Loomis Dredger rod for backpacking.

"Look . . . I'll buy a new shooting head and backing line if you will put two more ferrules in this rod so I can backpack with it. It will not screw up the action!"

Willis, the proprietor, was just as adamant. "Look, I've been doing this for a long time. If you cut this rod up and put ferrules in it, you won't be able to cast right. I got some backpacking fly rods that will work fine. I'd much rather sell you one of those than tear up this Dredger! That is just . . . nuts!"

Mike was in a hurry and really didn't want to argue with the old beat up, stubborn, proprietor. "Ok already. If you have a rod that will work with my Skagit River style of casting I'll take it, but I don't have all day. And it better fit my Nautilus NV spey reel or I'll turn my dog loose on you!"

"No problem. The Nautilus will fit. That's one fine lookin' dog but he looks more like a wolf than a pet. I don't think I'd like to dance with him." Willis said sarcastically.

"Very perceptive. Dog's name is Varmint and the ladies think he is . . . cuddly. Let's trade, even-Steven: your rod, a shooting head, clear backing line, and two dozen forty pound salmon leaders, solid tied, for the Dredger."

"Throw in a Texas-ten and you have a deal." Willis wanted to barter; Mike was losing his patience.

"I'll give you a pair of twenties . . ."

"I've gotta walk all the way to the back of the store for those salmon leaders; make it fifty and we have a deal."

Mike considered a counter offer but time was running short. "Sold! But you probably have a secret spot for steelhead or kings. I'll need that too . . ."

"Jesus! You want my shirt? Ok, ok . . . A little south of here, on Pennock Island, is a cove. The water is shallow and clogged with seaweed. Steelhead and kings hang out there before heading up the rivers. You can't miss it, there's a big house with a long pier to the north. Fish the south side of the spit with a big green and white Clouser right next to the weeds at low tide. I always hook-up a steelhead but the real fun starts when a thirty plus pound king hits! Good luck." Willis lowered his voice to almost a whisper and said, "Oh . . . and keep an eye on Varmint. A couple of guys with Rotties come snooping around most every time I fish there. They scared the shit out of me the last time and ran me off their property! I haven't been back."

Mike thanked Willis, as an afterthought, gave him his cell number, and extended an invitation to spey or deep-sea fish with him any time. Having a local with you always improved days on the bay and usually changed a day of *fishing* into a day of catching.

Opening day of fishing season started wet, windy, and cold. This was a typical late spring day in the Alaskan rain forest. Chicken fried steak, eggs, and cottage fries were finished with a bit left over for Varmint and the galley was nearly squared away.

"We're goin' over to Ketchikan to get some fuel and then we'll see if we can't hook up a salmon or two. Why don't you run and fetch Deputy Dawg for me? He should be here by now . . ." Varmint closely watched Mike put the last of the dishes in cupboards but appeared more interested in scamming more scraps than doing favors.

"Permission to come aboard Skipper!" Huck, dressed head to foot in foul weather gear, carrying a beat up wicker creel and decrepit split bamboo boat rod with an old left-hand, Penn Senator, reel announced his arrival.

"Permission granted but you might want to leave that garbage your carryin' on the pier!" Mike gave Varmint a harsh look. "You goin' soft on me? You're supposed to warn me about people sneakin' up on us."

Varmint wagged his tail in anticipation while Huck drug his compilation of ancient fishing gear in to the salon and plopped it down on the table. Ever since Mike's arrival, Huck carried handmade, gourmet, dog treats with him. Varmint learned that fact quickly and looked forward to his visits.

"'Sup dawg? You lookin' for a Scooby-snack? Mornin' Mike you ready to go kill some kings?" Huck drawled in his unhurried Southern manner.

"Definitely! Since you're dressed up for the weather how about untying us so we can get the fuck out of here?" Mike started Springer's engine while Huck slipped the mooring lines from cleats and jumped back aboard.

"What's the plan Skipper? Best fishin's up north off the mainland rivers." Huck checked his gear while Mike idled Springer out into the open channel.

"Fuel first then I thought we'd troll around Pennock so I can do a little recon. Tomorrow I'll do a little fly fishin' down near Mr. Star's place and snoop around a bit. You know anything about the dogs there?"

Huck thought a moment before answering. "Couple of nasty Rotties there. I run across them every once in a while on my rounds. I don't know who's meaner, the hounds or the two assholes with 'em! If ya'll are thinkin' 'bout snooping 'round there; go armed!"

That gave Mike something to think about for the rest of the busy fish catchin' day.

Yesterday's catching was much better than this morning's poor excuse for fishing. Mike was running out of patients; he could not get into the groove.

"Fuckin' mother fucker!" This was the third tangle and the worst of the lot.

Mike's timing was off and his *'D-maneuvers'* were not working all that well. Today's twenty foot tide was rushing back in and Varmint was whining because Mike was chest deep about thirty feet out from the shore.

Mike waded near shore to a flat rock, sat down, untangled the shooting head from the backing line, and prepared to try spey casting again.

This time, rhythm was good, timing was good, and the shooting head placed the line right at the edge of the sea weeds. He let it drift and took in the slack. Water swirled and splashed in the subdued sun light near the Clouser. Mike's line exploded and snapped as his new fly rod bent into a 'U'. He let the line fly out between his index finger and thumb until it came on the reel's drag. The fight was on. Varmint growled and barked to get Mike's attention.

"What the fuck Varmint! Not now!" Black Cloud's sixth sense said 'see what Varmint wants'.

Water exploded forty feet away. A bright silver monster broke the surface, sailed two feet into the air rolling and showering water. It reentered the water with a sizable splash and line peeled off the reel; Mike used his index finger and gently supplemented the drag. The first run subsided and he looked over his shoulder. The line went slack; it only took a fraction of a second's inattention for Black Cloud to lose his trophy salmon.

The scene behind him riveted his attention. Black Cloud turned and reeled in his line while slowly wading ashore putting the beached Zodiac between him and the newcomers. Two men with a pair of large snarling Rottweilers on leashes were desperately trying to get them under control. Both men were armed with what appeared to be scoped AR-15s. Varmint was standing his ground; he was in a fighting stance, hackles up, all teeth bared and a vicious snarl escaped his salivating jaws.

Black Cloud, ten feet behind Varmint, issued an order. "Heel!"

Varmint deliberately backed away maintaining his fighting posture. He stayed alert even though he took up position on Black Cloud's left side. The two intruders, twenty feet away, barely had their dogs under control. Both strained at their leashes to the point it took two hands to keep them from breaking free.

Black Cloud slowly stooped down and laid his rod and reel in the Zodiac while unsnapping his wader straps giving him easy access to his shoulder rig and 44 Auto Mag. Varmint was no match for the two beasts. If they broke free or were deliberately released, one would die immediately but the second might slip by. That would be Varmint's job . . .

"Hope those dogs don't get free. It would ruin my day of fishing." Black Cloud said that slow and easy with both hands at his side; one rested gently on Varmints head.

A burley, unshaved, ugly man, the obvious leader, dressed identical to his partner in head to foot cammo barked back. "This is private property. You and your mutt get back in your boat, get the fuck off this land, and don't ever come back!"

Flinty, deadly, sniper-eyes stared daggers sizing up the situation, but Black Cloud replied calmly, "You might want to spend a dime to post this land so tourists don't get offended. Fishin's good here. What's the beef?"

Four sets of steel hard eyes stared back ignoring the question. One guard spoke and made a clear demand. "I won't tell you again. I'll turn these dogs loose. Now get the fuck out of here!"

Black Cloud raised both arms as if surrendering; snapped his fingers and ordered Varmint: "Boat!"

Varmint jumped into the Zodiac still on alert, still ready to defend and kill. "I'm out of here. Sorry to trespass," Black Cloud said in a low menacing voice that left no doubt as to his meaning, "but if you let those dogs loose I'll kill 'em both and probably you too."

Black Cloud deliberately unsnapped the restraining strap on his shoulder holster and slowly backed the Zodiac out to knee-deep water before boarding. He never once broke eye contact with the two guards. One pull of the starter cord brought the kicker to life. When reverse was engaged Black Cloud and Varmint whispered away. Both guards freed their dogs and un-slung their rifles. The Rotties made a frenzied, barking, snarling dash toward the rapidly receding

Zodiac stopping chest deep in water. Fifty feet away Varmint just stared them down. Black Cloud continued backing the Zodiac south and out into the channel until the guards recalled both dogs, re-slung rifles, and skulked back into the woods.

"That answers the guarded compound question. We will have to be careful of those dogs even half a mile away . . . Might have to see if I can arrange a visit to the vet for them next week. . ." Black Cloud was thinking in overtime while looking for a likely place to even the score with the fish population.

Chapter 32
A SHOT IN THE DARK

The pungent aroma of alder smoke reminded Black Cloud that five days of fishing and scouting had filled Huck's walk-in smokehouse with fresh king salmon and steel head trout. He would take some along as a supplement to MRE (Meals Ready to Eat) selections already packed. A camp with more traditional supplies was set up on the west side of Pennock Island. Great care was given to the camp's location its appearance and most of all its seclusion and difficulty to spot.

Mike fished with Willis, the owner of the Tongass Trading Company, on Saturday and let him know he would be backpacking and fly fishing the west side of Pennock for a week starting today. That was probably a silly precaution but one did everything one could to cover all the bases. Sunday was another profitable fishing day but today, Monday, was a do-nothing day dedicated to making sure everything was well prepared for the mission. All equipment was packed, checked, and rechecked. Mike assembled and tore down the Barrett twice and checked and rechecked his ten rounds of ammunition before stowing it precisely in the backpack. The only thing left to do was stay out of sight and wait until dark.

Mike and Varmint stayed in the Ranger Station last night with all their gear. They were checked in on the station log with notes stating they would be backpacking, hiking, and fishing along Pennock's west coast. Today was spent laying-low, out of sight, and studying last minute details. If all went according to schedule, Mike and Varmint would slip into the forest and take up station under the cover of darkness. And dark it would be! The forest was dense and the sky was gray bordering on black in anticipation of a medium sized blow descending on them from the north.

Mike snoozed and Varmint paced. Huck left half an hour ago to make his normal rounds and try toexecute a plan he devised to get the vicious Rottweilers off the island. A friend of Huck's, a State retained vet, laced steaks with something that would emulate salmon fever. Huck would drop them off at the periphery of the compound knowing that each evening the hounds were allowed to run free for an hour or so.

A low growl from Varmint alerted Mike to arriving company. Mike saw a young couple enter the station lobby, look around, and then press the button to summon the Ranger. Varmint was getting annoyed at the persistence and length of the ringing by the third press of the button; he emitted a menacing growl.

The young woman cupped her hands around her eyes, pressed them to the one-way window, and tried to peer into the living quarters. She gave up after a few seconds and joined her companion who was just finishing the sign-in process. With one last forlorn look around, they picked up their backpacks and disappeared into the mid morning gloom.

"Wonder where they will be hiking? With any luck, they will be going north. . . Not only are we going to be wet, but we might have company. Shit!" Varmint sniffed. He was just glad the annoying bell was silent and plopped himself down on his favorite spot in the middle of Brownie and joined Mike for an afternoon snooze.

Mike and Varmint woke from their pre-deployment nap late in the afternoon. Huck still wasn't back, but Mike could hear the drone of an outboard engine and assumed it was Huck on his return trip. Just to be certain, Mike verified the Zodiac was still tied snugly to the dock and the station's bright red Duckworth was not.

When dinner was finished, Varmint laid on the kitchen floor working over a pair of t-bones: the leftovers from one of Mikes' famous meals. It was time to go over last minute details. Once Huck left to finish his rounds, the countdown clock would start ticking.

"I'm surprised . . . Wasn't there any new intel from Gman?" Mike asked Huck when he entered the living quarters. "Gman is what my friends in Seattle call Billings. I'll take that as good news. On the other hand, the couple hiking in the interior isn't. I'm hoping the weather will drive them back to Ketchikan but you may have to give them a little push . . ."

Huck gave that a bit of thought before commenting. "I'll keep my eye on them the best I can. It's going to be miserable for the next few days. I'll bet they give up before long. Camping in a rain forest is just as challenging as snow camping! Not only is it wet but it's cold to boot. Ah . . . leave the dishes. I've gotta finish my rounds and deliver special treats to your friends at the compound before it gets too dark. I'll see ya'll in a week or so . . ." Huck let that hang in the air more as a question than a statement.

"Yeah. That's about right. We'll be two days in the woods and three or four days on the coast depending on how good the fishing is or how bad the weather is. I put the cover on the Zodiac and set security on ***Springer***. The monitor and key fob are on the counter. My iPhone will be off so if anyone comes snooping around use your own discretion." There really wasn't much else to say or do and Mike wanted Huck to be on his way. Those Rottweilers were a worry and the sooner he took care of them the better.

Full dark descended at sunset. By 2100, Black Cloud and Varmint stole into the dense forest. "Time to get to work buddy." Black Cloud put on night-vision goggles, made one last check of the vox unit, and then sent Varmint scouting ahead.

Black Cloud followed the trail scouted earlier. He picked up each discrete trail marker that was nearly invisible in day light but shown like a beacon in the night-vision goggles. He kept careful count; there would be no telltale signs of his passing left for anyone to discover.

"*0049 . . . Fifteen down ten to go.*" Navigating through the dense forest was difficult. The narrow field of view afforded by the night-vision gear didn't make things any easier. On two occasions a low growl from Varmint reminded Black Cloud that they were not the only critters on the prowl.

"*Marker #24 . . . This is where Varmint's cache goes.*" Without the night vision gear Black Cloud could, literally, not see his hand in front of his face. He switched on the two small, red, led lights under the bill of his ball cap. Three short puffs on the dog whistle brought Varmint to his side. His MREs were contained in biodegradable pouches. He would eat what he needed when he needed it. Water was not a problem here! Black Cloud placed the cache under a fallen cedar tree he and Varmint had selected while scouting and marking the area. Black Cloud's scent wasn't on them, the pouches were sealed and odorless, and that would keep curious critters from Varmint's chow.

"Ok now for the fun part . . . Ugh! Marker #25 and my tree are just ahead. Two hours until sunrise. It will be close but I should be settled before it's light enough for anyone to see anything out here."

Climbing a large Sitka Spruce tree in the day light was difficult enough. Climbing one in pitch black during a rainstorm with night vision gear was a near impossibility! The initial twenty feet to the first limb took a lot of time. Climbing was not difficult with spikes and a wide belt; what took the time was taking care not to leave noticeable marks. Once the first limb was conquered the next sixty feet was just a matter of carefully squirming between limbs and hauling the backpack up every ten feet or so.

Black cloud snaked into his cliff climber's tent and sleeping bag to the sound of a floatplane idling into Mr. Star's dock. *"Tuesday morning . . . right on time."*

Black Cloud switched the vox unit to 'transmit' and spoke. "Rest." Varmint would return to his cache, eat, sleep, and wait for further orders.

Sitting in a tree was not the best of circumstances but a sight better than spending weeks on end in the Iraq desert. Pissing in a bottle wasn't all that tough and a liberal dose of Imodium AD negated the immediate need for toilet paper. . . at least for a few days.

Just before dozing off Black Cloud thought about life in a tree.*"FMTT! sleeping in this harness sucks . . . Real food and sleeping horizontally will be nice once this job is finished. These Pillsbury Space food sticks are ok but sizzling bacon, coffee, and hot cakes would be much better!"*

Black Clouds backpack was lashed to a pair of close-growing limbs. It was at a perfect height to bench-rest the Barrett while he sat on a limb below. The sleeping bag/tent made a suitable pillow to sit on and was quite comfortable. He rehearsed the mission while paying strict attention to not being spotted. He checked his ballistic tables for the fifth time and wrote the figure beside the hourly, temperature, humidity, barometric pressure, and wind speed and direction information. *"Ok . . . windsock shows between five and ten knots. Up here, I have ten knots steady. That means I have an average three knot differential . . . I can stay in this position for several hours at a time. With this forest ghillie suit on I'm nearly invisible during daylight hours. Especially from this range: 878.8 yards... All I need now is my target."* Black Cloud made a slight adjustment for windage and elevation, sighted the handle on the floatplane's front door, took a deep breath, and slowly let it out while applying steady pressure to the trigger.

'Click!' The firing pin struck the snap cap. *"Good, not so much as a millimeter of movement and I had no idea when the sear released the firing pin. It will be dark in a couple hours, there are no guard dogs anywhere near, and Varmint is on the job. I'm ready! Getting out of this fuckin' tree and back on the ground tomorrow morning will be . . .heaven!"*

A low growl in Black Cloud's left ear alerted him that Varmint noticed something or someone. Four short puffs on the dog whistle sent him to 'shadow' whoever or whatever aroused his curiosity. Several minutes later, the distinct but faint tinkle of bear bells mixed with light banter came through the vox unit.

"Shit! Tourists. Just what the fuck I need . . ." The banter grew louder and louder as Varmint stalked his prey.

"Hey Jude . . .you get the feeling someone or something is watching us?" Two bear bells sounded off noisily as both hikers shook their walking sticks.

"I do. It creeps me out. This place reminds me of the movie "Twilight"!" The soft but nervous female voice shook a bit. "We should have gone kayaking like I wanted . . ."

Black Cloud could picture one or both hikers furtively glancing back over their shoulders, even turning around, and walking backward now and then. *"I should have Varmint growl."* He smiled and decided against it.

"There's still time before it's dark to go back to the ranger station. If he's there he might give us a ride back to Ketchikan . . ." Jude punctuated her rising fear with a loud sustained shaking of the bear bell.

"Don't be a woos there's no. . . ." Varmint's growl was loud enough to be heard.

"I'm going back!" Jude whimpered, "I'm going back right now . . ."

Black Cloud hoped the bear bells reminded Varmint how much these two annoyed him ringing the bell at the ranger station and not that someone else was in the area.

Black Cloud squirmed, and finally gave into the temptation to exercise; he needed to work the kinks out. Tai Chi was martial arts practice and a good sniper workout. It's slow precise movements would not be seen. The ghillie suit was hot and confining and Black Cloud worked up a sweat after an hour's exercise. Nothing in the compound half a mile below changed. That was expected and the mission was set for early tomorrow morning. It was getting close to sunset and it was already pitch black eighty feet below on the forest floor.

Black Cloud switched the vox unit to transmit and ordered Varmint: "Rest." Both would nap and conserve energy until 0300. If Mr. Star stayed true to his routine, he would board the floatplane between 0400 and 0430. Sunrise was 0503 and it would be light in the forest by 0600.

"I hope this dick head is punctual. It's gonna be a bitch getting out of this tree and clear of the area before someone comes looking! It'll be dark in an hour . . ." Black Cloud mapped out his escape in fine detail before dropping off to sleep.

0300 came around in a hurry. Black Cloud was up twice after dark. The ghillie suit, and all non-essential equipment was lowered to the base of the tree. The backpack would be dropped and the Barrett lowered on shot line right after the job was done. It would take seven or eight minutes to descend to the ground. The last limbless twenty feet would be accomplished with a repelling line that was already in place.

"0345 . . . That shot line comes in handy. Wonder where the fuck Kensey got all those rolls? Satellite phone on; check. Round chambered; check. Safety off, check. Wind at target, zero; check. Wind here two knots; check. Windage corrections made; checked and verified. Varmint ordered to return; check. People up and lights on in the house; check. Come to papa asshole!" Black Cloud's right index finger itched . . .

At 0410, a shaft of light illuminated a path down the pier as the cabin door opened. A man with a high power flashlight meandered down the pier and entered the floatplane. A moment later navigation lights came on and the engine coughed to life. Two additional men entered the shaft of light cast by the open door and started down the pier toward the smoothly idling floatplane. One man, the target, marked by his lucky Jets ball cap worn backward, stopped momentarily to flip the butt of his cigarette into the water.

"*Bingo! Intel's spot-on. Profile matches, and ball cap matches.*" Black Cloud exhaled and started applying slight, steady, pressure to the trigger. The target spun around, sped up, caught up with his companion, slapped his back, wrapped his arm around his shoulder, and proceeded toward the floatplane.

"*Sombitch!*" Black Cloud eased pressure off the trigger. "*Looks like dickhead's buddy told a whopper of a joke. Won't be so funny in a minute!*" They walked past the dock cleat marking eight-hundred-fifty yards. Black Cloud made a minuscule elevation adjustment.

"*Come on . . . Come on . . . A little further. Don't stop now!*" Black Cloud led the target ever so slightly while steadily applying pressure to the trigger. Dick Head's buddy suddenly broke free, stopped and kneeled down in front of him.

"*How the fuck could your shoe come untied? No matter it's gonna be a twofur!*" Black Cloud's breath was two thirds of the way out when the Barrett roared. The night scope optics completely went black for a millisecond with the light from the suppressed muzzle preserving night-vision. Black Cloud was still on target when the optics cleared.

"*No need for a second round . . . Time to get the fuck out of here!*" One last glance verified the Winchester, two-hundred-fifty grain, match round did its job. Mr. Star, the dick head, was writhing in agony while holding his right leg. "*Winged the fucker! Payday's a go!*" Dick Head's buddy was not so lucky. The round that winged his friend caught him in the neck. There was a clear gap between where his body came to rest and his head. The pilot bolted from his floatplane and ran to give assistance.

"*Fool! Damn good thing I'm in a hurry . . .*" Black Cloud pressed the satellite phone's call button. One ring barely finished when a gruff voice demanded, "Report."

"Done."

Chapter 33
Escape

The voice on the other end of the satellite connection did not sound like Gman but Black Cloud's job was to immediately report when his mission was complete, not second-guess anyone. He disconnected the call, shut the phone off, removed the battery, carefully zipped it into his jacket pocket, unlashed his back pack from the tree and pushed it off the limbs, securely tied shot line to the Barrett, lowered it until it stopped, and then, as quickly as he could, followed it down the tree.

The Barrett wedged itself between two limbs thirty feet below. Luckily, it was easy to free it and lower it the rest of the way to the ground. A yip from Varmint confirmed it was all the way down and probably landed on his head. There was no time to worry about that now. Six minutes were already burned and it was still fifty feet to the ground. *"Wonder what's happening' out there on the pier? Hope no one is calling the authorities. I haven't heard the plane take off yet; That's a good thing."*

Black Cloud slipped and dropped five feet to the next layer of limbs. He desperately hung there with his feet flaying for a purchase on anything. He contacted a limb in the crook of his right knee but his tenuous grip gave way and he found himself upside down hanging there. His night vision gear slipped up his forehead completely blocking any vision. *"Slow down . . . Think!"*

A few seconds of carefully rocking to-and-fro with arms full extended found two closely growing limbs about three feet below. Black cloud solidly gripped the branch furthest from his chest and carefully straightened his right leg. He took as much weight as he could on his arms but still managed to bang his knee before coming to a secure, upright, rest. He finally had a death grip on a good-sized limb and his feet were firmly ensconced on another five feet below. *"Nine fuckin' minutes and I'm still up a tree!"* A slower pace found Black Cloud repelling the last twenty feet, thirteen minutes after the shot. Varmint was there, itching to go, even before Black Cloud's feet hit the ground. All gear was gathered within a matter of seconds. Black Cloud limped off for the first marker to what he now referred to as 'fish camp #1', with Varmint close at his side.

"Hope you had a nice day . . . Next time you climb the fuckin tree!" Varmint trotted along happily saying nothing. Every once in a while he nudged Black Cloud's hand just to make sure they were really on the move away from this dark, dripping, moss-infested forest.

"Ok. Be that way. Don't answer. I'm going to call Kurten if we ever get cell phone reception again . . . "

Rain cascaded down in buckets. Black Cloud could hear it in the trees sighing like a banshee. Little rivulets of water streamed everywhere making travel slow and tedious. *"Must of missed the first marker . . . Fuck! I can't afford to wait until it gets light to get out of here."* A quick consult of the compass verified they were traveling at 285 degrees magnetic. *"Fuckin' marker should be here somewhere . . . Aha! There it is just ahead to the left. Thirty-three left to go."*

Sunrise, supposedly, occurred more than half an hour ago but it was still darker than the inside of a cow amongst the tall trees. Black Cloud gave up worrying about pursuit; no one in their right mind was out hiking in the woods in this wet, muck! The camouflage issue was no longer a concern either. Three falls, especially the last tumble down a twenty-foot incline had him covered in mud from head to foot. Even Varmint was irritated. He growled his displeasure after shaking mud and water off his fur for the umpteenth time. *"Marker #19. 0541 . . . Thank God it's lighting up . . ."*

The trees were thinning. The pouring rain subsided a few minutes ago. Fish camp #1 was less than a mile away. Black Cloud halted under the drooping limbs of a large cedar tree. Varmint was glad to get out of the soaking rain and plopped himself down to watch. Black Cloud removed the night vision gear and turned the two small red led lights under the bill of his ball cap on. He unrolled the tent /sleeping bag, smoothed it, laid the Barrett in the middle, and rapidly disassembled it and stowed the pieces in the backpack. The night vision gear was stowed next. Varmint's vox unit followed along with the ear bud. Lastly, Black Cloud removed the satellite phone from the zipped jacket pocket and smashed the circuit board and sim card with the butt of his survival knife and then placed the pieces in a zip lock bag and stowed them away.

The small ultra violet light was still snugly zipped into an inside jacket pocket. Black Cloud fished it out, turned it on, and shined it on a handful of trail markers. They blazed purple.

"Ok. Let's get a move on it." Black Cloud shook his head in bewilderment. Varmint was sound asleep.

"Yo, Mutt . . . I'm leaving you here if you don't get your lazy ass up." That was loud enough to wake Varmint. He rolled over, stretched, squiggled around on his back, and then rolled back over, stretched, and finished with a yawn big enough to unhinge his jaw. Black Cloud searched around in his jacket pocket until he found the last of Huck's gourmet Scooby Snacks. That got Varmints attention.

"Here; you deserve this!" Black Cloud and Varmint set out at a good clip in the gloom. Varmint took the lead. He usually found the trail markers before they glowed purple. It was a game they played that pretty well precluded leaving any markers behind. *"Marker #33. Two hundred yards to the camp."* Three short puffs on the silent dog whistle brought Varmint to his side. Black Cloud unzipped his jacket and freed up the Auto Mag. Next, he removed the Smith and Wesson from the hollow of his back, jacked a bullet into the chamber, set the safety, and then put it in his jacket pocket.

"I don't hear, see, or sense anything but . . . they don't call me Black Cloud for nothing!" Two silent predators entered an abandoned and unmolested camp from opposite sides. When the tension broke, Mike Smith breathed a sigh of relief and went about hiding all gear associated with this morning's ambush in three different locations. They would be retrieved later and given a burial-at-sea where no one would ever find them. He noted and memorized every landmark. Black Cloud made certain that he knew where each piece of gear was hidden and in his mind created a detailed map that he could quickly recall and transmit to Huck if needed. Once that was completed to his satisfaction, Mike broke out coffee, bacon, eggs, pancake mix, and happily started the propane camp stove.

CHAPTER 34
TAKING CONTROL

Black Cloud, perched on a log, watching rivulets cascade off the makeshift canvas awning, warmed his hands over a small campfire and complained to no one in particular. "One more day of this shit is about all I can stand. What say we call it quits and see what Deputy Dawg is up to?" Varmint vigorously shook the accumulated raindrops from his rain soaked fur. Black Cloud interpreted that as an enthusiastic affirmative.

Fishing was great but the dismal, all-day, gloom that progressed into a never-ending deluge made it difficult to distinguish all too short days from all too long nights. Black Cloud gave that some thought. *"My primary mission is accomplished. For whatever reason, bad weather, or lack of interest, yesterday's sniping didn't generate much excitement. One helicopter and a bush plane made aerial searches for several hours and I spotted two patrol boats searching along the shore. Hell . . . a Homeland Security patrol boat stopped and two officers checked my credentials. All they said was Ranger Cooley asked them to check and make sure I was ok. I gave them a slab-side, Chinook, and told them to bring some decent weather with them when they returned . . . Fuck it!"*

"Come first light we're out of here. I'll bet Huck cooked up some Scooby snacks while we've been trompin' around in this muck." Varmint scooted a little closer to the sputtering campfire and smiled.

Sometime during the night Ketchikan's incessant rain subsided. Mike whole-heartedly approved. He threw the last rashers of bacon into the frying pan and coaxed last night's campfire to life. Varmint sauntered over, sniffed the pan and wagged his tail in approval. Coffee burbled into a slow perk and the eastern sky showed streaks of subdued light. Mike scampered about breaking camp. He planned on starting back to **Springer** shortly after finishing breakfast. The ranger station was a mile and a half east as the crow flies but skirting swampy areas and small streams made returning a five-mile hike.

A mug of steaming coffee rested on log used as last night's camp chair and Mike flipped two large salmon fillets over into the sizzling bacon grease. "Well Varmint, all we have to do now is eat, kill the fire, scatter the ashes, and take down the tarp. We should be back to civilization by 1000. I don't know about you but a nice hot shower is first thing on my agenda!"

Varmint eyed the salmon fillets thinking, "Two thin rashes of bacon do not a meal make."

Breakfast finished, fire tended to, and the tarp rolled and secured to his backpack, Mike set off at a brisk pace with Varmint scouting the trail ahead. They slogged through swampy patches and forded small streams, to save time. Three grueling hours brought them to the clearing adjacent to the Ranger Station. Mike signaled Varmint in close and scratched his ears while studying the area.

Nothing was stirring; ten minutes passed. Mike, satisfied all was in order, spoke softly to Varmint. "I'll bet Deputy Dawg is still sleepin'. We'll find out soon enough." Black Cloud sent Varmint ahead; he took off like a shot knowing goodies were stored in Huck's quarters.

No one greeted Mike when he approached the back door. **Springer** and the Zodiac rested securely beside the dock. Mike dropped his backpack and looked around for a hose to wash the mud and muck off of himself and Varmint. Once that chore was completed, he spun the 'use other door' sign around, retrieved the spare key, and entered the ranger station. It was just as he left it several days ago but the lingering aroma of biscuits and bacon said Huck had been here some hours ago.

Mike ordered Varmint to stay outdoors and he whined to come in. Mike looked around for his iPhone, spotted the charging cord trailing out from under a pile of books on Huck's end table, rescued it, buttoned it to life, and signed onto Springer's wireless connection. No security alarms were tripped; everything was in order. It was time to find some old towels, dry Varmint off, let him in, and take a much-needed Hollywood shower.

Mike, fully refreshed, sipped a generous shot of Elijah Craig, single barrel, bourbon. Huck left the bottle on the coffee table atop a pile of books with a thoughtful note: You will probably need this after all the rain and fog!

Mike called Huck's cell phone; he answered on the first ring. "Hey, I see you are back from fly-fishing. Any luck? Bet you wish you didn't forget your iPhone." Huck sounded upbeat but a little out of breath.

"Must be someone within ear shot . . ." Mike thought before answering. "Fishin' was good; rain sucks and damn sure wish I had my phone with me. I could have checked the shitty weather if nothing else! You comin' back to the station any time soon?"

"Don't know when I'll be around. I'm out here with Homeland Security. We had a little excitement the other day and we're goin' over the island inch by inch." Black Cloud started the conversation on guard and was now at full alert.

"I talked to those guys a day or so ago. They didn't say anything about excitement . . . Hey, if you are anywhere near where I camped would you look for my Garmin GPS; I dropped it around there somewhere." Black Cloud's mind raced in overtime. *"I need to know where those guys are if I'm going to retrieve my equipment . . . Shit!"*

"We went by there a few hours ago and are up north. You want me to go back and look for the Garmin?" Huck knew how to play the game and now Black Cloud knew where Homeland Security was and what direction they were searching.

"No that's ok I'll have a look-see on the way out. Fly-fishin' was good over there and I want to try some trolling. Thanks anyway. Oh, that bourbon you left out is most excellent; I might leave you a shot or two . . ."

"Yeah, that *is* some good stuff; if I don't get back before you get underway, take the bottle. You headin' back to Seattle?" That was Huck's way of saying he had no more useful intell.

"I want to be in Prince Rupert tonight. There's an interesting woman who owes me a rain check on dinner. I'll be up on HF when I get out of cell and VHF range if I you want to get a hold of me. Thanks for letting me stay. I'll be back later this summer or next year." That gave Huck the information he needed to pass on to Gman.

"Got it and there's a bag of gourmet dog treats on the kitchen counter; make sure you take them with you. Catch ya'll next time around."

Mike took one last look around, shook the bag of Scooby snacks to get Varmints attention, departed the ranger station and replaced the door key behind the 'use the other door' sign. He took a long look around thinking, *"I like it here. I wonder if Gman could get me a gig like Huck's."*

It took an hour to stow the Zodiac and make all preparations to depart. Varmint was asleep in his favorite spot under the galley table when Mike finished checking all of ***Springer's*** systems and was satisfied with the gentile loping sound made by her idling engine.

"Yo! Hound. We are officially out of here." Mike backed away from the Ranger Station dock with great skill; three fenders, one white and two blue, attached to the port side rail with granny knots, gently swayed in time with the ground swell.

"With Huck and Homeland Security up north you and I'll swing by Fish Camp, fuckin wet, dreary Fish Camp One, and recover our gear. I'd have Huck do it but Gman was pretty explicit about deep sixin' the gear used to wound Dick Head." Varmint did not flinch. He did not hear Mike or really care what he was rambling on about.

It took Mike the better part of two hours to retrieve all the cashed equipment and get moving toward Prince Rupert and Kurten. Anchoring ***Springer*** and lowering then retrieving the Zodiac burned most of the time. Gathering the gear and departing without leaving a trace turned out to be the easy part.

Mike trolled for salmon until he was well out of sight of Pennock Island. He secured the fishing gear, kicked ***Springer*** up to fifteen knots and set a beeline course for Prince Rupert. One detail of his assignment remained to be completed and the time for that was now.

"This is it buddy; this is where we dump the last equipment that can tie us to the events on Pennock Island." Varmint opened one eye, emitted an SBD and went back to sleep.

Mike engaged autopilot, donned a pair of surgical gloves, fished the last pieces of disassembled and smashed satellite phone and the last five rounds of custom made ammo from the back pack and tossed them into Hecate Strait. He placed three cannonball-sized boulders into the backpack and then pitched it over the side.

"Wake up you lazy hound! That's the last of it. Anything connecting us to North Star is scattered over fifty miles of ocean. Two hours more and we should be moored in Prince Rupert. As soon as I get a couple of dots on the iPhone, I'll call Breakers Restaurant and make reservations for two at 2030. Sorry buddy, you have to stay and guard the boat." Varmint barely opened one eye and slipped back to sleep in his favorite warm, dry, spot under the galley table.

Mike dialed up channel 73 on the VHF radio. "Prince Rupert Rowing and Yachting Club, this is *Springer*. Do you copy?"

The response was immediate. "*Springer* this is PRRYC. What can we do for you?"

"I'm about ten minutes out; do you have moorage available for a Nordic Tug 37? I plan to stay ten days."

"Affirmative. Slip M61 or M62 are available. Radio us when you are a few minutes out; we'll send a tender to guide you in. PRRYC out."

"Thanks. *Springer* out."

The radio chatter woke Varmint. He paced a bit, went out on deck, and used his special scupper on the windward side.

CHAPTER 35
TRYST AND TREPIDATION

A cold, May rain drizzled from a darkening gray sky. *"This would be depressing if I was still slogging through the rain forest on Pennock Island."* Mike thought and happily saluted the crackling log fire in the Breakers lounge with his ice cold Kokanee. He checked his watch for the fifth time in the past six minutes, *"Kurten should be here shortly. Wonder what the Squid is doing? I'll bet he's on the Willamette fishin' Springers. Maybe I can talk him into riding back to Seattle with me?"*

Mike retrieved his iPhone from the inside pocket of his North Face jacket, thumbed it to life, cycled down to 'Old Goat' in his contacts, and punched the talk button.

"What the fuck; you sink that scow? Where the hell have you been?" Bob Kensey could not believe his long-lost fishin' partner finally called.

"No . . . put a few holes in her but nothing that a case of Flex Seal couldn't fix. And Varmint and I are just fine, thank you! I'm in Prince Rupert waiting for my dinner date and wondered if you want to fly up here and spend a week or two fishin' back to Seattle?"

"Dinner date? You run into Sasquatch up there? No can do the fishin' thing. I have a little job to do and it will take a few months but I should be back in time to catch Humpies. What the hell are you doin' in Prince Rupert, British Columbia?"

"Like I said, dinner, and Venus just walked in. I gotta go. Say hi to the guys at the Haven." Mike broke the phone connection, stood up beaming from ear to ear, and motioned for Kurten to take the seat beside him on the plush, red, leather chesterfield polished by thousands of fellow travelers. He barely noticed the tall, well dressed, man entering the lounge just behind her.

Mike stammered slightly. "I am very glad you could make time for this short-notice rain check. My iPhone," Mike pointed to his phone sitting on the drink table. "Doesn't have very good service up here or I would have called sooner."

Kurten smiled while she shed her shapeless, full-length, navy, bridge coat to reveal a stunning frock best described as a 'Little Black Dress'. "I know what you mean. Pirates, no dots on the iPhone, bad weather, gotta feed the cuddly K-9 . . . A girl can't expect a busy guy to drop everything and call."

Mike reddened slightly. He suddenly felt out of place dressed as if he just fell off the ***Time Bandit*** following two weeks of Bearing Sea crabbing. "Well . . ." Mike's mind raced looking for a plausible excuse but Kurten's dancing eyes said she was teasing not scolding. "The dress code at WCMR has improved, a lot. I approve!"

Kurten smiled, batted her eyelashes, handed Mike her heavy coat and small 'Coach' clutch and then made a show of gliding onto the ottoman.

Mike waved a waitress over and slid in next to her." We have a few minutes before our table is ready, would you like something to drink?"

"That pint looks good. I'll have a Sleeman Original and I only had a few minutes after work to throw something on. If you are going to be here a while I can dress for a proper date."

The waitress arrived with RCMP Special Agent Angus McKinney in tow. Mike ordered another Kokanee, Kurten's Sleeman Original, and glared at Angus who pulled a chair opposite the chesterfield.

"Miss Kellogg, Mr. Smith may I join you?" Angus ordered a Kokanee and watched while the waitress receded out of earshot.

"Ah shit." Mike said. "Angus, I didn't recognize you dressed in that fine fitting suit. Where is your bright red Smokey the Bear outfit and what are you doing back in this part of the country?" A feeling of foreboding dampened Mike's mood.

"Maybe Angus is here by coincidence or maybe someone found a fishing boat adrift. Regardless, come hell or high water, I'm staying here for ten days!" Mike was determined until Angus broke in on his thoughts.

"I hope this doesn't interfere with your plans too much, but I've been ordered to escort you to the airport and a waiting jet."

Black Cloud remained calm outwardly but Kurten noticed a subtle change. She peered into his eyes and saw a jungle cat looking back. Her interest rose with noticeable goose flesh.

"If I can sit in a tree for two days I can outwit this Mountie."
Mike considered his next move carefully. "I'd love to go with you but I can't just up and leave Kurten, and I can't leave my boat at the marina, and, sure as shit, I ain't leavin' Varmint behind! Whatever *'it'* is can wait until I return to Seattle."

"I'm afraid that is not possible. Mr. Billings insists. He says a herd of old goats needs protecting and you would understand. Arrangements for ***Springer*** are already made. She will be moved to WCMR, given a new color scheme, and refitted. Now Varmint . . . He's another story altogether. I thought I would pick him up on the way over here. He was very uncooperative; I'm lucky to be alive! We can stop and retrieve him on the way to the airport." Angus made a point of looking at his wristwatch. "We need to leave shortly." The waitress deposited drinks on the table and Angus gave her a credit card to pay the bill. He said no when she asked if we wanted to run a tab.

Kurten sipped her ale and gazed at Mike over the schooner's frosty rim. That made him anxious and unsettled and his mind raced in overtime. *"Well . . . I guess this is goodbye Kurten. Probably forever! Thanks Gman! I will get even."* Mike was torn between staying or jetting off to help Kensey and a herd of old goats. The old goats won out.

Mike sighed, resigned that he would have to leave and help the Squid. "Yeah, Varmint would not take kindly to anyone trying to board ***Springer***. Ok, Angus, if Kensey and his raggedy-ass band of old goats need a hand I can help out. Do we have time for dinner?" He gave Kurten a hangdog look and hoped she was not too upset.

Angus hesitated and Kurten spoke up. "Mike, who is Kensey, and why does he need help with a herd of smelly old goats?"

Mike realized his error and ignored the daggers Angus stared at him. "Kensey, the old goat, is a retired Navy Master Chief. He and some of his Goat Locker friends crew a three masted schooner. They're probably all too old to climb the rigging and need help sailing her. You have any vacation time? The schooner is in Baja, California."

"Mike, we don't have time for dinner and you need to leave Prince Rupert within the hour. I don't think Miss Kellogg has time to pack but she can ride to the airport with us." Angus squirmed and Mike smiled at his discomfort.

Kurten suspected there was more to this than Angus or Mike was letting on. She sat her ale down and then picked her coat and handbag up. "Thanks for the offer. I'm ready to go."

"To the airport or Baja?" Mike asked innocently.

"Just to the airport; someone has to make sure the work on *Springer* is done correctly."

No one spoke. The silence said volumes while Mike and Kurten followed Angus to the parking lot and a nondescript, black, Denali. Mike noticed an airline travel kennel in the back and smiled to himself. Angus unlocked the Denali and Mike escorted Kurten into the back seat and climbed in beside her.

"I brought a travel kennel for Varmint. I think he will be comfortable in it." After his most recent encounter, Angus wanted nothing to do with Mike's dog running loose.

"You aren't going to put that cuddly puppy into a cage all the way to Mexico are you Mike?" Kurten sounded genuinely upset.

Angus physically whitened at Mike's answer. "Hell no! Varmint goes first class or we aren't going at all."

It was a short drive to *Springer*. Angus pulled into the marina parking lot and asked Mike if he needed any help getting things for the trip and again reminded him time was critical. Mike declined the help but did not object when Kurten slid out of the Denali and joined him.

There was a commotion in progress alongside *Springer*. Three men in coveralls were cowering atop a WCMR shipyard jeep. Varmint, looking anything but cuddly, held them at bay.

"John, Steve, Gregg . . . what are you doing? Kurten spoke with authority and the three atop the jeep looked relieved.

The one addressed as Gregg spoke up. "We were ordered to move this Nordic Tug over to the yards Miss Kellogg. No one said anything about a guard dog!"

Mike ordered Varmint to stand down and boarded *Springer* to gather the few things he needed for travel. Kurten stayed on the pier obviously giving orders to the yard crew. When Mike and Varmint came out on deck all three jumped into the jeep and slammed the doors shut. Mike handed a set of keys to Kurten who in turn handed them to Steve through a partially opened window with two minutes of explicit instructions.

Mike and Kurten went over details about what he did not want messed with aboard Springer. They finished just before reaching the Denali and Angus waiting with tailgate down and kennel open. Mike wandered to the rear of the Denali feigning a close inspection of Varmint's intended travel cage. He bumped into Angus and surreptitiously slipped a Scooby snack into his suit pocket. Varmint's head immediately snapped around; he zeroed in on the Scooby snack in Angus's jacket pocket with keen interest. Angus noticed Varmint's intense stare and nervously moved a step away from Mike.

"Do you need a hand getting Varmint into the kennel? Eh?" Angus sounded apprehensive; Mike smiled.

"No. Don't think so." Mike innocently replied and strode around to the passenger door with Varmint close at heel. Varmint's eyes never leaving Angus.

Mike opened the car door with a flourish, snapped his fingers, and Varmint jumped into the Denali and assumed his favorite shotgun seat.

The drive to the airport was tense for Angus. Varmint stared at him the entire way and every now and then bared his fangs and emitted a low menacing growl. Angus gazed at Mike in the rearview mirror and asked if he could calm Varmint down.

Mike's reply was instant. "Hope you can get the deposit back on that kennel." He flashed Angus a payback, shit-eating grin.

Angus was relieved when they pulled to a stop next to the boarding ladder of a dark gray G-550 jet resting on the tarmac.

Mike exited the Denali and opened the shotgun door. Kurten mistook Mike's hand signals for a nervous twitch until Varmint jumped out of the Denali and started an obvious and systematic security sweep of the area.

Kurten, minus her bridge coat, was next out. She snuggled up next to Mike and asked him for his iPhone. Mike gave her a quizzical look but complied. She then asked Angus to come take a photo. He was focused on Varmint's antics and idly took the iPhone.

"Is Varmint working? Will he be calmer when he returns?" Angus was genuinely worried.

"Yes! And he won't bite. He rather likes you but I ordered him on alert to bug you. Payback is a mother! Kensey taught me that." Mike smiled and Angus breathed a deep sigh of relief.

"There are ten cases of beer left on board ***Springer***. They are yours for your trouble; just don't tell the Old Goat I gave away his San Magoo!"

Kurten gave Mike a peck on the cheek and Angus took several photos. Before Angus could hand Mike's iPhone back, Kurten turned the peck on the cheek into a long sensual kiss.

She gently pulled away from the embrace and whispered tenderly. "The photo is to remind you to call, and the kiss is to remind you why."

The pilot slid open a cockpit window and yelled down to the little gathering. "Hey! Get a move on it. I have a schedule to keep!"

Kurten pushed away and reluctantly whispered, "I guess you have to go. You will be back . . ."

Mike, never at a loss for words, answered from cloud nine. "I do . . . I will. For sure!"

He quickly regained some composure when he noticed Varmint zigzagging toward the gap between two hangers. He turned to Angus and muttered low so Kurten could not hear. "Take Kurten out of here now! Varmint is on alert and found something he doesn't like and I'm not armed."

"Call Varmint in and get on the plane. I have men here keeping an eye on suspected Cartel activity that you stirred up in Old Bella Bella. I'll get Kurten out of here and let Mr. Billings know if his jet got the wrong people curious. "Angus was all business and Mike had no doubt Kurten was safe.

He fished in his pocket, retrieved his keychain with the silent dog whistle attached, gave three short puffs, and started for the waiting jet's boarding ladder. Varmint nudged his dangling right hand with his wet, cold nose, two steps from boarding the nondescript jet. Varmint stood in the jet's doorway and glared down at Angus. He sighed in disgust; Angus was leaving with his Scooby snack!

Mike punched up 'Old Goat' on his iPhone while Varmint paced the isle checking behind each and every seat while they taxied toward the runway. The message, *'Sasquatch my ass, you old goat!'* went out with two photos attached . . .

CHAPTER 36
TRIALS AND TRIBULATIONS

Jim Billings, ensconced behind his desk, sifted through reams of reports generated by Black Cloud's recent mission in Ketchikan and nodded with satisfaction. He smiled at the sheer amount of operable intelligence gathered before him. He sorted information into a logical order and confirmed what he surmised all along was fact. Kensey's operation in San Diego was being closely monitored by at least one major drug cartel.

A key player in Cabo San Lucas, now identified as Paymaster, ran an operation from a ranch near **Goats On A Roof** in Descanso, a dusty village located in the high desert east of San Diego, CA. Paymaster's soldiers already had one altercation with Kensey, Boats, and Masters in a hotel parking lot, the Vaquero. For now, they mostly stayed in the background watching and gathering information. *"I wonder if they ran José off the road in Harbison canyon?"* crossed Jim's mind.

Jim perused the latest bits of information and formulated plans. In typical chess master thinking he considered scenarios at least four moves ahead. *"Paymaster placed several calls to San Diego. He said his man, Feo, would arrive shortly and take over operations at the ranch. Paymaster is either stepping up surveillance and/or planning to interfere with Kensey and crew."* Jim sighed and even though he did not like it, he settled down and changed strategies in 'mid game'. *"That cinches it; Black Cloud's primary mission just changed from running down the assholes who shot up* **Derdrake** *to eliminating Feo and associates."*

"Oh oh! Better inform Gemma Grace that Mr. Smith will be in contact and she will brief him mission details." Jim laughed out loud at that thought and decided to send Gemma a Marine for backup.

****

The sun slid behind Gaskill Peak casting long shadows across the Vaquero Hotel parking lot; Black Cloud was bored with waiting. He and Varmint sat in a dusty pick up cab itching for something to do. Thinking about the surprising sprinting speed displayed by a gangly picture taker after taking one look at Varmint helped pass the time.

"Jesus Varmint, you didn't have to give that kid a heart attack! Hope he has a change of drawers. There goes our guy now. Let's see where he hangs his hat."

The blue Ford pickup entered the Kumeyaay highway and sped east. Traffic was modest and following entailed no more than maintaining a discrete distance. They exited the highway at Kitchen Creek and continued east on old highway 8. Following was still easy. Black Cloud hung back and almost missed his query turning north on the La Posta Truck Trail. The rising dust cloud saved the day. The blue Ford pickup turned onto a smaller gravel road and continued north. Black Cloud hung back and studied the terrain.

This was typical southwest high desert country. Creosote brush, Manzanita and cholla cactus lined the ditches on either side of the road. Numerous trails led off in all directions and signs of quad and motorcycle activity was evident. Cottonwood trees grew along winter watercourses and massive prickly pear cactus grew among moonscape boulder heaps. Black Cloud spotted a ranch complex down on his left and from his vantage point he could see the pickup speed on past and continue north.

"Inhospitable looking place Varmint. GPS says this is Thing Valley but I don't see a fuckin' *thing* I like about it. Another quarter-of-a-mill ($250,000) for this job . . . I'm not sure it's worth it. I'll round up the old goat when we're done here. For some reason, Kensey always liked San Diego. Must be something interesting to do in this desert. Here we go . . . Hope no one is awake at that ranch." Varmint sat up and looked around; something piqued his interest.

Black Cloud passed the ranch house and out buildings in the waning light of dusk. He came to an area with close growing, large, cottonwood trees but the settling dust said the pickup was still on the move. Nightfall was fast approaching; headlights would soon be needed and that would put an end to following anyone undetected.

"Let's stop here and go on foot. You look like you need to water the cactus anyway." Black Cloud pulled his truck off the road into a clump of trees, shut the engine off, and listened for a second before opening Varmint's door. He jumped out and quickly set about scouting the area.

Black Cloud stepped out of the truck to the *'sssssssssssss'* of what sounded like a flattening tire. He bent down to examine the left front. "Shit! Fuck! Sidewinder!" He jumped back with his 9mm ready but thought better of using it.

"You live this time you piece of shit snake . . . Don't be here when I come back." He blew three short blasts on his silent dog whistle and started up the road.

Varmint fell silently into step beside Black Cloud. They emerged from the cottonwoods after negotiating several tight switchbacks up a short, steep, grade. From this vantage he could see a good-sized ranch nestled in a valley below. There was activity and a blue Ford pickup parked in front of the ranch house. A quick scan with the field glasses revealed three men present. Two sat on the veranda drinking cervesa and a third was retrieving something from the pickup bed.

"This is it Varmint." Black Cloud consulted his GPS and quadrangle topo map. "Right here." he pointed to an elevation west and a little south of the ranch. "That's where we set up and we can hide the truck somewhere along the La Posata Truck Trail. Let's go check that out before someone spots us." Black Cloud approached his truck cautiously making sure the sidewinder moved to safer ground.

Black Cloud back tracked to the turn off and started up the La Posata Truck Trail. It took less than half an hour to scout out a suitable place to hide the truck. A large mound of boulders, fifty yards off the road, surrounded by a grove of cottonwood trees filled the bill nicely. Three short blasts on the silent dog whistle brought Varmint back from a quick scouting mission.

"That's it for tonight. It's too dark to do much else. We'll camp out on the high ground tomorrow and see what's what . . . I still have a few Scooby snacks back at Cibbets Flat and I have rib eye steaks to BBQ. Let's go!" Mike opened the passenger door and Varmint jumped into the cab.

Half an hour of easy driving brought them to Kitchen Creek road; Mike was deep in thought planning his mission and the next few days. *"This isn't going to be simple . . . At least I don't have to worry about wingin' some shit-bird!"*

Cibbets Flat campground was deserted except for the thirty-one foot Airstream Classic trailer prepositioned by Gemma. Black Cloud pulled into the campsite but sat a moment contemplating his next move. He let Varmint out to scout the area while he planned. *"Time to drag the artillery out of its hiding place. That should be under the cross bed-toolbox according to instructions left by Gman.*

Mike sat at the Airstream's dining table and carefully assembled a twin of the Barrett rifle he used in Ketchikan and remembered the remorse felt at deep-sixing that cannon. Once the assembly was complete and the action checked he set it aside and studied the included ballistic information and test firing report. Twenty rounds of custom-made ammunition sat on the dining table nestled in their plastic case. They looked wicked and Mike knew they would do the job at hand.

Varmint scratched at the door breaking Mike's concentration. "Alright already. I know it's dinner time. Keep your hair on; I'm coming!"

Mike opened the door, stepped out, and idly lit a small Weber propane BBQ. He started a mental list of the things he needed and began outlining a plan of action.

"I need a small, quiet, dirt bike. I'll drive up Fred Canyon Road and then ride east, cross-country, to the next canyon about two miles from the ranch on Thing Valley Road. I'll travel from there to the stand on foot. I'll have to hide out until full dark before returning to Cibbits Flat . . . I'll need night vision gear and will disable all lights on the dirt bike . . . Humm . . . I'll have to reconnoiter when I get the dirt bike. I think this should be a middle-of-the-week hit."

The BBQ was heated and ready for cooking; Mike retrieved a pair of rib eye steaks from the fridge and slapped them on the grill. The sizzling beef soon brought Varmint back to camp. He managed to get soaking wet but waited until he was next to Mike before shaking the last drops of Kitchen Creek from his sodden fur.

"Jesus Varmint! I thought you had enough of being soaked. I'll get Gman to ship your soggy ass back to Ketchikan if you can't behave."

Varmint positioned himself downwind of the broiling steaks and shook again before laying down in the gritty, dusty, high desert, sand. He fixated on the rib eye steaks wanting to make sure Mike did not overcook his.

Mike muttered something about over trained K9s, fished a secure satellite phone from his cargo pants pocket, and punched number two. *"That should connect me to my San Diego liaison, Gemma Grace."*

After one ring the gruff old woman answered. "Mr. Smith is this an emergency?"

"Ah . . . no." was all Mike could think of to say.

"Then why in God's name are you calling me at this hour?" The gruff, old, irritated person grew stern and impatient.

Varmint growled deep and barked his displeasure. His steak was done and Mike was not paying attention.

"Did Varmint just alert? Do you need assistance?" The voice was still gruff but changed from annoyed to alert.

Mike had no doubt he we speaking to the Gemma and decided to tweak her a little. "Varmint's just letting me know his steak is done. Hold on a second." Mike plucked Varmint's steak off the grill with a pigtail skewer and dropped it in his dish. "Sorry about that but you don't want to be on the bad side of Varmint."

Gemma interrupted, annoyance turning to peevish anger. "Mr. Smith! Get to the point before I send a platoon of Seals up there to straighten you out!"

"Yes Mam! I need a small, quiet dirt bike, a 175 cc, four stroke would do nicely, night vision gear, and a folding trenching tool, and, ah . . . a Kbar Becker Crewman knife, and . . . a vox unit and collar for Varmint."

"I'll have those items to you by 0530." The phone went silent leaving Mike standing alone in the dark wondering if Gemma Grace had any friends in this world.

CHAPTER 37

PREPARATION H

Varmint growled and jumped off the bed telling Black Cloud something he already knew; they had company. Black Cloud rolled out of bed onto the floor, slipped into a pair of khaki colored sweat pants with 'ARMY' printed in bright yellow letters down the right leg. Next, he slipped a pair of tennis shoes on, secured the Velcro straps, and clicked the P-9s safety off.

Varmint growled low with excitement and menace; he was impatient with Black Cloud and the twenty seconds already burned. Black Cloud slid up next to Varmint, stroked his bristling fur, and whispered orders. Varmint grasped the trap door's rubber t-handle with his teeth, opened it, and disappeared into the darkness beneath the Airstream. Black Cloud followed and took up position behind the dual wheels. He had a commanding view of the campsite opposite and the Chinese-Fire-Drill in progress.

"Shhhhh. Quiet John! The old battle-axe said there would be hell to pay if we woke the wolf up and his master is supposed to be worse."

"FOAD (Fuck Off and Die)! That old cow ain't no Ava Braun and I ain't no delivery boy! I don't even get up this early to go fishin' so don't shush me! How the hell do these tie-downs work? Ow! Fuck!"

The motorcycle handle bar John was leaning over jumped six inches when the tie-down was released catching him squarely on the bridge of his nose. Blood gushed and he air-stepped off the side of the bike trailer holding his bleeding nose. He landed in a heap grinding desert sand into the back of his hand, forehead and chin. When he rolled over groaning Pete thought his bloody partner had been shot.

Varmint took that opportunity to let the sleep-wreckers know he was present. A loud vicious growl stopped the bickering. Both men drew weapons and took shelter behind the bike trailer. With only one tie-down holding the motorcycle in place it overbalanced and fell denting the trailer's left fender. The handle bar and clutch lever thumped John on the back of the head; he dropped his piece and howled out another Ow! Fuck! Varmint barked and snarled, two feet behind the pathetic pair adding to the turmoil.

Mike, unable to contain his laughter any longer, came out from under the trailer and ordered Varmint to his side.

"I assume you two noisy clowns are here to deliver my dirt bike and other toys."

John, holding his nose pinched shut with one hand and rubbing the growing lump on the back of his head with the other, stood up and nodded yes.

Pete stood up slowly and confirmed his partner's nod. "Gemma Grace sent the bike and some things. Can you give me a hand getting the bike off the trailer? My partner appears to be occupied."

Ten minutes later Pete, John, and a black Denali were nothing more than a dust cloud on Kitchen Creek Road.

"This bike ain't exactly wimpy Varmint! You ever hear of a Christini AWD-450? Hope this stealthy fucker came with some instructions!" Mike may as well be speaking to himself; Varmint was occupied chasing a gopher snake back into its hidie-hole.

It was still dark when Mike and Varmint started up Fred Canyon Road but morning dimly glowed in the east. A hasty breakfast and hurriedly packed rations combined with several quarts of water were soon forgotten; Black Cloud was concentrating fully on his driving. He motored down the dusty gravel road showing no lights checking out his night vision gear. He listened for the telltale beep letting him know when the preset GPS waypoint was reached.

Varmint flashed ahead. Mike wanted to have his running done before the brutal, high desert sun, heated things up. Sustaining ten miles an hour was an easy dogtrot in the cool mountain air and it would last less than an hour. Once they started cross-country the pace would slow to a crawl and Varmint staying hydrated would cease being a worry.

Gloomy morning light found Black Cloud picking his way down a treacherous dried up watercourse. This was the second time he dumped the bike in crumbling granite and marble sized pebbles. *"Should have kept up on trials riding! This aint't no fuckin' ISDT,*

(International Six Day Trials), bike," crossed his mind. A little further down the trail a flat spot looked like a perfect place to take a rest.

He stopped and whistled for Varmint to return. It was too light for the night vision gear to work effectively and still too dark on the canyon floor to continue without seeing where this perennial streamed petered out. Thing Valley was still over a mile and a half to the east and this looked like a good place to take a rest and check Varmint's pads. If the terrain got to rocky he would have to wear booties to protect his feet. Varmint's feet were in fine shape and the rapidly brightening morning light and steep canyon afforded Mike a good opportunity to test the accuracy of the Barrett.

Mike removed the inconspicuous looking tent roll from the bike's rear parcel grid and inspected then assembled the Barrett .338 Lapua Magnum. He ranged on a light splotch of granite seven-hundred-twenty-three yards up the canyon. He laid in a comfortable prone position with the Barrett resting on its bipod, took careful aim and slowly squeezed the trigger. The Barrett popped like a two-inch salute. The muzzle brake and flash suppressor mitigated the recoil and muffled the expected deafening boom. Less than a millisecond later the scope optics cleared and Mike clearly saw his bullet splatter six inches below and barely right of his aim point. Movement on the dark granite ledge above his intended target, now bathed in glaring, hot sunlight, caught his eye then disappeared.

"Not bad. *Whoever dialed this rifle in knew his shit.*" Mike made a minute adjustment to elevation and left the windage setting alone. He jacked another round into the chamber and took careful note of where the expended cartridge landed and then sighted in on the chipped, discolored, granite splotch where his last round hit.

"Well, son of a bitch!" Mike's exclamation was lost on Varmint who could not see the large Diamondback sprawled out on a dark colored ledge soaking up the sun's warmth. The snake's presence reminded Mike to be ever on guard.

"Die motherfucker!" Black Cloud squeezed his second round off. Two Diamondbacks wriggled around aimlessly until the head-half tumbled from the ledge and out of the scope's field of view. "Nice piece!" Mike said to no one in particular.

That concluded all equipment checks and it was time to move out. The sun climbed above the canyon walls making it easy to navigate the last half mile to the planned bike cache´. Mike took a long drink from his hydration backpack and poured half a quart of water in a collapsible bowl for Varmint. When Varmint finished his water Mike sent him on orbit, policed their resting place and made certain the two expended cartridge cases were securely zipped into a vest pocket. Last thing before moving out was to check and double check the Barrett, ensuring it was secured to the bike's parcel grid and all gear was packed and accounted for.

It took less than an hour to reach the predetermined stash point for the bike. The chosen canyon was thick with cottonwood trees and creosote bushes. A slight trickle of water still flowed through a rock and boulder strewn streambed. There were few signs of bikers or hikers and no trash strewn about to indicate illegals used this canyon to hide out. Mike selected a thick tangle of a creosote bush to hide the bike. Black Cloud removed the equipment he and Varmint needed, turned the gas off, laid the bike on its side and covered it with camouflage netting. Finally, he broke a branch from brush twenty yards away and erased all tracks within fifty feet of the hidden bike.

Three short blasts on the silent dog whistle brought Varmint to his side and they set off for their stand a mile and a half to the south and east. Two hours of picking their way through cactus, brush, sand washes, and boulders brought them to their destination. Mike searched the area for a suitable place to hole up and keep an eye on the ranch without being spotted himself. He found an excellent shooting stand just over the crest of the hill that was suitable for nighttime shooting. He found another site thirty yards away. Overhanging boulders afforded some shade and Manzanita and creosote brush would keep him from prying eyes.

An hour of watching the ranch revealed some peculiarities. The blue pickup was parked close to the front door but no one ventured out until well after noon. No horses, goats, cattle or sheep could be seen anywhere near. About two dozen chickens wandered around near the ranch house looking for scratch. No dogs were spotted and that made Mike very happy.

Two men exited the ranch house, lit cigarettes and seemed to make a security sweep of the grounds. Mike mentally tagged them as Poncho and Leftie. Following their security sweep, they went directly to the truck, revved it up and left in a cloud of dust. Another hour passed before a third man exited the ranch house, chased the chickens, caught one, rung its neck and carried it to a chopping block at the end of the house. Mike tagged him as Cookie.

"Must be dinner . . ." Mike mused while stroking Varmint's ears. "None of those assholes look ugly enough to be our primary target. I don't think much is going on down there for a while so . . . It's siesta time."

Before drifting off, Mike conjured up a memorized likeness of his primary target. The oddly named man, Feo, identified in the intelligence package given to Mike on his initial briefing by Gemma Grace shortly after his arrival in San Diego was not at the Thing Valley Ranch.

A low growl and gentle nudge from Varmint instantly awoke Black Cloud from a sound two hour, power-nap. He slipped out from under the camouflage netting and carefully surveyed the panorama spread before him. Spotting nothing he eased around the pile of boulders and checked the La Posta Truck Trail. He spied a blue pickup with three people in the cab moving slowly north, and a mutt of some sort prancing around in the bed.

"Looks like a security sweep and Poncho and Lefty picked up some extra help and a fuckin' mutt. I wonder what's up." Varmint laid patiently listening to Mike's prattle; his recent stealth training kicked in when he heard the pickup truck and he would not move until ordered.

The pickup continued north until turning on Thing Valley Road. It stopped at the ranch house and let out one passenger. The mutt, a mangy Heinz-57 variety, jumped out of the truck bed barking. He chased chickens until the newcomer caught him with a vicious kick followed by a brutal beating. A low growl registered Varmint's displeasure.

Poncho and Lefty continued driving south until meeting up with the La Posta Truck Trail. Once their security sweep was complete, the driver raced back to the ranch raising a cloud of dust.

"Wonderful . . . Four men and a dog. This assignment just keeps getting easier and easier. Lucky for us that unfortunate cur isn't a guard dog." Varmint agreed but ignored Mike as usual.

Four men sat on the veranda. The mutt climbed under the front steps after his beating and had not been seen since. One man poured charcoal into an oil-barrel-BBQ while another plucked two recently slaughtered chickens. Two men sat drinking cervesa while the sun disappeared behind the mountains.

Mike decided it was time to return to Cibbits Flat, contact Gemma for an intelligence update, and make solid plans based on today's reconnoitering. Mike already determined he and Varmint would have to sit and watch the ranch until Feo showed up. That could take a day or two. Mike started planning what he and Varmint would carry if extra water and rations were needed to sustain a long vigil.

The return trip was quicker than this morning's trial and error learning experience but the trail was steep, slippery, and dangerous. Disaster struck within the first five minutes. On the first narrow, steep, climb up a trickling streambed the bike suddenly sputtered and quit running.

Black Cloud swore and struggled to get out from under the bike that toppled over and now rested atop him. "What the fuck! Varmint you're supposed to remind me to turn the fuckin' gas on!" Varmint was concerned and tugged on Mikes' pant leg to help him slither out from under the bike.

The remainder of the up-hill trail ride was uneventful but painstakingly slow. Finally, Mike stopped on the hill above the Airstream and sent Varmint ahead to scout for interlopers or signs of trouble. He returned in less than ten minutes and everything appeared peaceful and quiet.

Mike rode on past the Airstream leaving Varmint on guard. He road all the way to the Cibbits Flat entrance. The construction crew was long gone but all the barricades and Camp Ground Closed signs were in place. A six-foot wide and ten-foot deep trench cut Fred Canyon Road off from traffic. Mike assumed something similar was in place at the other end of Fred Canyon Road and returned to the Airstream satisfied that Gman was on the job.

CHAPTER 38

TERMINATION

All preparations for tomorrow completed, Mike made the dreaded call to Gemma for the latest intelligence. It was late by civilian standards, 2123, but Gemma answered on the second ring. "If this call is interrupted by Varmint checking on the status of his steak I'm sending the Marines! What do you want?"

"Me and my partner just got back from a grueling day in the dessert and are in no mood for bullshit. Target one is not on site, extra help including a K9 arrived and I need updated, information. I'll be at the objective from tomorrow, early AM, until completion. Thanks for the toys! They are perfect."

"Ah . . ." That was unusual for a Gemma response. "Target will definitely be in the area tomorrow or the day after. I'll have a backup plan in place by the time you are on site. No bullshit Mr. Smith."

"Ok. I'll check email before I depart but I *will* be dark and silent until the mission is completed."

"Understood. I will have the latest intel in your mailbox before you depart." Gemma ended the call in a most unusual way. "Be careful Mr. Smith."

True to her word Gemma emailed updated intelligence including satellite photos showing infrared signatures in the mountains near the Tecate Border Crossing. *"Probably two legged Coyotes and their flocks of illegals,"* Mike noted their position relative to his stand and dismissed them as neither threats nor witnesses.

He checked and rechecked his equipment and rations for the last time and wished he did not leave his .44 automag back in Prince Rupert aboard ***Springer***. He verified that he carried three extra M9 magazines and fifty rounds of hyper velocity, hollow point rounds for the Henry, AR7, survival rifle. Before leaving the Airstream, Mike zipped the last half dozen Scooby snacks, made by Huck in

Ketchikan, into a vest pocket, looked around, switched the dimly glowing red lamp off, and closed and locked the door behind him.

Three short blasts on the silent dog whistle brought Varmint to his side near the dirt bike. "You look pretty spiffy in your Kevlar cameo vest! I know you don't like wearing the vest and carrying water but it is the only way I can be sure you can get out of the desert if things go south. Let's roll!" Hand signals sent Varmint coursing ahead.

It was the third time Mike traversed the narrow, steep trail in the dark. He made good progress and arrived at the bike cache´ with red streaks appearing in the eastern sky and a feeling of general unease. *"What does Kensey always say and where is that old goat anyway? Oh ya, red sky in the morning sailors take warning. Thanks for that tidbit Kensey!"*

Mike sent Varmint ahead to scout the gloomy canyon and busied himself erasing all signs of their transit within a fifty-yard radius. That took time and morning was in full progress when they approached the La Posta Truck Trail. Mike chose a well-hidden spot among the moonscape boulders where he could keep an eye on the truck trail and called Varmint to his side. Varmint sneaked in and Mike did not notice his approach until he nudged the back of his left hand with a cold, wet, nose.

"Fuck!" Black Cloud spun around, M9 on the ready, completely surprised. "Jesus Varmint! I was thinking about that diamond back I plugged yesterday. You damn near gave me a heart attack." Black Cloud checked the VOX unit and switched it from off to on.

Black Cloud and Varmint drank half a quart of water each, made sure the coast was clear, and then scurried across the truck trail and disappeared into the brush and boulders on the other side. Varmint growled and stood looking south down the truck trail. Black Cloud crouched low and found shelter in the boulders where he could look south. A quick scan with the compact, twenty power, field glasses found the now familiar blue 4X4 pickup slowly driving north. Two men rode in the cab and the mutt, chained to a tie down, slept in the bed.

"Security sweep. I'll bet they do this several times a day." Varmint ignored Black Cloud but growled as if annoyed when the truck passed two hundred yards away.

Black Cloud was wary. He kept Varmint close and slowly worked his way to the stand. Nothing seemed out of place and none of the hidden tells left behind on the last visit were disturbed. Black Cloud slithered into his ghillie suit, sent Varmint to scout their back trail and settled in waiting for Feo to appear.

Morning wore on into early afternoon. Nothing unusual took place at the house. Black Cloud passed the time by identifying each of the four ranch hands until he was certain he would not mistake one of them for his ugly target, Feo.

Every forty-five minutes, the chicken slayer Black Cloud tagged as Cookie, came outside, walked the veranda, or pranced around the grounds, cell phone held high, searching for a signal. At various times one or two others would come outside and try the same maneuvers with their cell phones held high. Black Cloud dubbed the one wearing an overly decorated, large, sombrero as Cisco. He hung the moniker 'Idiot' on one pathetic ranch hand and watched Idiot's routine antics with amusement. First he staggered to the pickup, climbed into the bed, faced north, spun in slow circles looking for bars and eventually unzipped and took a leak over the side of the truck. Black Cloud mentally kept track and bet himself that Idiot would fall out of the pickup bed before his sixth trip.

"Better have your prostrate checked Idiot! No one has to piss that often." Black Cloud chuckled to himself. *"Maybe I can take care of that problem for you when Feo shows up . . ."*

Black Cloud paid particular attention to Jerk, the hand who beat on the mutt. When Jerk emerged from the ranch house, Cur, as Black Cloud dubbed the mangy dog, hurried out from under the veranda with hackles bristling, fangs bared, nose to the ground, and tail tucked between his legs. Jerk would make faints toward Cur who backed up a few feet but never relaxed, cowed or ran.

Following Cookie's 2000 cell call attempt, he and Cisco got into the pickup and drove south. *"Probably another security sweep, the third today,"* crossed Black Cloud's mind. They returned from the south an hour after sunset. That piqued Black Cloud's sixth sense and he paid close attention. Another vehicle, a white Escalade, followed well behind the pickup avoiding its dust plume.

The Escalade made its way to the ranch house and parked beside the pickup; no one emerged. Black Cloud could not see inside the heavily tinted Escalade windows. Finally, a single man got out and hurried up the steps and into the ranch house. Black Cloud's intuition told him it was Feo, his target, but he could not be one-hundred percent certain.

Cisco and Idiot emerged from the house and took up chairs on the Veranda. They passed a bottle of clear liquid between them. It was nearly full dark and Black Cloud missed the lingering twilight of the northern latitudes. Muted light sneaking through faded curtains supplied plenty of light for the riflescope optics. Black Cloud could plainly see his targets but he was invisible lying in wait dressed in a full ghillie suit.

Varmint sat impatiently waiting for orders. He eyed half a Scooby snack, sniffed it, savored its aroma, gave into the temptation, grasped it in his jaw and then chomped it into scrumptious bits before swallowing. That did not quell his excitement. He sensed action was just around the corner and he was rearing to go.

The ranch house door burst open. The newcomer charged out, spied Cisco and Idiot, spun in his tracks, and then kicked the legs out from under Cisco's leaned back chair. Cisco jumped up from where he sprawled on the veranda ready to fight; Idiot followed suit and leapt to his feet.

Through the riflescope, Black Cloud could see the rage filled ugly, by any definition, face of his target who brutally stabbed his index finger into Idiot's chest and shook his fist at Cisco. Varmint came to his feet, ears tilted forward toward the threesome. Varmint had no trouble hearing Feo screaming seven hundred twenty eight yards in the distant.

"Target confirmed!" The Barrett roared twice in rapid succession. The shots were so close together it was hard to tell how many rounds were fired. Feo threw his hands up and crashed into Idiot dragging him to the deck in a deadly embrace. Black Cloud instantly switched targets and fired two quick rounds at Cisco. He tumbled backward and crashed through the window. Black Cloud could see his legs dangling from the windowsill; what was left of his torso resided indoors.

Idiot scrambled out from under Feo. He was covered in blood from head to toe. Consistent with his name, he rushed for the door. He and a Barns, two-hundred-fifty grain, match bullet arrived at the same time. Idiot's rush was halted when he suddenly gained a third eye and crumbled into a heap one-step inside the doorway.

Black Cloud ejected the Barrett's magazine and slammed another home. All lights but one went out inside the ranch house and an eerie silence fell over Thing Valley. Within two minutes the single light winked out.

Five minutes stretched to ten and then fifteen. Black Cloud grew apprehensive; two men, Cookie and Jerk were still out there somewhere. He ordered Varmint to orbit. Varmint was off like a shot. If anyone was within a quarter mile they were in for a nasty surprise.

Half an hour passed with no change. No one emerged from the house and Black Cloud spotted no movement in the dark. It was time to move out. He squirmed out of the ghillie suit, packed it, and sanitized the stand. Last thing before bugging out was calling Varmint back from his orbit. Three short blasts on the silent dog-whistle accomplished that.

Black Cloud swept back and forth one more time with the rifle optics while waiting for Varmint to return. Movement at the southern end of the ranch house caught his attention. He zeroed in applying ever so slight pressure to the Barrett's trigger. Cur slinked out to Thing Valley Road and gazed in Black Cloud's direction.

"Well shit, dog; you are free. Run like the wind!" Varmint's wet, cold, nose nudged the back of Black Cloud's neck shutting off any more thoughts about Cur.

"Jesus! I wonder if I can send you to un-stealth training. You are going to give me a heart attack yet." Black Cloud rolled over and stroked Varmint's ears. "Let's get the fuck out of here. I think you better stay close. We still have two shitheads unaccounted for."

Black Cloud quickly broke the Barrett down and packed it for travel. He eyeballed the diminutive AR7, put it back in his backpack, thought better of it, removed it from the backpack and assembled the small rifle. *"I just might run into a piss-ant or horny toad. This thing is nearly as quiet as my old Red Ryder BB gun . . ."*

Chapter 39
EXTRACTION

"Turn that light out you fuckin' fool!" Poncho, the one named Cookie by Black Cloud, barked his order to no avail.

"Fuck you! It's dark in . . ." Carlos, the only other survivor, emerged from the bathroom and was half way down the hall before he spotted his friend crumpled on the floor with half his head missing surrounded by a rapidly expanding pool of blood.

He scrambled in retreat and forcefully snapped the bathroom light off. Poncho heard scuffling low on the floor and surmised that his partner was crawling toward him in the dark.

"Where the fuck are you?" Carlos asked no one in particular in a wavering, loud whisper.

"Back here in the kitchen beside the refrigerator. Hurry!" Poncho was scrunched into the smallest profile he could manage and was not about to move. He was thinking in overtime.

Carlos crawled into the kitchen, flattened himself against the wall beside Poncho, and started jabbering. "We need to vamoose out of here. Who's out there? Where did those shots come from? You got the truck keys? What are we going to . . .?"

"Quiet! Let me think." Poncho formulated a plan and knew Carlos would not like it. "I need to contact the boss in Cabo. Feo was his man and he needs to send us some help. I will sneak along the truck trail until I get a cell, make the call, and then come back for you."

"Fuck that! Let's get the truck and get the hell out of here." Carlos had no desire to stay alone in or near this death trap.

"You do that . . . imbecile. The instant you open the truck door, if you make it that far, you are a dead man. No Carlos, you are going to take the shotgun and hide out in the boulders near the north end of the ranch house, and I'm going to get help. Let's go." Poncho scooted to the back door, reached up, turned the doorknob, held his breath, and pushed the door open.

Poncho did not pause to see if Carlos followed orders. Once the door swung open he got to his feet, crouched low, and broken-field sprinted to the brush and boulders twenty yards behind the ranch house. He sat behind good cover, heart pounding, stopping only long enough to take inventory of useful items. *"Cell phone, truck keys, Ruger Black Hawk, ten extra bullets, and Buck, folding, hunter knife . . . If I stay twenty or thirty yards off the road I should be ok. Where the fuck is that shooter?"*

Poncho picked his way through the brush and boulders. The going was excruciatingly slow in the dark. He brushed against the second cholla cactus in half an hour and felt the barbed spines penetrate his left shin. He was less than one eighth of a mile from the ranch house and had no cell phone reception. He came to realize traveling on the gravel road was the only option. The moon, when he could see it through the gloom, was a ghostly sliver. He decided the road would be a safe avenue to travel if he took care.

Poncho checked his cell phone every five or six minutes desperately hoping to see some reception bars. He rounded the one-eighty bend on Thing Valley Road three phone checks ago and cautiously proceeded south on the La Posta Truck Trail.

"At last!" he silently said a prayer, turned in a slow circle until he got two bars and then picked his way uphill, through the brush forty feet until he got three bars. A slight but chilly high desert breeze snaked down the hill and through the canyon.

"Fuckin' burrrrrrrrr! Wish I had a serape or a poncho." Poncho smiled at his own pun, noticed the time was 2213, and scooted around to the downhill side of a boulder pile to make his call and get out of the nippy breeze. He felt rather than herd something, grudgingly shut the cell phone off in mid ring, slowly slid down the boulder, nervously sat in the sand behind a creosote bush, readied the Ruger for action, and waited.

****

The night vision gear made traveling through the brush, boulders, and cactus faster and easier but not as fast as Black Cloud wanted. He and Varmint stopped fifty yards from the truck trail and made sure nothing was moving along the gravel road.

"Something isn't right . . . I should send Varmint on a few orbits . . . Fuck it, don't have the time." Black Cloud dismissed his sixth sense and rapidly proceeded to the edge of the truck trail through thin, scrubby brush. A sliver of a moon briefly shown through a crack in the gloomy marine layer dimly lighting Thing Valley. Varmint growled, leapt from Black Cloud's side and streaked back up hill and up wind.

Black cloud spun around, M9 on the ready. Two shots roared from the brush thirty or forty feet away. One .44 slug caught him squarely in the chest and the other grazed along his right side. He was knocked unconscious and dropped to the ground like a sack of potatoes.

Forty feet up the hill dark fury slammed into Poncho's left side missing his neck but crunching through the bone of his left shoulder. He yelled out in fear and agony. Reflex and adrenalin brought his right hand up and he fired twice blindly. The crushing pressure in his left shoulder subsided but his left arm was a mangled, useless mess. He lay there a moment before wriggling out from under one-hundred-twenty pounds of wolf.

Poncho did not bother reloading. He distinctly heard the 'thunck' of two solid hits and knew whoever lay beside the road would not be moving again. For all practical purposes, the dog with a vest and water bottle laying bleeding in the sand was done for and would not be a problem. He sat there shaking for several minutes before retrieving his cell phone, placing it on his lap and dialing the man he only knew as Paymaster. He stood up trying to shake off the increasing agony radiating from his left shoulder.

Black Cloud moaned and felt the dent where the .44 struck his vest. He was groggy but reflexes kicked in when his night vision gear flared from a light thirty feet away. Black Cloud could not find his M9 but the little survival rifle was lying beside him in the sand. He grabbed the AR7 and came to a classic sitting position. He winced from pain low in his right side and carefully aimed at what he could clearly see was a man holding a cell phone. The small .22 spat four times in the blink of an eye.

Poncho's last words were, "Yes, ambushed . . ."

Black Cloud puffed three time on the dog whistle and waited. Varmint did not come to his side; he feared the worse and hurried up hill, rifle on the ready.

221

"If this isn't a Black Cloud moment I don't know what is!" Varmint lay on his left side blood trickling out from under his vest, down his left, front leg, into the sand.

"Cookie, you motherfucker! If you weren't dead I'd torture you to death!" Black Cloud angrily kicked the Ruger Blackhawk away from Cookie's dead body and knelt beside Varmint and checked for breathing.

"You're alive! Let's see how bad it is." Varmint's eyes flashed open; he growled, bared his fangs and painfully gained his feet. "Easy old friend. Let me get this vest off you." Varmint recognized his master, quit growling, and stood there wobbling on three legs while Black Cloud removed the vest.

One bullet gutted the hydration pack on Varmint's back. That probably stung but did not do any significant damage. Once Varmint's vest was off Black Cloud started to worry. The second bullet went under the vest. It must have hit the shoulder bone, turned ninety degrees and exited about four inches back along the ribs. The entrance wound was weeping blood and all the fur was burned away. *"The Ruger's muzzle flash must have cauterized that wound."* Black Cloud thought while putting a battle dressing on the oozing exit wound and cinching it tight.

Varmint yipped and nudged Black Cloud's hand with his teeth each time a tender spot was touched. Black cloud signaled Varmint to lie down and used a painkiller/sedative Syrette followed by an antibiotic to calm and sedate him.

"You stay here. I'm going to the ranch house and get a truck. I'll be back in half an hour." Varmint drifted off to sleep and Black Cloud rifled through Poncho's pockets. He located the truck keys and the folding knife. He picked up Cookie's cell phone and zipped all three items into a vest pocket and hurried back to the gravel road. It took three minutes to locate his M9. Black Cloud checked the pistol's action, verified it was in working order, turned north and started a fast jog up the truck trail ignoring the nagging pain in his right side.

After seven minutes Black Cloud rounded the hairpin corner, spied the ranch house and slowed to a double-time pace across the desert. Less than fifty yards from the truck a dog started barking.

"Fuckin' Cur! This just keeps getting better . . ." Black Cloud zigzagged toward the truck using every piece of cover he could find. Cur confronted him twenty feet from the back of the pickup.

"I'm not Jerk! Shush Dog." Black Cloud extended his hand holding one of Huck's gourmet dog treats. Cur inched forward, sniffed the treat, snatched it from Black Cloud's hand, and backed away one-step before wolfing it down. Black Cloud offered another Scooby Snack. Cur cautiously took it and allowed Black Cloud to scratch her ears.

"Take it easy boy . . . girl. I'm just going to borrow this truck for a while. Black Cloud dropped three Scooby snacks next to Cur, crouched low and made a beeline for the driver's door.

"I hope Jerk hauled ass." Black Cloud flipped his night vision goggles up, crouched below the window and jerked the pickup door open. A shotgun opened fire from the north end of the house the second the courtesy light flashed on. The truck's driver door window shattered pelting Black Cloud with glass. He felt the sting of half a dozen pellets spray his legs after bouncing under the door. Black Cloud slammed the door shut and rolled under the truck, assumed a prone firing position, flipped the night vision goggles down, and searched for movement at the north end of the ranch house.

Cur flashed past and went straight into the brush where the shots came from. Black Cloud heard screams and vicious growling and snarling. He rolled out from under the truck and sprinted to where he heard the last scream.

"Easy girl; he won't beat you ever again." Cur relaxed and shook six inches of Jerk's jugular free of her jaw. She backed away from her kill, looked at Black Cloud and then padded back toward the truck.

Black Cloud ran back to the truck and started it. Before he could peel out Cur jumped into the pickup bed and laid down. "Hope you can hang on girl. This ain't gonna be no joy ride!" Gravel, sand, and dust flew as tires spun wildly. Getting Varmint to a vet was the only thing on Black Cloud's mind.

It did not take any time at all to fetch Varmint and get him situated comfortably on the front bench seat. Cur was not happy with the situation and paced and growled but would not leave the pickup bed. "Better sit down girl or you're gonna be on your ass in the middle of the road." Black Cloud gently accelerated and cur laid back down.

They exited the La Posta Truck Tail and turned south toward a small village called Boulevard. Black Cloud pulled into a dusty side street, parked, waited a moment and then speed dialed Gemma Grace on the secure satellite phone.

Gemma answered on the third ring. Report."

"I know you are better looking than Mr. Billings but you sure as hell sound like him. I have a situation. Are we secure?"

"Yes. Proceed."

"Mission accomplished times five. Varmint is badly wounded and immobile. He needs a vet now! I have a few shotgun wounds and probably a fractured rib. Transportation is hidden in desert and I had to commandeer a pickup truck to extract Varmint. I'm in Boulevard and will stay here awaiting instructions." Black Cloud took a breath and waited for an answer.

The line was dead less than a minute. "Proceed west on highway 94. Once you pass through Campo look for a remote pub called Dog Patch. Park at the north end of the parking lot and wait. Help will be there or they will arrive shortly after you."

"Thanks and oh . . . I have one extra passenger and she isn't very friendly." Black Cloud heard a sigh before the line went dead.

Dog Patch was not much to write home about. The flickering Coors sign in the front window barely cast enough light to see twenty feet into the parking lot. Black Cloud pulled off the road across the street and studied Dog Patch. Nothing moved or approached on highway ninety-four.

"Typical government employees . . . It takes ten to do the job of two and they can't even do it on time." Black Cloud's thoughts were unflattering before he spotted headlights coming from the west. A black Denali approached, slowed, turned into the Dog Patch parking lot and then proceeded to park under a large tree near the north end of the lot. Black Cloud started the pickup, cruised slowly next to the Denali and parked next to its right side with M9 ready and the AR-7 propped between him and Varmint on the driver seat.

The Denali's passenger window silently glided open and Black Cloud immediately started a conversation with the Blues Brothers. "I'm Mike Smith. You two here to see a man about a dog?"

"Yes sir. Your ride will be here shortly. We are here for Varmint and Gemma says to get your ass in gear and get lost." Cur growled evilly getting everyone's attention.

"Varmint is here beside me and he is hurt bad. Sweetums, in the truck bed, belongs to Gemma. Tell her I'm really sorry about getting her all dirty and bloody. Take her to a doggie spa, get her cleaned up, and return her to Gemma. She will be forever in your debt for doing that."

"We can do that. I'm Doctor Rhinard the Vet." Doc Rhinard exited the Denali, opened its back doors and extracted a gurney and then wheeled it around to Varmint's door.

Six Harley Davidson motorcycles could be heard speeding toward them. Three bikes passed by; three turned into the parking lot and stopped behind the Denali and pickup truck.

The Denali's driver spoke in an undistinguishable monotone. "That is your ride and your security team. Varmint and Sweetums will be well taken care of and a sanitation team is already at work. Do you have anything for me Mr. Smith?"

Mike thought a moment. "This is a cell phone the asshole who shot my dog was on just before he bit the dust. It might be of some use." Mike stepped out of the truck and handed it through the window. "All my gear and a few odds and ends are in this truck. The gear and truck need to disappear."

"Taken care of. You really need to disappear yourself Mr. Smith." That sounded like the final word from the disjointed voice.

"Hi I'm George. Put these on and let's get the fuck out of here." A burly Hells Angel biker handed Mike a helmet and leather jacket. "We ain't got all day." was his final word.

Mike watched Varmint being wheeled to the back of the Denali on the gurney and laughed at Doc's partner trying to coax Sweetums out of the pickup bed. He fished the last Scooby snack out of his jacket pocket and tossed it to the Blues Brother in distress.

"Here, coax her with this Scooby Snack." Mike yelled

"You ready to roll?" Gruffly barked by George interrupted anything else Mike had to say.

"Yeah. Let's get the fuck out of here." Mike answered but thought, *"Hope no black clouds roll in. These fuckin' motorcycles are dangerous!"*

225

EPILOG

Jim Billings listened to the message one more time just to make sure he heard it correctly. In all these years of working with Gemma Grace he never saw her lose her composure or, come to think of it, swear. Gemma was in rare form and it appeared that Black Cloud managed to get her goat.

Jim paused the playback at an especially high-pitched tirade. "If I ever see that shithead again I'll treat him like a rattlesnake. I'll blow his fuckin head off!"

Jim smiled in rare good humor; he remembered what Kensey told him when he suspected Black Cloud was in Gman's employment. "Shit happens and all kinds of weird shit happens around my friend Mike Smith!"

Jim closed his eyes and restarted the playback savoring Gemma's dilemma. "Fuckin' Sweetums! Fuckin' Sweetums? You are payin' for the tetanus shot and doctor bill! I thought Varmint was vicious until your assholes dropped fuckin' Sweetums off at my house compliments of Black Cloud! And what the fuck are Scooby snacks and where can I get them? I will get ahead Mr. Gman. I might even ship Sweetums to you . . ."

Jim emailed Gemma, "Have no idea what Scooby snacks are. Ask Black Cloud." He smiled wickedly and turned his thoughts to dividends earned during the past few months.

Jim Billings was highly satisfied with the conclusion of Black Cloud's mission, code named **Storm Cloud**. Wounding North Star, identified as Richard Kopf, triggered the desired effect and provided a bonanza of information. Gman grinned remembering "The A Team" leader, John 'Hannibal' Smith's, signature line. "*I love it when a plan comes together!*"

Following operation **Storm Cloud**, HF radio chatter, cell phone calls, and emails from Kopf identified several important drug cartel operatives. One major player, Paymaster, was located just outside of Cabo San Lucas in Baja. Perhaps the most important player, South Star, was located on the border between Salinas, Ecuador and El Bendito, Peru.

Gman broke into a rare full smile and low fived his desk with a slap. *"Got ya now fuckers! You do not know it yet, but I have your radio frequencies, cell phone IDs, and email addresses. As Kensey would say, the game is afoot! Phase two starts today.* Boeing delivered on their promise and Kensey and crew pick up **Goat Locker** in a few hours.

Gman squirmed at the funding required to purchase, modify, and outfit **Goat Locker**: Kensey's new Suparmarine 10 hydrofoil. The ship itself was only half the price tag. She was fitted with new technology from the bottom of her keel to the top of her pyramid mast and that more than doubled the total cost.

He spent months convincing his hesitant, government superiors that his ship with Kensey's crew would more than pay for itself. Three-hundred million dollars was not a drop in the bucket but Gman had a plan and a target generated by intelligence gleaned from **The Raid*** and bolstered by new information acquired from operation **Storm Cloud**.

Gman settled into pleasant thoughts. *"This calls for a double celebration."* He unlocked the lower desk drawer and extracted his favorite single malt carefully wrapped in a bloodied pink apron. *"Salute you old farts! I met you at* **Goats On A Roof** *in Descanso, California and discussed prospecting for gold."* Gman drained his tall shot glass of Laphroaig and poured another. *"Let us see . . . Boeing delivered my ship on time,* **Scrap Dealer***,* **Goat Locker's** transportation and mother ship, *is modified and ready to carry out operations anywhere in the world. My spooks are tracking when, where, and how the payload will be shipped, and I have FISA (Foreign Intelligence Surveillance Act) Court issued warrants so I can roust and jail an entire drug cartel on two continents. We will start with Paymaster. In all likelihood, he orchestrated the attack on* **Derdrake***. That should give Kensey and crew some satisfaction."*

Gman took a long sip of his scotch and continued his train of thoughts. *"Kensey completed a successful recruiting mission and Katy arranged schooling on the new Strales modified 76mm. A few weeks of at-sea training will knit everything together nicely."*

Gman tapped his fingers together in deep thought before taking a tentative sip of scotch. *"Gemma, an old goat in her own* right, has everything at Point Loma and Thing Valley under control. Earlier this evening she informed me that operation **'Bite the Dust'** successfully concluded. There were a few glitches, but there always are when Kensey's friend Black Cloud is included in an operation. If they are not already scratching their heads, it won't be long until the Cartel starts wondering just what sort of blivet (200 pounds of shit stuffed in a 100 pound bag) they created!" Gman chuckled at that thought.

He poured one last shot and merely sipped the fine Scotch whiskey speaking and thinking between nips. *"The double agent at work in my organization doesn't have much time left! I am sure I know who he is . . . He may have an appointment with Mr. Smith in the very near future. In the meantime I can use the leak to my advantage. I just might let Kensey handle that problem."*

A long pull on the shot glass signaled the formulation of a parallel plan. *"Kensey may need a sniper on his mission. I suspect the target I have in mind will be closely guarded, heavily armed, and well defended. Mr. Smith is going to be pissed: it will be some time before he gets back to Prince Rupert. He will get over it; after all, he earned his name, Black Cloud, for a reason . . ."*

FALCON CODES

Usage: typically via voice radio, e.g. 'Falcon one one five.'

Code	Meaning
1	Sheeeeit!
10	Shit Hot!
100	If CAG saw that, he'd shit!
101	You've gotta be shitting me!
102	Get off my fucking back!
103	Beats the shit outta me
104	WTFO
105	It's so fuckin' bad, I can't believe it!
106	I hate this fuckin' place
107	This place sucks
108	Fuck you very much
109	That gawd damned SOB
110	Beautiful, just fuckin' beautiful

111	Here comes another fuckin' CAG brainstorm
112	BFD (Big Fuckin' Deal)
113	Let me talk to that SOB
114	Get your shit together!
115	You bet your sweet ass
116	Fuck it
117	I love you so much I could just shit!
118	WETSU
119	Get this aircraft out of Delta; it has more fuckin' down gripes than the USS Arizona.
120	That's a no-no
121	That gawd damned O-Club
122	You piss me off!
123	Fuck off, mate
124	FUBAR
135	Adios, Motherfucker
136	If you ask me for a low pass one more time, you're not gonna get launched for a week!
137	You may NOT have any fuckin' fuel!
139	I have a prostate over-pressure light

140	COMEX, motherfucker
141	That motherfuckin' CIC is dreaming again
142	The fuckin' helos are all fucked up.
143	It's the Air Boss's fault
202	You may not like the fuckin' staff, but the staff likes fuckin' you!
221	Fuck you and the horse you rode in on!
223	Get your head out of your ass
224	You say 'I don't know' one more time and I'm gonna shove a sonobuoy up your ass!
225	You must have shit for brains!
226	Would you like a kick in the ass to help you get airborne?
227	What does it take to get a clearance out of this fuckin' place'
228	Just fly the bus and leave the ASW to us
229	You're so fuckin' stupid, you're a menace to society
230	This bastard has more downing gripes than the USS Arizona
231	Comments and recommendations, my ass
232	Just out of curiosity, NAV, where the hell are we'
269	Excuse me, but you have obviously mistaken me for someone who gives a shit!

500	Those fuckin' carrier pukes!
600	Those fuckin' ASW pukes
641	Hang it in your ear
700	Fuckin' grunts
728	If I hear 'CV concept' one more time, I'm gonna shit
750	That fucker runs like a well-oiled machine
775	Your old lady wears Boondockers
800	I love this so much I could just shit
901	If this is such a fuckin' good deal, send Crew Two
902	If I called for shit, you'd come sliding in on a shovel
1000	Cool it, the Chaplain's here
3000	Hay for my horses, whiskey for my crew, and a plate of flies for my toad
3001	He's so light, he's a menace to aviation
3003	He hasn't had his lobotomy yet

CPSIA information can be obtained
at www.ICGtesting.com
Printed in the USA
FSOW03n0136290416
19792FS